Grand Slams

a coming of eggs story

by
Timothy Gager

ISBN: 978-0-9969887-4-2
Printed in the United States of America

Cover Designed by: Christopher Reilley
Author Photo: Teisha Dawn Twomey

Also by Timothy Gager:
The Thursday Appointments of Bill Sloan
The Shutting Door
Treating A Sick Animal: Flash and Micro Fictions

Big Table Publishing Company
Boston, MA
www.bigtablepublishing.com

Thanks to Gabe Gager, Caroline Gager,
Teisha Dawn Twomey, my mother and my father,
Peg and Charlie.

Mignon Ariel King, Rene Schwiesow,
and Cheryl Devitt for their editing eyes.

Also to Colin, Bill, Gail, Dottie, Dino, Joe, Mario,
and Kenny, for two summers of food for the story.

Chris, like
nothing
eggs and syrup
at 7 am Sunday

Tid

Part One:

"Don't think we don't know
what you're doing, because we do."

1. Happy Birthday from Grand Slams

Woody Geyser was born on April 17, 1965—the same year Grand Slams introduced their Double Home Run Breakfast. His full name was Woodrow Wilson Geyser, after his father Herbert's favorite president.

His father was very much a progressive. President Wilson enacted many policies young Herbert favored: the Federal Reserve Act, the Federal Trade Commission Act, the Clayton Antitrust Act, the Federal Farm Loan Act, and an income tax. Child labor was temporarily curtailed by the Keating-Owen Act of 1916. Wilson also averted a railroad strike and an ensuing economic crisis through passage of the Adamson Act, imposing an 8-hour workday for railroads. At the outbreak of World War I in 1914, Wilson maintained a policy of neutrality.

Woody didn't care too much about any of that. All he knew was, it was difficult to be named Woodrow, even in progressive Lexington, Massachusetts, a town known for some famous history of its own. Upon further review, Woody discovered that Woodrow Wilson's first name was really Thomas, and Woodrow was actually President Wilson's middle name. *Who the fuck does that?* he thought, considering his parents poor naming idea. Often, he wondered if his life would have been easier if he'd been named Thomas.

On his seventeenth birthday, Woody Geyser took the family wagon and headed just over the town line, to Bedford, where a Grand Slams was open 24 hours. It was midnight when he drowned his sorrows in the Double Home Run Breakfast: two pancakes, two eggs, two bacon strips, two sausages, two slices of toast, and two scoops of whipped butter. The breakfast's name, even in baseball terms, made no sense. Who's ever heard of a double home run in baseball? The hash browns cost extra, but he ordered them on the side because he admired the way the flannel-shirted trucker in the booth next to him sucked the thin, greasy, litmus-paper-looking sliced potatoes down his throat. Woody was served by an old, salty-looking waitress named Maura. He knew his cute-as-can-be, former high school classmate, Sugar, worked here, but she was nowhere to be found.

Instead, Maura was the server. She was at least fifty, with baggy stockings and a spare tire around her middle that Woody compared to his old stay-at-home, pretzel and beer-drinking dad.

"Is this free?" he asked Maura. "It *is* my birthday."

"Of course," Maura said, not without her cutting frown, already worried that 15% of nothing would be nothing, especially with a kid looking like Woody in front of her. "First time here?" she snapped.

Woody was nervous. In fact, his voice sounded awkward and odd. He rubbed the back of his hand against his oily face then flipped his hand over and ran it through his short, spiked hair. "Well, sort of, you know, it's my first time out here on my own. How long have you been here?"

"I've worked here for twenty years," Maura replied, pointing to the gold, racy-looking *GS* on her one-piece, brown polyester uniform with the number *20* centered smack in the middle of it. "Best job I ever had," she said. Woody saw her smile.

He ordered a coffee to go. He didn't like coffee but figured it was about time he learned to get used to it. It was some kind of horrible birthday, but it was about time he got used to doing the things that everyone else did—to try to blend in. First, he had to wash his face. He left a dollar on the table, heading to the bathroom before he left.

Woody felt the April chill of the Massachusetts weather against his still-wet face as he exited the front door of the restaurant. After five strides he was grabbed and tossed to the ground by a kid who, he would learn later, was nicknamed Kayak Kenny. The kid looked sick, with a sort of greenish-yellow tint to him, which usually means the suffering and grinding of two or more vital organs. Kenny acted strangely excited as he yelled out urgently for someone with a name that sounded like "Cheating" or something. Woody grit his teeth as

2

Kenny's full body weight pressed on his back, his arm twisting at a weird angle, his other hand pushed down on his dark, spiked hair.

With his skull pressed against the blacktop, all he could see was a pair of plastic-looking black shoes in front of the cement curb from the sidewalk in front of Grand Slams. The shoes reminded him of the shoes a Ken doll wears. The man in the shoes, standing above him, finally spoke, "You didn't forget to pay for that, did you, college boy?"

Woody tried to shake his head, but the weight of Kayak Kenny's chest on the side of his own left him immobilized while his nose filled with the aroma of fried eggs and sickly sweet syrup roaring from the skin and rank clothes of Kenny. "Tell you what," the man with cheap shoes said. "Come back in a few months and you can have a job for the summer. How does that sound, punk?'

Woody hadn't yet landed a summer job, and the spring semester had been rough on him, academically and financially. Without much thought about anything further, he opened his mouth and grunted out the word, "Yes," while the bouquet of dish swill coming from Kenny caused him to dry heave.

The next day the skin on Woody's face was raw, making it uncomfortable to the touch—which was new, since Woody always felt raw on the inside rather than the outside. It was that inner-tenderness that drove him toward the bottle and the need to experiment with other substances as he discovered the vast potpourri of kicks and tricks he depended on to change the way he felt. Despite the fact that Woody had been late to the game, not indulging in partying until much later than most kids his age, drinking made him feel warm and confident. Even if he was a little awkward, he no longer agonized over every conversation. Finally, he was granted relief from caring so much about how he was perceived, opting for playing the role of King Pig, amongst the garbage and slop.

Nights like last night reinforced how simple social interactions often went straight to hell when he was involved; how he failed at reading social cues; and how the rest of the world reacted to it. Yet somehow, amongst this inadequacy, Woodrow Wilson Geyser had landed a summer job.

2. Geyser's Grand Slams Glossary

Bus Tub: Molded, sturdy plastic basin, with built-in side utensil compartment.

Swill-(n): The liquid or solid remnants removed from a bus tub to the dishwashing work area. *(v)*: The act of washing dishes.

Swill Station: Dishwashing work area.

Bus Apron: Brown, leather-like apron worn when you're working on the floor, clearing tables and helping the wait staff.

Dish Apron: Green plastic apron which is waterproof, but tends to have dish water run down, soaking your pants.

Grand Slams Top 40: Any song where the lyrics are changed, or imply a change, by employees to reflect a Grand Slam menu item or employee. i.e., "Sugar, Sugar" sung directly to the waitress named Sugar or "Born to Swill" sung to Springsteen's "Born to Run."

Clippie: Black clip-on bowtie, which male employees are required to wear when assigned to the front restaurant area, unless there aren't any available because aforementioned employees threw them behind the dishwasher or ice machine.

Scrubbie: (1) Sponge-like cleaning pad with rough side to rub dried egg off dishes before placing them in dishwasher. (2) Person who performs the job of dishwasher.

Country Club: Pool area for The Super 8 Motel, the chain attached to Grand Slams restaurant, Store #506.

Egg Wash: Pre-prepared, ten-gallon bucket of uncooked, whisked eggs, ready to be poured for omelets and scrambles.

Nursing Home Special: The $4.99 open-faced turkey sandwich covered in gravy, served before 5 PM to people over aged 65 with dental issues.

The Ayatollah or Pope: The shift's Head Chef who wears the white, starched, and standing tall chef's hat.

The Giant Snake: High-pressure water hose that hangs over the dish area to power-wash old food and crud off plates before entrance into dish machine.

Bag and Boil: Any sauce, gravy, melted cheese, or vegetable not found
in a can which is heated via boiling water through a
plastic pouch.

The Convoy: Supply and shipment truck, full of Grand Slams food
and supplies.

The Drug Dealer: Driver of above truck, usually importing and
exporting recreational drugs.

Woody Geyser's stomach and head are slow-boiling from a
hangover. If only he can get through his shift, his very first at Grand
Slams, he will be fine. He walks to the dish area, and the odor of grease
and sulfur-smelling egg remainders, combined with that damn syrup
smell, makes his stomach tighten in pre-retch anticipation. He is nearly
paralyzed. It's 6:45 AM and his peers are here early, with way too much
energy for this time of morning. Bees are dormant at night, but during
the day they buzz around in a frenzied turmoil, hustling to complete
their tasks. This is what it feels like as two boys, about his age, swoop
back to claim two brown, fake-leather busing aprons, before racing to
the front of the restaurant to work. An older pock-marked man,
named Marisimo, is sliding and slamming brown plastic tubs toward a
large overhead faucet the size of a small showerhead. He wears a
different apron, one that is stained, green, and waterproof.

"Hello, I'm Tribuno, a manager," a stocky man with a black
handlebar mustache, suit, and heavy accent says, walking up to Woody,
interrupting his sickness. "I'm the Assistant Manager of Grand Slams
#509, Bedford store. Let's head over to the break area and fill out
some paperwork."

Woody imagines the break area being a comfortable, living-room-
type space or a cafeteria setting, but is disappointed by the cramped
area with a conference table pushed against a crumbling wall that holds
a time-clock, mounted and perfectly centered. To the left and right of
the punch clock are two racks with cardboard cards that have the
printed and alphabetized names of each employee. Tribuno grabs a

blank card and writes *Geyser* on it. "Punch in, like this, and sit down. I'll bring you some papers to sign," he says.

At 7 AM, Sugar walks in, looking to have aged between five and ten years since graduation. "Hey, Sugar," Woody says shyly.

She tilts her head, face scrunching in a way that matches her dry, blonde, crimped hair. She is obviously trying to place him.

He refreshes her memory. "Woody Geyser. Remember we had algebra together, and I helped you during the final?"

"Oh, yeah… Woodrow," she says dryly. "I'm late. Gotta get on the floor now."

She looks much rougher, Woody thinks; the combination of too much makeup, the deadness of her eyes, and her inability to recognize him throws him for a loop. He suddenly realizes that during the past ten months, while he's been away at college, she's just been here, working. "Slinging hash," his father might say.

"Get to work," Tribuno returns to bark, totally out of habit.

"But I'm waiting for you to bring me papers."

"Oh, that's right, never mind. Here's your W-4 Forms, a consent to be treated if you get injured at work, the Workman's Compensation Policy, and the Sexual Harassment Policy. Read and sign."

Woody signs without reading as Tribuno juggles a handful of video tapes. He drops the top one onto the break table along with a trifold pamphlet titled, *Hot, Hot, Hot*, which trains employees about the temperature of coffee and other hot beverages. "I'll be back with the video player," Tribuno grumbles.

At 10:00, the dishwasher with the wrinkled face and clothing, Marisimo, joins Woody at the table, eating a glazed muffin. He asks Woody what's on TV, then volunteers that because he's blind in one eye, he can't watch. He also volunteers that he's on a fixed income. Woody tells him the film is called, *Diner Amongst Friends*, but Marisimo points to his right eye where there appears to be a large, round, and bulbous cyst-like formation. The cheesy music in the video is annoying, perfect for a training video, which creates a surreal feel to the video's portrayal, one that stresses the importance of being courteous and friendly to everyone, no matter what the circumstances. Conclusively, customer-to-server conflict resolution in the film is resolved by the Grand Slams Team with an over-the-top amount of ass-kissing.

One of the busboys Woody saw earlier hustles by with a tub full of smelly dishes, covered in a one-inch thick sludge of swill, which sloshes, left to right, as he makes a sharp turn towards the dish area. The bile in Woody's stomach mirrors the motion of the liquid throwaways. The busboy is a large man with dark hair pushed slightly over his large forehead. "Bobby Maloney," he bellows as he sprints by, "Nice to meet you."

"Leave those there," an agitated Marisimo directs, pointing to the dish station counter. "Can't you see I'm on my break, you asshole?" he shouts at Maloney's taillights.

On the way back, Maloney mockingly hums the music of the training video and repeats the line, "*It may not be your way, but it's the Grand Slams way, and you always want to hit a Grand Slam with your customers*" verbatim. "Here it comes—the laugh. Here it is. Brace yourself for the laugh." Sure enough, the Grand Slams Team on the video lets out a boisterous group laugh, complete with additional chummy back slaps. All is right in the Grand Slams world.

Tribuno hears Maloney and Marisimo talking and enters the back area. "Maloney, get to work. Marisimo, get to work," he says rapid fire, then, "Geyser, there's someone outside to see you."

Woody pushes through the swinging doors and sees his mom at the counter. "Excuse me, sir, may I have some coffee, please?" she asks with a wink and a smile. "Just wanted to check in to see how my boy was doing on his first day," she adds at a volume not hushed enough for Woody's liking.

"Oh, fuck," Woody says under his breath, easily drowned out by Sugar introducing herself to Woody's mother and saying that she is her server. Woody is relieved, knowing that Sugar has saved his ass, and retreats thankfully back to the break area. This feeling is short lived, as

8

Sugar comes back rolling her eyes, taunting, "Oh, Woody, dear, I'd like some coffee, please," then to Maloney, "I just wanted to check in on my little boy… " After about the third go-around, his co-workers overhear the mocking and begin to notice what's going on. This is not a stretch on Woody's part, because Sugar always gets noticed. When the chuckling dies down, Woody fixates back on the video, cranking the volume, which is now lecturing new employees about proper restaurant etiquette.

Each Grand Slams employee who passes him now eithers says out loud a partial quote from his mother or gives a running commentary on his mother's current actions at the counter. *Mommy is ordering pie. Mommy is paying. Mommy has left a dollar tip. Mommy says to tell you she said bye-bye.* It feels like torture, but Woody tries to remind himself, it's all part of the work environment and all part of the bullshit he gets paid for. Just four more hours to go, he counts down, eager to be free to finally go home. He grits his teeth and mentally prepares himself for the no-nonsense lecture he intends on giving his mom.

3. Honor Thy Maura

"You know, I wouldn't worry too much about anyone who works here. We have a strange crew," Maura says to Woody. "Not like any other that I've worked with in my twenty plus years. Much less professional." She looks down at the training video Woody is watching. "These videos are good. The workers that stick around… what I mean… good workers are the ones that take pride in Grand Slams and stick around. It's the Grand Slams way. You getting this?" She takes a sip of orange juice from a large plastic tumbler.

Woody has his head down on the break table. "I'm on break. Check the time-card."

"You know, I know who you are. You're the kid that tried to run out on the check a few months back. You should be grateful you didn't get arrested."

"Run out on the check? I thought it was free. Isn't that the policy on someone's birthday?"

"You should be grateful that Grand Slams gives you another chance in life. It saved *my* life. You could have spent your birthday in jail and the day after in front of a judge."

"You know, I'm just here for my summer break. I go to school at UMass."

Sugar has stopped by, raking her bag for a cigarette. "Yes, big college man. We're all proud of you," she scoffs. "UMass. Great parties there. Bobby Maloney went there too." Woody doesn't recognize Maloney from campus, most likely because he went back to Grand Slams to work on the weekends. Sugar taps Woody on the top of his head and struts into the walk-in refrigerator to smoke, "I'm allowed… "

Maura raises her eyes at her. "I'll talk to Mr. Keating about it. Not that he'll do anything about it, but at least he'll say he will. Honestly, I don't understand why he is still here, while hard-working Tribuno is waiting in the wings, like a dog sitting loyal next to his master.

10

Sometimes, I wish I had taken over one of these franchises. Now *that* place would be amazing."

Tribuno strolls by. "Break's over Geyser," he says. "Did you learn anything?"

Woody pauses, shifting his gaze toward Maura. "Yes, I learned a lot about Mr. Keating."

"No, no, from the video."

Maura downs the rest of her juice, "He learned about how courteousness pays off, both for the company and for the employee."

"Good. Good, Maura. You'll have a successful career here," Tribuno says. "Now, Geyser, watch the next one till you can answer like Maura"

"I need to get back to my tables," Maura says. "It does pay off, remember that."

The gold-colored metal of Maura's twenty-year pin wasn't made from any precious metal of any innate value, so Maura only needed to polish it with whatever was in the cleaning bottle full of orange liquid. It wasn't the pin itself she valued, but rather what it represented, along with the number *20*, inserted inside a script *GS*. The number could have been written on a paper towel with a green crayon for all she cared, it represented change for her—how her life had changed and how working here saved that life. She remembered the day she was hired by Grand Slams. It was the same day she'd removed the cross she'd always worn around her neck.

In the early nineteen-fifties Maura, trapped in the ideals of "the fifties," had nowhere to go. Those values did not include someone like her, pregnant in her early twenties, living off the charity of her strict Catholic parents who were so uncomfortable with her life choices that they wanted her to disappear. The mortification of this alone caused them to struggle for breath, heavy-chested, wondering what to do with

11

their swelling and husbandless daughter. Disowning her was out of the question, but still the facts were, sinners and non-perfectionists from their belief system stick indecent thoughts about their daughter into their heads. If they were honest with themselves, they'd realize that women like Maura just weren't ready for life in general. It was a time in California when most young people were supposed to be free and easy. It wasn't that way for Maura.

After Bridget was born, Maura passed a "Help Wanted" sign posted on the window of a Homer's Donuts in Lakewood, a town of pronounced growth. At the interview, Maura was surprisingly impressed by the manager/owner Mike Homer, who would end up becoming the CEO of the entire Grand Slams franchise. She loved that the place was always open; in fact, it didn't even have a lock on the front door. There was something comforting about a place always welcoming those who needed it, that no one would ever worry about being turned away.

Douglas Aircraft Plant was nearby and there was always a steady stream of customers and money to be made. For a single mom, who relied on her parents to watch the baby, it allowed her the flexibility to work whenever she wanted and whenever the restaurant needed her. She even filled in, when Mike asked, as a Night Porter during overnight shifts. Even Homer had to admit that Maura was second, only to him, as the hardest worker he'd ever known.

Mike was self-made, a trait Maura appreciated greatly, as she yearned to make it on her own. Maura was still there when the name changed to Homer's Coffee Shop and, later, she was there when the name became Grand Slams Coffee Shop. This change was necessary as a nearby competing chain, Homer's Coffee Shop, was named after its owner, Homer Jones.

Maura worked relentlessly, saving every penny, as Grand Slams grew and franchised, each building looking virtually identical to the last. This presented the opportunity for Maura to relocate, as her young daughter Bridget was approaching school age, and Grand Slams was popping up in new locations all over the country. The chance to move on and no longer feel the shame and the guilt from her parents, which was as thick as the tan gravy ladled over Grand Slams powdered mashed potatoes. It all seemed logical, the Gold Rush in reverse: moving from California to make her way to the East Coast, with all the hope in the world. Besides, her daughter, she believed, would be better off being raised by her parents anyway.

Mike had hoped that one day a solid worker like Maura would become a manager or owner of a new franchise. However, it turned out that waitressing was good enough for Maura, mostly because she enjoyed the work and she made a lot of money. There was nothing in this world better for Maura than doing something she enjoyed.

4. Keating's Barter Economy

Based on an old method of exchange, used long before money was invented, the Super 8 always had a room available for Joe Keating. If Keating bartered items that were expendable, like Double Home Run breakfasts, he could get the things he wanted. It worked so well that sometimes he wished money had not been invented at all.

Jimmy Pudlow manages the Super 8 located no more than twenty feet from the back door of Grand Slams. Keating has no idea why the place is "super" or why it has the number eight attached to it, but that doesn't stop him from getting a room nearly every night. Each time he thinks of the same tired old joke about an ad campaign he might pitch: *The Super 8 is the perfect place to share a super eight-ball.*

Jimmy comes into Grand Slams every day Keating works, and when he gets sick of the free breakfasts, he comes for free lunch and dinner. The entire staff know Pudlow's a customer Keating serves, which suits them fine because Keating usually sits him in a section that's closed, or in Keating's "executive" table in Section 1. It's the table of utmost importance.

The Super 8 would buy into Keating's slogan, or into the fact that a customer like Keating can call and get a room for an hour, midday, for whatever reason he wanted. Jimmy obliges Keating with the room furthest away from the closest overnight guest. It's not that Keating would be loud; it's just that Jimmy knows most substance abusers tend to want their lives to be under cover from the general public.

Keating is alone tonight in Room 124, having struck out with his invitations, but he is too wiped-out to drive all the way home. Cocaine hangovers are the worst. Sugar was here last night, but all they did was talk, and talk, and talk. A few times when they had fooled around, Sugar always felt bad afterward, shamed and riddled with guilt. She finally confessed to him that she felt obligated to be physical with him because he'd paid for the room as well as the other things.

Keating snorts a line and takes a spin around the channels. He stops at *Scarface,* a movie he's seen before. Near the beginning of it, Al

14

Pacino, a drugged-out gangster, takes in Michelle Pfeiffer, who's the girlfriend of Robert Loggia. Keating can remember the actors, but keeping track of the names of the characters they play takes too much brain power. Pacino plays a power-hungry sleazeball, and Keating relates a lot more than he cares to admit, so he shuts off the TV and flips through the restaurant section of *The Yellow Pages* instead.

Sometimes Keating looks at the pictures and drawings of the restaurants he could be running, an activity he enjoys as much as the toothache he suffered through a few months ago. His mind wanders back to his graduation day at Endicott College, where he was the top of his Hospitality Administration class. Man, was his father proud. So, how did he fall into the grasping arms of Grand Slams? He thinks some more, with further regret, and rolls onto the opposite empty pillow and concludes that many times in his life he's made the best of bad situations. What he's doing now is not all that bad—a free bed anytime he needs it, a young woman, and enough drugs. Things are in control, right? He then questions the logic of all of this. Keating tosses and turns until 3 AM, but before finally drifting off to sleep, he dials Sugar's number too many times, leaving a series of increasingly desperate messages on her answering machine.

Keating wakes up late for shift. Where is he? What day is it? He hasn't been home in days. Who is opening today? Then he remembers. *I am. Shit, I am.* His panic is short-lived as he pauses to consider the schedule. Maura is there for the 6 AM shift, and she can handle anything. He trusts her more than Tribuno, anyway. Besides, Maura knows the combination to the safe, whereas Tribuno does not. *What else do I need to note?* New kid, the college boy, there on his first day, paired with Maloney. Sugar is on, but will pretend not to know him the way they really know each other. *What else? Can I go back to sleep?* Keating reaches into his shirt pocket for the triangle of paper he keeps there. He pours out some powder. *Sleep is a luxury.* He combs his thinning, sandy-colored hair, then pulls out his can of Lysol, giving his suit a couple of perfunctory sprays.

Forty-five minutes later, Keating saunters in like he's feeling like a hero, smiling strange and reptilian, shouting, "Okay, everybody, I'm here… Joe Keating is here." The black overlapping rings circling his eyes are as thick and dark as coffee-colored rings from a cup's liquid, absorbed on a white tablecloth (a nicety you'd never find at a place like Grand Slams.) The rest of his employees never think of him in the grandiose manner; rather, they view him as slithering in or perhaps sliming in. Keating is wearing the same powder-blue suit he wore during his last shift, two days ago. At least it smells of lemon freshness from the Lysol. Sunday is the busiest day at Grand Slams, and Keating is about to swim into a pot of coffee, his sandy mustache flavored by the coffee, cream and seven sugars.

Maura shoots him a smile, but Keating can tell she is stressed out, perhaps even angry. Sugar had called in late again this morning. Keating plays it cool, as he knows Maura, after it's all said and done, won't mind; she'll have picked up extra tables, making extra money. When she counts her tips at 3 PM, all will be well in Grand Slamville.

After his first pot of coffee, Keating brings his briefcase into the men's room. He yanks down the metal flap of the paper towel dispenser to see if Kayak Kenny has restocked product. He takes a towel and polishes the *GS* logo embossed in the rack's metal. He then walks into each stall. The toilet paper should have three rolls in each unit; when one is finished and the roll pulled out, a new one should drop down to replace it. In stall three, the handicapped unit, there is only one roll of toilet paper. Usually this is where he starts, stall three; being that it's meant for a wheelchair, it's big enough for him to settle in, to pull a mirror out of his briefcase, and to pour the powder out of the triangular piece of paper and snort it up. No need for him to carry any dollar bills, as Grand Slams supplies him the plastic straws.

His briefcase carries a cache of important sprucing items. There's a smaller sized Lysol spray can, which he again sprays his blue suit with, some wet naps to wipe down his plastic shoes, a bottle of Secret roll-on deodorant, which Sugar left behind, and a 16-ounce bottle of Listerine, which he sloshes a mouthful of before swallowing the shot for good measure. They don't sell beer or booze on Sundays in Massachusetts.

Kayak Kenny is in the dish room helping Marisimo. Together they do the work of half a man.

"There is only one roll in stall three," Keating says as he whirls past with a smile pasted onto his face.

"I did it," Kenny counters, pulling the curl of his hair, resting on his forehead, out straight. It looks like a cursive *G* or *S* hanging the way it does. "Look at the checklist."

"I don't care about the fucking checklist," Keating yells. "Some guy in a wheelchair will use the last square and there will be nothing left to wipe his ass with. Kenny, complaints from the handicapped are not the kind of shit we need around here."

Kenny looks confused, child-like, reaching back into the deepest parts of his brain, but not responding.

"Well?" Keating urges.

"I swear, I did it."

"I swear, you're a bit slow," Keating says sarcastically, waiting. "Well?"

"I might not be smart, but I'm a good worker," Kenny says, defending himself.

"You're a good worker, huh? Well, then, fix it!!"

He follows Kenny, past the supply room where Kenny grabs only one, rather than two, rolls of toilet paper, the white wrapper gleaming against the greenish-yellow skin of his hand. They then pass the break area, where Kenny pulls a piece of buttered toast off a plate and takes a bite.

"Did you put that on your time card?" Keating says, smiles, because he knows he has him.

17

"I will, I will," Kenny scowls, thinking *The nerve of this guy.*

Toast is not a free item, Keating thinks, *but even dumb people need to feel big enough to cut corners.*

"Hey, Joe?" Kenny asks.

"What? Call me Mr. Keating."

"Mr. Keating? When I save up and buy a kayak, do you think Sugar would like to go out with me? Then we could sit somewhere after and have a picnic. Do you think if I asked her, she would say yes? I would say, 'Hey, Sugar, would you like to go out with me in my kayak. You wouldn't even have to paddle.'" Kenny ponders the possibility, committed to his daydream. "I'd do all that for her. I'd paddle and we'd ride around in my kayak and I'd ask her if she liked me. I like her sunglasses. Do you think she'd say yes? Do you, Joe?"

"Hey, Kenny."

"Yes?"

"I think she would never do that. Now can you do me a big favor," Keating adds with a transparent sarcastic smile, "if you want to get paid, just shut the fuck up."

5. Sugar, The Insider vs. The Outsider

What people think of Sugar is not what Sugar thinks of herself. People think Sugar is gorgeous. Sugar is worthwhile. Sugar is social. Sugar is fun. Sugar is ditzy. Sugar has got it together. Sugar lives for the attention from men. Sugar is from the South. Sugar is a "cocaine whore." These are all false, except she was born in the South; but only lived there for less than a year. Sugar does not care what others think about her.

When Sugar pals around with her friend, the boss, Joe Keating, it's mostly out of convenience. By staying local to her job, Sugar does not have to drive the back roads for thirty minutes to her house, but the most important factor is, she likes drugs and she likes hotels. Even motels are a worthy stretch. Even hanging out with Joe is a worthy stretch, though others think she is a bad person, just trading companionship for his drugs.

Truth is, the hours and hours of conversation she has with Joe, except for the sexist cracks he makes about her smallish breasts or anything else he can think of, are fairly interesting. Joe, after a few lines, can be very optimistic. He tells her what can be, rather than what could have been, such as college in her future. She tells him that she enjoys his optimism and that he is one of the few people who believes in her. Sugar is careful to build him up because an all-nighter, when Joe feels sorry for himself, is pure torture. What people do not see is that Joe, when he is happy, is a gentleman, and Joe, thank God, would never put a move on her when she doesn't want it. It's all on her, and when anything happens it's kind of a pay-back for the money and the attention Joe gives to her. She feels bad, immediately after, and even worse the next morning when she needs a full two hours to get her shit together before she can face her co-workers. It is time needed to place her head in a space that she can convey proper swagger and attitude, the kind that people are used to out of her. It's the only way she can survive. Without the "I don't give a crap what you or anyone thinks" attitude, Sugar would probably stay in her bed, depressed, for weeks.

19

By and by, Sugar is intelligent. That's what she reminds herself when her old classmate Woody is hired. Keating calls him "college boy," which he uses as a deriding label, but it also cuts Sugar deep into her soul. Sugar likes to disparage Woody by calling him "Woodrow" instead.

She still wants to continue her education at some point, if only she can get out of this cycle of work, party, get paid, spend money, and so on. She never gets ahead, but by getting ahead, it would only mean working to save money and sleeping. Eating is optional. She has problems with that. Her co-workers joke that no one has ever seen her eat at the restaurant.

Last night she tried to change the pattern. She went home to her small apartment in Billerica where she lives by herself. No one questions the circumstances that caused her to live on her own as an eighteen year old. Everything has led her here.

Today she came to work late because she had to condition and blow-dry her hair. Her hair is always softer when she washes it at home because the motel shampoo is of extremely poor quality. Lately, her hair has felt brittle and harsh; a different kind of brittle and harsh than the looks Maura gives her when she walks in at 7:30. Sugar tells her friends it's salty old Maura's "shaming look." Even coming from home this morning she receives this guilt-by-association stare from her connection with the boss who she knows had a rough night next door. He'd left three sad and lonely messages from the Super 8 on her answering machine. It had pissed her off. "Deal with it," she'd spoken back to the first recording of his pathetic voice, without fully listening to the last two messages. Now Maura's eyes are hawking her, and this morning Sugar barely can tolerate it. She'd rather deal with Maloney sexualizing her with his flirting, and shooting down Woodrow before he can start with something as simple as a "Good Morning." To deflate a guy like Woody, it would only take one single bitchy look. She didn't even need to put out the energy it takes to straight-up ignore him, as that simple look which she does so well, with her eyes, works exactly like her hand brushing off Woodrow like a fly from her arm.

Sugar hears Maloney and Woody's voices on their way back to the kitchen area, stops, and softens briefly, thinking maybe she is being a bit harsh; Woody is harmless, perhaps too nice...he'd never hurt a fly or brush her off in any way.

As Maloney and Woody hustle, two hands on bus tubs, kicking open the swinging doors to the back, their dishes clamor and rearrange themselves from horizontal to vertical within the plastic tubs.

"Hey, sexy," Maloney says, while scurrying by. Sugar and Woody share a look then, as if synchronized, roll their eyes with tight-lipped pressed grins, towards one another.

6. Woody Geyser And The Members of Grand Slams Country Club

Often when the days hit 90 or 100 degrees there's a pool party after the 3-11 PM shift at the Country Club, a.k.a. the pool area at the Super 8. This is a club that only accepts awkward guys as members. It's not much of a party—a few six packs shared by the members of the dish staff, maybe a waiter and Gus, the young cook who only works two shifts a week. Jimmy from the Super 8 usually discovers the party around midnight. In the past he's tried calling Keating's room if he's there, to tell him to put a lid on it and break it up. This produces no result except the usual one: the party ends when it normally would anyway, fizzling out at 1 or 2 AM. The next day Keating will give the boys his usual sarcastic head tilt and a predictable jab, "Did you have fun boys? Any of you guys sneak a kiss? Because I can get you a room through my connection, you sweet bastards."

Woody doesn't know what to do when the boss makes gay jokes. His cousin is gay, but Woody knows he'd only stick up for him if his cousin was standing right there; and even then, there was no guarantee.

Woody also doesn't know why he goes to the pool parties. Parties make him uncomfortable. Sure, last night there were extra supplies: a case of Miller Beer, a boom box and some weed, but Woody is free to drink alone and listen to music at his parents' house, his place of residence for the next three months. He smokes pot on occasion, not very often, but last night he gave Bobby Maloney ten bucks for three joints because his parents are always asleep when he returns from the night shift and he is bored with nothing to do—smoking pot seems like a good idea.

Kayak Kenny shows up poolside after he finishes work, twenty minutes later than Woody and Maloney. It takes him awhile to get the end of the shift necessities completed, but he usually catches up to the others' progress at the Country Club when it comes to drinking. Kenny can down three quickly in about a half hour. The bright light inside the pool shines through the highly-chlorinated water, casting a blue hue over Kayak Kenny, making his coloring appear less yellowy green, or more precisely, as blue as everyone else.

"Hey, I asked some of the waitresses to come over," he grins. "But, they all said they had forgotten their bathing suits. Some said they had plans."

"Ugh, don't mention that you're hanging out with us," Gus says. "I don't want that association."

Maloney snorts out a laugh. "Well since it was you who asked, of course, they forgot their suits, and their plans were to do anything else but come back here."

"Huh?" Kenny said. "They smiled when I asked. It means they wanted to. Do you think they like me?"

"I'm sure it means that," Maloney adds, feeling a little guilty now.

Woody is sitting with his feet trolling in the water, admiring how the lights create blueish, yellow and green swirls beneath the surface. It's the only light besides the overhead ones in the parking lot, cutting into the night. Jimmy shuts the deck lights off at 10 PM.

When Woody was in junior high, the night he took all those pills, the lights in his head, when he lost consciousness, looked almost exactly like what he's looking at now. Then he woke up at a hospital. That was the end of the story, no questions asked by his parents, no follow up therapy, just be left with your own thoughts and go back to school on Monday, please.

"Ah, they don't like you, as in *like you*, Kenny. They're just being nice. Sometimes women can act nice just to shut guys, like you, up," Woody reflects.

"Guys like me?" Kenny's voice has an added incredulous trill to it. "What the fuck do you mean? You've only been here a week and I've worked here for three years. What the fuck do you know?"

"Chill, Kenny. They do it to me too, and you admitted yourself, that you might not be too smart… but you're a good worker."

Maloney is sprawled out across a deck chair with sunglasses on, pretending it's daytime, the glasses splitting his face and forehead in near equal parts. "Pass the sunscreen Kenny."

Kenny starts walking around the deck to look. "I can't find any, Bobby."

The boys let out a laugh and Gus says, "Keep looking, Kenny. You don't want Bobby to get sunburn." Then Gus turns to Woody, to needle him: "What about it, Woodrow? You sleeping with anyone?"

The hairs on the back of Woody's neck begin to stand up, as if his instincts are kicking in, preparing him for a fight. "It's Woody," he says, aggravated. "No one calls me Woodrow."

"Relax," Gus says. "I'm just busting your chops because I've heard Sugar call you that. I think she's calling you that for a reason."

"Yeah, it's because she's busting my chops too. It's her way of saying, *I knew you when, and when I knew you, you were this way, so please remember what the pecking order is*. Girls like Sugar want to keep the power structure from high school exactly the way it was at the time of their senior year, when they were on top of the social ladder."

"No," Maloney says. "It's not about being on top and keeping the pecking order. I think it's about preventing you from thinking you're better than her, I mean, going to college like you are, and all. Last winter, over break, I used to talk to her all the time. She felt left behind. All her friends were in school and it made her feel bad about herself."

"Did you guys smooch?" Kenny asks.

"No, retard. We're friends. I see how others would find her pretty, but she's not my type. I'm not fond of that All-American, girl next door kind of look, but perhaps with bigger breasts... "

"Yes, you, peering through the blinds into the bedroom window of the girl next door, you should know about her breasts," Gus said, ending his own joke with what he usually ends his own jokes with—a manic laugh.

"She was, umm," Woody stops in mid-sentence, as they all stopped to listen to him. "She was the All-American type of girl. She had everything going for her. She partied too hard and by the end of high school, she hadn't applied to any schools except the ones she was reaching high for... the Harvards, Yales, and Dartmouths. She might have gotten into those schools if she hadn't fucked up, but after her senior year grades she had no chance. Of course she has regrets."

The sound of the pool filter kicking in replaces the sudden reflective silence. Kenny belches. "Anyone want to smoke another joint?" Maloney asks. Gus and Kayak Kenny walk over, but Woody stays in the deck chair. "I'm good," he says.

Woody's parents are asleep. He still has two joints left but he's too stoned to smoke anymore. He hits the bed at 5 AM, too paranoid, too self-attacking to sleep. In ten hours he has to go into work again and the switching from the early mornings to mid-afternoons is tiring him out.

Maybe if he gets himself off he can sleep. He has a small window of opportunity, because his parents will be awake soon and even though he's two floors up, the kitchen coming to life in the morning is a sound he has a difficult time blocking out. He starts having thoughts about Sugar, but not the current Sugar, his co-worker; he thinks about the one he knew in high school, the wholesome version he talked about tonight. *Yes, I am a douchebag,* he thinks, pretending to know all about her tonight at the pool—and to act more of an expert on women, in general.

In high school Woody had been an obvious virgin, ashamed of his thin body, which failed to reach puberty until much later than the rest of the boys in his class. Showering after gym was a nightmare, so he never did it, enduring the rest of the day covered in dried salty dodgeball sweat. He carried this awkwardness into college, and even when he had the chance to close the deal and have sex, he didn't know what to do, so any chance he had to gain experience was missed. Most

25

of the girls in his dorm figured it out and when Cyndi, who had slept with his roommate the week before, asked him to come over to her room across campus the night before Christmas break for a drink, he didn't think much of it.

She had a gift for him, which he unwrapped while sitting on her bed. In a small box was a cocktail glass, with a heart and #1 printed on the side of it. She kept filling it with rum and cokes, getting him drunk, while sitting closer and closer to him, until her legs were slung over his lap, and the back of her hand was resting directly on his crotch. Her other hand was tugging at his short, dark, spiked hair. She re-gripped and pushed the back of his head; pushing him in firmly, with eyes closed for a kiss.

After the sex was over, he went to the bathroom to pee, still erect and feeling such relief that he almost busted into laughter, which once started, he would have a difficult time being able to stop. Instead he held it, and went back for four more times with her, lasting until dawn. By the time morning came, he knew he wouldn't have a reason to ever see her again.

Woody slides his hand under the waistband of his pajamas, but nothing happens. He thinks of Sugar's mouth and something begins to stir, but quickly dissipates, like a not-quite-dead car battery. He tries again, thinking more and more graphically about Sugar, her petite breasts and small ass, but instead all he can think about is the need to hurry and how floppy he is. He hears the frying pan bang against a sauce pan as it is pulled out of the cabinet for the purpose of scrambling his father's eggs, and the image of Sugar disappears the way a match is extinguished when dropped into a cup of water.

Woody's parents' house is a nice, white-painted four bedroom house with black shutters. It has a large wraparound porch, in a neighborhood in Lexington with many other white houses with black shutters. Woody's dad, up at 6 AM for work, moves Woody's empty beer-can-filled vehicle to the street nearly every morning. The bottom of Woody's vehicle has started to rot out, so his father is never sure what is making the rattle sound, the car or the cans. Woody's mom debates on what she'll say to her son when he wakes up. Should it be, "We know what you are up to"? or "I'm worried about you"? Perhaps it's all because of the influence of his co-workers. She could casually mention that she doesn't like the people he's been hanging out with.

He's always been a good kid, drinking "normally" with friends, never experimenting with drugs; but then there was that strange incident at age fourteen, which she reckoned was just a cry for help. A car full of beer cans is concerning to her. What if he gets pulled over with all the empties in there?

After cleaning the kitchen and wiping down the table, Woody's mom sits with a cup of coffee, waiting. Woody is usually up after 10 AM, unless he has the early shift. When she hears the steps creaking, she straightens, preparing herself for the uncomfortable interaction. Before Woody can even say "good morning," and before he gets into the kitchen, she blurts out, "Don't think we don't know what you are doing, because we do."

7. Momma Maura Has Dreams

Waking up at 5 AM has Maura in bed by 9 every night. It's all about work ethic and doing the right thing. It's about getting enough sleep. The success that she is, a waitressing powerhouse, is not about partying, staying out late or dating. Not that someone her age is doing that anyway, but it's what she has been doing ever since she started waitressing.

Sigmund Freud's theory about sleep and dreams was that your dreams are an expression of what you're repressing during the time you are awake, while Carl Jung believed that dreams provide messages about "lost" or "neglected" parts of us that need to be reintegrated. Many dreams simply come from a preoccupation with the day's activities. Maura dreams more than the average person.

Last night she dreamt about Mike, her first boss, returning as the new CEO of the entire Grand Slams franchise. It wasn't a dream about Mike, per se, though she's had some very personal ones about him that she would be too shy to admit; no, it was more a motivational speech, spoken directly to Maura, in a supervision meeting:

Maura, even though you never picked up a franchise or region here at Grand Slams, it is up to you to promote the integrity and pride of the Grand Slams Corporation. Think of the two Bobs, out of uniform... oh, not in that way, but in this one: Even when they are off duty they think, act, and promote the corporation with the sense of pride and respect that I always attempted to emulate. They know that it's not just about profits, but instead, it's a way of life. It's like you, Maura— without Grand Slams you may not have had the wonderful opportunity to turn your life around and do what was best for your child. You thought of the Grand Slams way each and every time you awoke to a new day and proudly zipped up your freshly pressed, brown uniform. Someone like Keating simply isn't who we want the company to look like. We do not barter Double Home Run Breakfasts in exchange for motel rooms and narcotics. We don't show up for work with our mind in

28

the gutter, thinking of which one of our employees we are most likely to pursue sexually. Likewise, the kids on college break are not company people. They are too willing to trade minimum wage work for books, beer, and other frolicsome dorm-life expenses. Employees like Sugar are clearly in transition. They are still looking for themselves, what they will truly "be" in life. Chances are, when they find it, it won't be here, nestled soundly beneath our beloved red and yellow Grand Slams sign. The "Kennys" of the world are only able to labor in these types of jobs. They'll be with us much longer than the rest, but only with the simple purpose of cleaning. They will never learn to love, to live the Grand Slams way, and they must be brought down.

Maura, you are a power of example. You need to continue to make the customers think seriously about their breakfast and brunch choices, inspiring within them the desire to pick Grand Slams every time. It's up to you to take the employees, lateral to you in your job, under your wing. You must be a one-person pep rally, but do so in a reserved and prideful way, that quietly promotes others to follow your lead. Maura, you are the one I've chosen, same as out in California, to continue the mission of Grand Slams family restaurant.

"God," Maura mutters, and rolls out of her shallow sleep. She immediately jumps into the present and hopes Mr. Tribuno will be there with her to open the shift and make all the coffee. She knows Tribuno works hard and he's been someone that Mike Homer would have been proud of.

Barely awake, Maura falls through that dark fissure in her memory once again. She suddenly remembers a different scene almost twenty years ago, a scene from California, where Mike was her hero and her rescuer. It was after a shift when Mike walked in on his co-manager pressing her body against the wall, kissing her, while she, pinned, was unable to move or push him off to get away. Mike shouldn't have been there at the overnight shift, but he had forgotten something and had come back. When he yelled at his co-manager, the piece of slime

29

stopped what he was doing. Maura felt her skirt slide back down in position as her balled hand swing wide and hard. She felt almost nothing when her fist made contact with her attacker's sweaty face. The contact was strong but sounded like a faint echo, not louder than the buzzing in her own head which brought the scene completely to a halt. Mike told him to leave and never come back.

Maura rolls onto her back, wishes she could get better sleep for once. She wishes she never had to think of her work history and the importance it has in her life and the various turning points. The big one was in Colorado, the first time she began slowly crossing the country to the east coast. She reaches to the nightstand and begins to polish her pin with a tissue, suddenly remembering the day that Mike had died seven years ago and how she couldn't take time off to attend his funeral.

Maura doesn't understand why people conduct themselves in ways that they will regret later. She thinks, *Sugar doesn't know what she's doing with her life. Keating knows what he's doing and he doesn't care. The college boys, Geyser and Maloney, care what they are doing, but really don't know what they're doing. Worst of all are people like Kayak Kenny, who doesn't know where he is in the Universe and may never, ever. Why do they mess up, or set themselves up to be messed up?*

Maura doesn't know, because she grew up fast, but her daughter has grown up fast as well, without her. She tried to establish a relationship after Bridget's trip to rehab. Bridget ended up there very quickly, and Maura still can't get emotionally invested to any of that.

Maura works the early shift most every morning, and follows a set Grand Slams procedure. The only time it all gets done correctly, using the proper time and the proper precautions, is when Tribuno is working with her. On the mornings Keating strolls in an hour to an hour and a half late, looking like hell, smelling like stale cigarettes, he says such things as, "Yeah, I see everything has taken care of itself."

Maura finds her own high work ethic is more comparable to her successful customers than to her co-workers. It's always been that way, as Maura is always trying harder to do well, to be the most professional, and to show that when you are given lemons, you might as well make lemonade.

One of them, a return customer sitting alone, is an Egyptian man named Sayid. He is in his mid-twenties, and orders, coincidently, his usual lemonade this morning. Maura has waited on him enough times to know his name, where he works, and what he's interested in, because Sayid, open from the very first time he sat in Maura's section, also revealed that he is single.

Sayid works at the Air-Force base down the street. He shows Maura his base ID every time to get the 20% off his Double Home Run Breakfast, the name making no sense to Sayid for a different reason than it makes no sense to everyone else. For Sayid, it's a language issue rather than the poor baseball terminology. Every time Maura looks at the ID she thinks how handsome he is. When he's done eating he jumps into a black BMW and pulls away; a blur through the heat rising off the parking lot. He looks to be a good catch—handsome, well-off, successful, and certainly not a screw-up.

Once Maura teased him, musing aloud, if only she were 35 years younger, to which Sayid blushed strongly, visibly coloring his bronze complexion. For the rest of the breakfast, he appeared to be unable to say another word. On the following visit, he asked if she knew any women that he could be set up with. Maura told him that there were plenty of them who came in all the time, but perhaps she might know one or two that worked at Grand Slams. Sayid, shrugged. "No, seriously," he'd said. "Do you know anyone?"

Today Maura seats him in Sugar's section so she can be the one to bring him his lemonade. Sayid can't bring himself to introduce himself to the pretty waitress. He doesn't even ask for the 20% off his Double Home Run Breakfast. He does say something which makes Sugar take a step backwards, and her eyes bulge into a large, rounder form: "Can I see you again?"

Sugar's actions are cautious; the question is almost creepy, but then, suddenly realizing that it may be a cultural difference, she bursts out laughing. "I didn't realize we were on a date," she jokes.

Sayid's face turns as red as it had when Maura complimented him a few days ago. His mouth moves, but no words come out.

"I work mornings some of the time, but mostly, I work nights—never the overnight shift. Come in any time I'm on."

Sayid finds the invitation to be quite forward. He's not used to girls coming on so strongly, because in his country they hardly say anything—they just fall into their roles. He doesn't know what to do about any of this, but feels both smitten and intrigued. "Yes, I will try to come in again, so I can see you. Perhaps that is what I'll do."

Maura catches his eye from across the dining room and gives him a big old "OK" sign.

8. Kayak Kenny

Without realizing it himself, Kenny is easily daunted. The fiber of his character is naïve, almost childlike. Those who get to know him find him harmless, but those who do not often misconstrue him as creepy.

Kayak Kenny was hit in the head with a canoe oar by his father, causing a head injury which forced the schools to hold him back in third grade for two extra years; then reluctantly they advanced him every year after. As a seven year old, before the accident, he'd loved going to the beach and watching boats. Now he watches *Gilligan's Island* reruns but doesn't understand the most basic of gags that the show promotes. His mother yells at him for being so stupid.

Residents of The Commonwealth of Massachusetts have a funny way of distancing themselves from each other. Folks who live in New England notice this when they leave the area; on vacation they think how other people generally seem friendlier and warmer. Kayak Kenny also does not understand the social nuances of the Massachusetts residents or recognize why they act the way they do. Not being able to understand this is not Kenny's fault. Kayak Kenny hears Maura talk about the people here all the time, because Maura lived outside of Massachusetts for many years. Kayak Kenny thinks people should be nice and that everyone is trying to be nice, at all times. Kenny doesn't believe that people aren't nice. He interprets people as "laughing with him" not "laughing at him." For him, simple is a good way to be and a simple smile or a hello is misinterpreted by Kayak Kenny as a show of interest for friendship, or as in the case of the female, an interest in a relationship with him.

Kenny thinks that if he saves up and buys a kayak, women will want to date him. It's innocent enough: a trip out on the water, and a picnic. They would never want a thirty year old who washes dishes and sometimes buses the tables at a Grand Slams, but a man with a kayak is a different story.

Kenny often gets tricked into washing the dishes when he should have a turn working up front as a busboy. Maloney and Geyser always tell him that it's their turn, not Kenny's, and cite dates and times they recently had to wash the dishes. Truth is, it's never Kenny's turn to work up front, unless the old and slow Marisimo is on with him, but Keating and Tribuno never pair the two of them up on the same shift. Together they are so slow at their jobs that they can't keep up and the restaurant runs out of dishes, silverware, coffee cups, and water glasses. Kenny often starts his dishwashing shift pissed off, because even though he is a bit slow, he's fully aware that the closed-in dish station is the worst place to be in the entire restaurant. There are racks on his left stacked high for the dirty glasses to be placed into, and a massive, two-foot in diameter garbage disposal in front that looks like a giant serving bowl of swill. This monster is where everything uneaten gets thrown and ground up, washed down the drain. Kenny often forgets to run the disposal, which creates a river of reddish-brown stank that runs over the counter and through his work area. The color scheme is surreal and depressing; the red-brown of the dirty byproduct along with the green-yellow of Kenny's skin, gives the appearance of a cheap color television set about to quit working.

Keating passes and with an upward sarcastic nod and smile, notes the flooded area and says, "I think you need a kayak for back there." Kenny realizes that Keating is the only person laughing *at him* or at least the only one transparent enough that Kenny understands what is happening. Most of the time, near the dish area, people are laughing at or placing demands on the dishwasher—any dishwasher. It's a natural consequence. None of that matters to Kenny. His only focus is to get his paycheck, save up a little each time for his kayak—a red one, or perhaps blue. A blue-eyed girl would look good in kayaks of that color, but Kenny seeing the complete image in his head, of him, a girl, and a kayak, is unable to understand why.

9. Keating and The Two Bobs

Joe Keating sits at a table with Dino Tribuno and two humpty-dumpty gentlemen, both named Bob and both wearing tan shirts and matching ties with the Grand Slams logo scripted about a million times on the color-coordinated fabric. Unfortunately, that is the only thing on Keating's mind: how ugly those ties are. His is a blue Brooks Brothers, given to him on a long-lost birthday by a long-lost fiancée, which he needs to at some point get dry cleaned, as there is a series of very small grease spots on it. At one point Jimmy said that he could take it down to Super 8's laundry, but the last time that was offered the Haitians, as Keating called them, who worked there didn't know what to do with a silk tie and it was ruined. If this made Keating a racist, then he was a racist in the first degree.

Keating often thinks in this way. When he is overtired he'll say those thoughts out loud; for example, the people working at the Super 8, who he refers to derogatorily as "the Haitians" also work shifts at Grand Slams, filling in when needed as night porters. Keating refuses to learn their names and acts as if their names confuse him, but they are not that difficult: Mahalia, Manouchka, and Martine, who he once called Marty (which drew a blank stare.)

Bob is a name that he can remember, which is fine when he is presented with both of the Bobs, in Section 1, shoveling in their fried eggs and hash browns at the manager's meeting. The dirty-blond Bob is important to the chain as he oversees six Grand Slams in the New England Region. He has traveled two hours to be here. He's all business, and Keating knows he is the wheel that needs greasing.

The other Bob, Bob Boolay, has jet-black dyed hair and makes better jokes than Keating, but then again, the bar is set pretty low. Dyed-hair Bob Boolay oversees a few very well-run stores in Holyoke and Chicopee Falls, but his main location is in Chicopee. The other day, when Geyser slipped and fell on the wet mopped floor behind the counter, Keating told him if he wasn't careful he'd transfer him to Chicopee Falls. Then he laughed at his own joke.

35

"Hey, Sugar," Keating calls across the restaurant. "Bring us some more coffee over here."

Sugar slides in with a smile and two bulbous coffee pots, one with a brown collar for caffeinated and the other, orange topped, for decaf. Keating and the bosses take the caffeinated, while Dino requests the orange one, saying, "My wife says I keep her up all night."

Dyed-hair Bob cracks, "She'd rather not have to keep you up all night."

Sugar fakes a chuckle, "Good one, Mr. Boolay."

"Call me, Bob."

"Good one, Bob," she says before she hurries off.

"Oh, that Sugar," Dyed-hair Bob cackles. "I'd like some Sugar with my coffee."

"Is that actually her name?" Blond Bob asks. "I was about to say something about nicknames on nametags, but if that's her legal name, I guess GS Corp has nothing to say about it."

"Right," Keating says.

"This is what I'm getting at, Keating. We need to make sure Bedford, #509 is run by the book. We need to, as the company says, *Bring the Pride.* Our accountants are at wits end about some of the stuff going on at this store." Blond Bob pushes his coffee cup forward, sloshing a little over the lip of the cup, making a small brown puddle on the table.

"Geyser!" Keating shouts. "Come get this." Keating notices Kayak Kenny is standing much closer to them, but certainly not to be considered helping out with the Bobs here.

"Geyser, clean up the coffee geyser," Dyed-hair Bob jokes. Keating decides to laugh, but the other Bob doesn't, so Keating quickly silences himself.

Woody jogs in from the other end of the restaurant with a Handi-Wipe to absorb the mess. "He's right there!" Keating compliments, yet noticing that Blond Bob does not look happy, Keating scolds him, "Now, slow down! We don't need a Workman's Comp."

"Keating," Blond Bob says, peering over a quarterly report. "This free coffee you bring us is great, but you should account for it some way, just like the occasional free meal you might give out as a perk, or even a chef error that an employee eats. It seems like the Bedford store has a huge overall produce to profit loss margin in this area. Now, I'm not accusing anyone of anything, but something needs to be cleaned up. We have the ability to tabulate each of our portion sized meats and frozen foods and the amount of eggs used, per a computer program which calculates amounts and orders. All I have to say is that your store is one of the worst in the state. It's just one of the points I wanted to talk about."

Tribuno rubs and pushes down his mustache with the inside of his thumb and glances over to Keating. Jimmy from the Super 8 has entered the restaurant. He also looks over at Keating, who sternly nods, indicating for him to keep his distance. Jimmy approaches the table anyway, sweaty, quick and nervous. He's been using the same top-flight cocaine he sells to Keating.

"Joe, we need to talk about the room."

"Not now, Jimmy!"

"Well, there is a balance."

"Jimmy, I'm in a meeting."

"Okay, I'll just have my breakfast. Can we talk after breakfast?"

"Not now, Jimmy! Dammit, not now!"

The two Bobs freeze over their reports, not that they know what's going on, but the easily-perceived slime running off of Jimmy has left them feeling uncomfortable. Blond Bob grips the papers and dyed-hair Bob doesn't have a joke up his sleeve.

"Some folks won't ever listen," Keating says, rubbing over the spots on the front of his tie, before adding, "Welcome to the restaurant business." Both Bobs shuffle the reports around in their hands, as Keating's humor has gone flat on his critical audience. This is not going well.

"Get a new suit, Keating," Blond Bob says. He reaches into his briefcase and pulls out the same necktie he and Dyed-haired Bob have on. "Wear it tomorrow. Make everything you wear look like a fresh start."

10. Sugar On A Real Date

Sugar swears she can hear her phone at home constantly all the way from the downtown Boston restaurant she and Sayid are dining at. She'll return in a few hours and hear all the messages, the full range of emotions from Joe Keating: sad, upset, jealous, and then, out of the blue, upbeat. She'll roll her eyes as she half listens to the estimated ten voicemail messages. She doesn't realize she is making a sour face at the table until Sayid asks, "Don't you like that?"

"No, I'd rather not have a phone at all," Sugar replies, pushing her baked stuffed artichoke hearts around on her appetizer plate, appetite suddenly gone.

"No, I meant don't you like what you're eating?"

"It beats a Double Home Run, anytime, but I'm not really hungry."

Sugar's suppressed appetite is from knowing that Joe is probably doing a slow burn at the Super 8, and knowing that there'll be the fallout of many uncomfortable shifts at her job. She mashes one of the hearts flat against her plate, making the food look suddenly smaller.

"I have saved a picture that I took at the restaurant while you were working," Sayid says, pulling out his wallet and flipping it open, then closing it nervously, several times in succession. "Look." Sayid shows her a photo from the wallet of Sugar in her waitress uniform.

"Please remove that from your wallet," Sugar says.

"You don't approve?"

"Well, it's kind of soon, certainly it's too soon to have a picture of me. This is the first time we've been out!"

Sayid stutters out an apology and it seems a bit disingenuous to Sugar. "I'll throw it away," he says sadly. "I just want you to know that I'm interested in you in such a way, I can see us getting married, as it's God's will that we do."

Sugar laughs at the absurdity. "Can we talk about it? I mean, not now, but perhaps down the line. We haven't even kissed yet!"

"That would be lustful and sinful. The bible says we can do it all, as long as we are married, or at least planning to. I'm not against the planning of it."

Sugar files this under cultural differences and chooses to be kind rather than challenging toward him. "We'll see," she says.

After dinner, Sayid walks Sugar to his car and unlocks the passenger side door for her. Pulling the key out of the lock, he takes the free hand and wraps his arms halfway around her back. Then, with a quick, smooth movement, he pulls her in and plants a firm kiss on her lips. Although she is surprised by his action, her first reaction is the feeling that he is a pretty good kisser and has a little more experience in that department than he has led on. Her second reaction is that he may be kind of normal after all. He kisses her again, then a third and a fourth time. Sugar thinks of disengaging from him in order to catch her breath, but Sayid does so first. Unlocking his lips from hers, he immediately hangs his head and stammers, "I'm so sorry. I feel terrible and bad. I feel I've done something shameful and I've shamed you. I didn't mean to do that…"

Sugar takes her finger and brings it up to his lips to silence him. "But didn't we both want to do that?" she says with confusion, knowing that she'll need some time to fully process this.

11. Geyser: The Parking Lot is a Beautiful Place

No one is interested in the Super 8 Country Club tonight, so Woody and Maloney hang out in the back parking lot in Woody's Toyota Corolla, drinking a twelve pack, listening to the radio. Woody starts the engine every thirty minutes or so, to make sure the battery still has charge. What if it didn't? Maloney would just give him a jump, but the starting, checking, and testing is more about Woody's nervousness than anything else. His mother makes him nervous.

Woody mimics his mother's voice in his head, then imitates it out loud to Bobby Maloney. *"Damn, he's always been a good kid, drinking 'normally' with friends, never experimenting with drugs."*

"Describe normal?" Maloney says, "because where I grew up, drinking in the woods with a big bonfire is pretty normal...out of sight, out of mind, that sort of thing. But most of those kids will stay in that town and die in that town. I'm glad my parents moved here. How about you? How did you start drinking?"

"Mostly stole from my parent's liquor cabinet. They didn't drink hard liquor. They had no idea what was missing. And I didn't have any idea what I was drinking. Kahlua, Tanqueray, Frangelico. Hell, my dad was a beer drinker and that's it."

"Beer. That's what my parents drank and it's what they gave me as a kid," Maloney says. "They didn't make a big deal out of it, as long as I didn't take drugs, which of course now I do, but just a little."

"Me too. Just a little, but only if they're available." Woody rubs the back of his arm which feels gritty from working in the dish room hours earlier.

"Keating... "

"Shit!" Woody says. "Is he coming?"

"No, no, no. He's not out here, but they're available through him."

"He looks like shit lately."

"He's broken hearted."

41

"He's a druggie and he looks bad," Geyser counters, not putting two and two together.

"And he's broken hearted. Sugar is seeing that Egyptian."

"Keating?"

"Damn," Maloney says. "Are you the only person that doesn't know this? Keating and Sugar go to the Super 8 together. Sugar says that they only party over there, but there's a lot of coke and it's a motel, so I'm sure they might be doing other things."

"She's with him? I fucking doubt it," Woody says, turning out of the lot and onto Bedford Street, which is void of heavy traffic at this time of night. "There's no way she'd be with him."

"Good drugs. That's the reason. The Super 8 manager is a dealer."

"Maybe she's just using him for that?"

"Maybe. She's looking a little rough these days, but I think it's more than that. There's something not so good going on lately. Their vibe at work seems way off even if she's not that serious about that Egyptian. I overheard her talking to the other waitresses about that, but I think she's just making Keating stew a bit. Not that she likes either of them all that much."

"But she smiles at him," Woody says, now mimicking Kayak Kenny.

"That means she likes him." Maloney watches as the back door of the restaurant swings open and almost on cue, Kayak Kenny appears, pushing out a large gray trash bucket. "I might be stupid, but I'm a good worker," Maloney cracks, which makes them laugh even harder.

"I'm glad we hang," Woody says, hanging on the hard "g" too long.

"I can't believe I never saw you at UMass."

"Probably because I was working here every weekend."

When a BMW pulls into the lot with Sugar exiting from it, Woody tries but cannot see Sayid behind the tinted windshield. Woody turns the car on again, this time to drive away and avoid any interaction.

42

"That was certainly not Keating," Maloney says.

A little drunk, Woody drives slowly, focusing on the lit road visible over the front fender of his Corolla. "You know, Sugar used to be a pretty hot number. Well, obviously, she's still attractive enough to date now. I mean she's pretty, she just needs some rest. What do you know about that guy?"

"He might be a customer or someone from the Air Base. That's pretty much how she would meet someone."

"Could be an old friend."

"Picking her up at the restaurant when she wasn't scheduled tonight, I doubt it."

"Hmm," Woody adds to avoid a pause.

"I'll have to have a little talk with her tomorrow," Maloney says.

The bed at his parent's house was waiting at 2AM. When he twisted into it, the spin started loose and fast, then it tightened, causing Woody's stomach to leap, then to shudder. If he rides it out, he'll know that he'll be asleep soon, before he has to do something serious, like vomit, which requires a long walk down the steep attic stairs, to the second floor bathroom where he definitely would be heard by his mother and father. The cold tile floor would be perfect for his alcohol-fevered body to relate to—an iceberg floating down a water oasis in the desert.

He began drinking more at college. They didn't have bonfires there, just room parties with lackadaisical RAs who let them do whatever they wanted. Guys in his hall used to put wet towels under the doors and get high, thinking it would mute the smell. It was what college was all about: re-inventing yourself to cover up various bad smells in your life. It was what Woody wanted college to be about. He knew that it was the perfect time to become a new person, but what had he actually become? Whatever it was, he was growing further

43

removed and dissatisfied with himself. Even holding a summer job at a chain restaurant seemed to disappoint him, nothing he'd confess when the question of *Where are you working this summer?* came up. At Grand Slams no one questioned why he was there, because everyone was there. The elephant in the room was that you didn't want to end up there, and if you did end up there, there was a damn good reason, such as Maura's.

Woody thinks it a shame that Sugar is there when she could be at college. He knows she is living on her own, and her parents are out of her life, but what about Maloney, or even Maura for that matter? Maura would more likely want to guide Sugar to her own career choice: one at Grand Slams, which would justify the whole thing to her. Keating? Woody is pretty sure that Keating would rather she not advance herself one damn bit.

12. Keating's Duds

Joe Keating has bought a new suit, a cheap one—a seventy-eight dollar one—from Milton's, in a color which matches his official Grand Slams necktie. The suit and tie are both brown; the tie has the restaurant name raised and embroidered in red. The darker suit, no longer matching his blue eyes, makes him appear far less soft than he did in his old powder blue. Keating feels that it is incredible how easily a new suit with a few less stains can make a man look professional.

He feels confident too. He's been bossing the employees around all day. Maura shares quick pleasantries and knows enough to rush back to work. Kenny doesn't know how to do that; he lingers, waiting for Keating's approval, but instead receives orders from him: de-grease the dish area floor; scrub the cement around the dumpster with a stiff broom, then finish the dishwashing, as he will have fallen behind, which is what he does nearly all of the time.

Joe Keating does not want to run into Sugar during shift change. She had ignored all of his attempts to call her the night before—an embarrassing number of times. He is tired, and going home at 3 PM is an option today, rather than asking Jimmy to put him up in one of the vacant rooms.

Sugar walks in the back door at 2:45 looking happier than she has looked in a while, and Keating can't help resenting it. "You shouldn't leave your car in the lot if you're not working," he says.

"Sorry, Mr. Keating," she answers with a big smile and a tone that could be construed as either serious or condescending, depending on who is listening. Keating takes it in the most negative way. In less than a minute Sugar is surrounded by co-workers all wanting to know the gossip about one thing or another. *Damn, girls can be so immature*, Keating thinks as he intentionally doesn't make eye contact with her. Sugar is looking at him, though, mostly checking to see if he has overheard anything and if she should be worried about his reaction.

Maloney runs in, with his black bowtie clippie already on. "Hey, Sugar... and, Joe? Nice suit." he says, making Keating scuff at the use

45

of his first name but also making him smooth his brown suit and Grand Slams tie, one that would make the Bobs proud. He wishes he could receive a little respect from them, but at this point it seems too late, unless he busts balls.

"Sugar, I want you to clean behind the bus tubs in Section 1. Use a bleach bucket."

"Ewwwww, it smells back there… " she answers. "Disgusting." She rolls her eyes at Keating, who feels that she is saying that he is disgusting. Sugar catches the look on his face. "Stop," she says, "you're just being paranoid." She's right, he is exactly that way when he is overtired or has had a rough time the night before. Right now, all his icy eyes can do is stare straight ahead.

Maloney has known Keating long enough to not respect him and feel that he is disgusting, so he takes the opportunity during the awkward pause to smile and say, "So, Sugar, how was your date last night?" Maloney immediately feels sorry for Keating, who does not retort but returns to the office to give Jimmy a call for a pick-up. Joe Keating is not going home as early as he thought he was.

The dinner rush is unusually busy, wait staff is short, and Keating's silent treatment has thrown off Sugar's timing. A loud customer with his family has been waiting for his spaghetti dinner for fifteen minutes. Every time Sugar passes, he barbs at her, "Where's my spaghetti?" countered with Sugar's, "It'll be right up, as soon as it's ready."

Regardless of the large resentment Keating is holding, he still wants business to run smoothly. Gus is ringing the bell, indicating that there is an order waiting under the heat lamp on the stainless steel shelf.

"Do you need any help with anything?" he asks Sugar, while sniffing in the remnants of his last line of cocaine embedded in his nostrils.

"What?"

"Do you need any help with anything?"

She smiles the same smile she normally paints on for customers which gets her a little extra tip for her wallet. "That would be great."

"Hey, that's my spaghetti!" the man yells across the restaurant looking at the cook's line. "It's sitting there!"

"Want me to bring that to him?" Keating asks Sugar.

"You're a lifesaver," she says, arms full of plates and heading to another table.

"Yes, I certainly am."

Keating walks to the over-loaded shelf at the cook's line and surveys the family's order ticket. He touches one of their orders, then another of the plates, thinking of the right way to balance them to bring them to the table. Gus smirks at his process and sees by the order ticket who the waitress is. Keating restudies the ticket. There are three meals, one of them a children's chicken finger dinner with the chicken product molded in the shape of baseball bats. The Single Slugger. Smaller plate goes best in the hand of the server, as the larger ones can balance better in the forearm area. Keating is set, Diamond Slam Burger in the left hand, then with his right hand balancing the spaghetti plate on his arm. The Kids Meal, Single Slugger, is the last item he grabs with the right hand.

"About time!" the man shouts across the restaurant as Keating leaves the pick-up station and begins to walk over, feeling a little bit dizzy and needing another bump. As he leaves the carpeted restaurant area and gets to the linoleum floored area behind Section 3, he has to maneuver around Maloney. His foot slips a little, which causes the spaghetti plate to shift a little in balance on his forearm. He moves his arm to adjust, but he over adjusts, and the plate has begun to fall down the area between his arm and body. Instinctively, he catches the plate, trapping it spaghetti side in, against his new suit.

"HEY, THAT'S MY MEAL!" the man shrieks.

Maloney looks over at Sugar, who has begun to laugh, and then he begins to laugh.

"ARE YOU GOING TO BRING ME ANOTHER?"

47

"It'll be right up," Keating says, looking like he's caught a full round of rifle shot against his body. "Fucking asshole," he says under his breath, as he walks to the back of the restaurant.

13. Marisimo: The Eye Of The Boxer

As Marisimo scrubs the dried egg yolk off the white with brown colored edges Grand Slams plates, he frequently thinks of the American Dream. He thinks that he has been tricked and that there isn't much to show for the twenty-five years here; only a new difficult life, with little cash saved to send to his family. He is a partially blind and slow moving eighty-five year old dishwasher who needs a ride to get to his job, where he would snarl and growl at his co-workers all shift long. He hardly feels human.

As a young boxer in The Dominican Republic, Marisimo neither won a lot nor lost a lot. He was about even, but in the boxing world winning half your fights was a pretty poor mark. In some of those losses, Marisimo took a fierce beating, and now he's blind in one eye and has a cauliflower ear. Boxing made his father, Pedro, proud; win or lose, there was some extra money for the household. Pedro proved to be much better hanging onto this extra money than what Marisimo ever could.

People he didn't respect, like Keating and Tribuno, would yell at him to work faster. This he felt was impossible. The bosses treated him the same way they did with dim-witted Kenny. Maloney would sometimes come back and talk to him about boxing, tell him that because of his eye, he was Grand Slams Sugar Ray Leonard. "Beeg Headed Bobby," as Marisimo called him, with his thick accent, made him feel better about his shortcomings, made him feel more human. Bobby, a huge boxing fan, at least took the time to share conversation with him about the fight game. Marisimo loved boxing and he loved companionship, but unfortunately at his age, he had neither.

Marisimo has now fallen behind in the dish station. Again. The counter is eight feet long by four feet wide and is so covered with brown tubs overflowing with dirty dishes that the stainless steel cannot be seen. On the floor are five more tubs, and Marisimo is like boxer Roberto Duran—slumping on his stool in a stupor, unable to move or do much except say, "No más," to an imaginary referee.

49

Joe Keating and Dino Tribuno have discussed how to keep Marisimo caught up with his work, many times—and whatever basic psychology they've attempted has failed. If they act stern, Marisimo gets angry and can't work efficiently. If they are lighter and joke with him, Marisimo has no urgency and then, also, can't work efficiently. The only solution is to call in the cavalry without even discussing it. "Geyser, Maloney, get back there and bail out Marisimo!"

They know that this temporary help gets him on track, but Geyser and Maloney's neglect of their own jobs causes a backup from the front, so even if the dish station gets cleared, the second they go back to busing Marisimo's area will be full again.

Maloney and Geyser join Marisimo, who is slamming the brown tubs around and swearing in Spanish. When Geyser goes to the receiving end of the dishwasher, he pulls a brown bus tub, full of dishes and water, directly out of the machine.

"Marisimo, you need to unload the tubs and put them in the racks first," Geyser says poking at a bloated blueberry muffin floating in the gray swill. "You need to work faster so you don't panic."

"That asshole Keating!" Marisimo shouts. "How does he expect me to do anything?"

Maloney slides over next to Marisimo, trying to calm him. "Do you want one of your songs from The Dominican Republic? I'll put on your radio."

"No, Big-headed Bobby. I only sing when I'm happy," with his accent pronouncing "big" as "beeg."

Maloney, knowing how to cheer him up, changes the subject to boxing. "I bet you were pretty good in your day, even though your eye is messed up and you have cauliflower ear."

Marisimo thinks cauliflower ear is a vegetable, like an ear of corn, served in a Grand Slams medley, along with broccoli. "I wasn't too bad." He assumes a fighter's stance in front of Maloney, who haunches down, square shouldered, to meet him. Marisimo throws out a quick, crisp jab into an impressed Maloney's open palm, which causes Maloney to shift and shuffle his feet to stay balanced from the force of the blow. Marisimo knows Maloney can throw a right any time he wants over his bygone defense. Marisimo also notes that his dish room opponent's capable shift in footwork indicates that Bobby Maloney has had some boxing experience. Maloney then fakes a big, quick, overhead right, over a flinching Marisimo. It is the same type of punch that has left him partially blind, but this time, Maloney's balled fist stops inches short of his face.

"Hey, Marisimo, who was the best fighter of all time? Ali?"

"I think it was Sugar Ray Leonard," Marisimo says, cocking his brow.

"Not Duran?"

"We'll never know. They tried the last time. Duran said, 'Sugar Ray, I want to fight you again.' But he told him, 'No way. I can't because I hurt my eye.'"

Maloney laughs. "Is that how it went down? Just like that?"

Keating walks past, his jacket covered from the spaghetti incident. "No laughing. You're supposed to be helping Marisimo. Get to work."

"Hey Joe, did you know that Sugar Ray Leonard told Roberto Duran, 'I can't fight you because I hurt my eye,'" Maloney says in his best Marisimo accent.

Joe normally would love the banter but tonight is not a good night. "Get to work or you're fired. You'll both be fired."

Keating takes one step away and the shamed Marisimo yells, "You asshole!" to the back of Keating's brown suit.

Joe spins, jerks his head upward, grins and says, "Go fuck yourself and get to work."

Maloney laughs. He knows psychology more than the rest of the Grand Slam staff and that if Keating, like Marisimo, will snap out of his normal bad mood, everyone's shift will vastly improve. "Can I take your jacket to the cleaner on the way home?" he offers. "You'll have it back in an hour and you can meet Woody and I at The Web Brook after work."

Joe Keating pulls off the brown, stained-with-spaghetti jacket and tosses it on top of the bus tubs of dirty dishes, that sit on Marisimo's work table. "No, he can do it," he says. "He can do it."

14. Sugar Can Tell Him Anything

Sugar wants to be high on cocaine when she speaks to Keating about her dates with Sayid, because it protects her from the hurt in his eyes. Not that she was particularly sympathetic toward him, but his pain pulls the joy out of any evening and she's in it for the fun. The high absolves her of her guilt and blacks out his jealousy. When he is high, it's just him quietly wishing things were different between her and him. She's used to that song and dance, heard it so many times in her life. She knows he is amongst the many in her life who want to be with her based on how she looks. It is a given.

Sugar can be honest about the dating stories she tells Keating, because she and Sayid had not gone very far physically. Usually the dates are him complimenting her, mixed with his disbelief of being out with her. She and Sayid discuss religion and how he doesn't allow himself to give into desire, as that would be a sin. Sex must occur after marriage, he says, and boy, does he seem ready for that. In fact, he's even spoken to his father about her, but his father's response was less than favorable; a commitment with an immoral American was not in his plan for Sayid. Sayid told her that story just after he said he would like to take her to Egypt for a few weeks, bursting her bubble. Although she can picture herself as the wife of a well-to-do foreign man, the real truth is that it was only a picture, one you might faintly remember from a disappearing image from a dream. Still, the new fantasy of going there, of meeting a hateful father and marrying his son anyway, is a wonderful thought of a conflict to smash.

At the end of the date there are usually make-out kisses, a hand under her shirt or pressed firmly on her thigh. He, of course, asks if it's all right, and if she approves of him not doing the right, moral, and pure thing, he dives into it. Immediately after, he moans about shaming her as well as committing an evil act himself. She's too good for that, he says in guilt, and that's when she pushes him away. If she denies him and was the one monitoring his beliefs, she ends up feeling as if she'd done something wrong, even if she was the one protecting him from feeling terrible.

"It's rather fucked up," Keating tells her. "I don't understand why you would be made to feel bad."

"Part of me wants to dream about the marriage part, but another part wants to just screw him. I mean, can't I just have sex for the fuck of it?"

Keating knows he should jump in and offer himself to her, even jokingly, as a natural transition in this conversation, but he and Sugar have not had sex in a while. He justifies it as an unfortunate side effect of the cocaine, even if it was the drug which formed their mental bond, their excuse to get to know one another.

Sugar reads his pause, knowing what he is thinking. "You know there is no future for us. It just wouldn't work."

"I wasn't saying anything, but I think there isn't much of a future with Sayid either."

"Yes, I know. He's handsome, but he's not experienced with women. A woman needs someone with some experience before marriage, but there are so many good things he offers. Maybe that's all there is; a safe, predictable future with nothing else. Don't you think it's kind of fucked up that he spoke to his father about me and the father immediately didn't like me?"

"Yes on both counts. Usually parents dislike their children's choices immediately and then they settle into it. They have to."

"But it's cultural. Can you picture a pale-skinned blonde woman without shared beliefs fitting into that country and that culture? I'm open minded about other points of view, but actually having a life over there?" Sugar feels an odd longing and that she may begin to cry, immediately wondering where that was coming from. *It's my life*, she thinks. *That's what it is.* She shakes her head fiercely to dismiss the feeling, and grabs the rolled-up bill. Lowering her head, she takes a nostril full. "I don't know if I can do this anymore," she says, snapping her head up, in full upright position.

15. In Keating's Room Tonight

After Sugar drives off, Joe Keating strips down to a white undershirt and his work pants in Room 107. His newly stained tie sits alone on one of the queen-size beds while Jimmy Pudlow sits on the opposite one with Keating. Joe shifts through the channels, 1 through 28, about a three-minute distraction before he begins the channel surf again. There is an empty bottle of vodka on the night stand and a quart thermos of Tropicana, that Joe brought over from the restaurant. Jimmy is not his companion of choice, but sometimes company presents itself and one should take it. Also, it's Wednesday and the Grand Slams food truck arrived earlier from Baltimore, which meant the driver was carrying something extra that Jimmy wanted to buy.

Keating pretends that he doesn't know this; but in truth, this knowledge makes him paranoid that everybody knows what's in the truck and what he is up to. He's not sure if they know anyway. When Maloney and Geyser help unload the food truck, while singing the song *Convoy*, Keating feels that the lyrics are somehow drug related, and orders them to stop.

"I may want to have some people over in the next few days," Keating says to Jimmy as he passes him a straw. "Just so you know." Keating is as casual as one might be if they were telling their neighbors that there might be a party next Saturday night.

"Not too many," Jimmy says. "Just in case Super 8 corporate comes in and does an audit. Your usual guest is fine but if there are six people coming out at all hours of the night... "

"Corporate comes at all hours of the night?"

"When they do a surprise audit, yeah they do. They're not going to catch any wrong doings if we know they are coming."

"I think it's safe. I actually invited some people over tonight, but it wasn't pre-planned. Everyone had something to do."

"All I can say is, you're getting a room for some breakfasts. I think you are getting the better end of this arrangement." Jimmy pauses, produces a tied plastic corner from a bag with powder in it.

"I give you other business," Keating adds, looking at the white powder on the mirror then looking back to Jimmy.

"So you want to have a few of the girls over?" Jimmy asks, changing the subject, hoping for an invite if that is the case.

"Well, of course there is Sugar, but she's not always available. She's gotten very busy in her life," he lies, rubbing his fingers through his greasy mustache.

"I haven't seen her come here in a while."

"Well, I thought of bringing over some people, you know, whoever wants to come. It won't be a *party* party, but just a few people. It will be quiet, you know, whoever wants to come. You've met everyone. They are good people, right?"

"I guess, as long as it's not too loud and that includes cars coming and going with their radios on. Also, the pool as the no use of the pool after hours has been violated often." Jimmy says. "You're getting a pretty good deal here. Remember that."

16. Geyser's Shattered Night

The muscled man stretched into the white polo shirt with the words WEB BROOK SECURITY stenciled on the back, scrutinizes the driver's license.

"Woodrow, huh?" he mocks. The bouncer is standing just inside the door on a rain-soaked summer night. Woody, still outside, water falling onto him from the overhang, spikes his wet hair with his right hand. The skintight-shirt bouncer's wheels begin to turn as he visibly is adding and subtracting in his head. This is not going well. Finally he looks at the sign on the wall that lists the legal birthdates of those born before April 18 and those born after. He flips the ID the long way, checks the back, and rubs his thumb between the separation in lamination at the corner of the license, where it peels back. Maloney is already two steps into the Web Brook, sliding past the bouncer and calling him "Brian".

"C'mon, I'm legal," Woody pleads. "Hey, could you not peel that back any further? It's hard enough to get into places sometimes without you ruining my license." Woody turned 18 on April 17, but still looks like a middle-school student. On April 18th Massachusetts raised the drinking age to 20, grandfathering all that came before, which included one Woodrow Geyser.

"April 17th is awfully suspicious and convenient," the buffed bouncer adds, again pulling at the separating plastic found in the upper left hand corner. Maloney takes a few steps back into the club's entryway, where Woody and the inflated bouncer are debating.

"Brian. Let the kid in. He's of age."

"Sure he is."

"He's legit, Stevie. Let him in."

"Listen, Bobby, I'm just doing my job. I may not want him in, especially if something happens and he's illegal," Brian aggressively states.

"Quit getting off on that and let him in." Bobby is about a full body smaller than Brian, but his directness always demands respect.

"Okay, Bobby, Jesus," he says, poking Woody in the chest. "If any trouble happens, you need to run out of here. Understand?"

"Thanks asshole," Woody says under his breath, after nodding to Brian the bouncer and walking in.

Woody knows places like The Web Brook. He's been going to bars to see bands for a few years with an altered ID, and this hole in the wall in Billerica is exactly the same as any hole in the wall that he's ever been let into. The band, Shattered, is your typical setup: two guitar players, bass, keyboards and drums. There is a spandex-clad female singer that Shattered rolls out when they need to do a Pat Benatar, Bonnie Raitt or Joan Jett song. She runs out for "Promises in the Dark." Woody and Maloney must yell into each other's ears at three inches away to be heard over the band's sound.

"I invited Keating to come out with us," Maloney says.

"You did? Why?"

"I'm just kidding. But he's the one that actually invited some of us to hang out with him at The Super 8."

"What?" Woody yells, and Maloney repeats it by shouting an inch closer to Woody's ear, who responds. "To hang out with him and Sugar?"

"No, just him. Sugar wasn't working tonight, so he invited whoever was on. I don't think anyone went. They all had to go home."

"I don't think anyone likes him that much, plus it's weird partying with your boss in a motel room."

"I feel bad for him," Maloney says. "You know, he's not a bad guy if you can see past all the bullshit."

Woody pauses. "So you think Sugar and Keating aren't seeing each another?"

"What?"

"Do you think Sugar and Keating are still... ?"

"Why? Are you interested?"

"What? Maybe... "

"I think she is openly dating. I know she is still dating that guy with the BMW, but according to the grapevine, it's nothing special, and

58

Sugar thinks there is a lot of weirdness between them and their belief systems."

"Bobby Maloney, insider to the waitress grapevine."

"That I am."

"No wonder I saw that uniform, the brown zip-up dress in your trunk earlier. It's how you infiltrated."

"What? I can't hear you."

"Never mind," Woody says.

Woody and Maloney stay until closing, suffering through Skynyrd's "Saturday Night Special" because, according to Shattered, "Every night is Saturday night!" and then the encore because Joan Jett "loves Rock n' Roll and we do too!" Maloney swears he is okay to drive and guns his large car out of the lot, leaving dirt swirling and gravel shooting back in their wake. Maloney knows all of the back roads less traveled, from Billerica to Bedford, all the way into Boston, if necessary, just in case he's in a set of circumstances where he doesn't want to run into a police cruiser. Maloney has the station set to WAAF, whose current playlist mirrors what Shattered had played all night. Woody reaches over to change the station, but Maloney pushes his hand away. "I'll find something," he says. As Maloney twists through the dial, a possum is brightly illuminated in the headlights. Maloney, still fiddling, doesn't see it until Woody yells, "Possum!" Maloney swerves around the animal, but the car can't recover, and it skids into the left lane, which luckily is empty of cars going the opposite direction, and swerves back across and into the ditch on the original side of the road. Woody and Maloney are sitting at a thirty degree angle, Woody lowered in his seat below the elevated Maloney. Maloney guns the Dodge Monaco, but the car bucks a few times without being able to advance out of their predicament. The car seems to be fine, just pitched at an angle in the soft muddy ground, spinning without traction. Maloney swears a few times, cuts off the ignition and then swears once more. "We have to call someone," he says.

They walk for an hour to a main road where Maloney knows there is a gas station with what he describes as one with "a stupid fucking dinosaur logo" and a pay phone. When Keating doesn't answer after Jimmy forwards to his motel room, they ask Jimmy to wake him for an emergency. Maloney and Geyser have strategized as they know Jimmy knows someone who has a truck in Bedford, which is ten minutes from the spot in Billerica where they are stuck; a spot out of the way of traffic. If they play it correctly, they won't have to ask Jimmy. They will ask Keating, who will ask Jimmy, who will call his friend for them. At times it's better to be offered help than to ask for it.

"Why should I help you? Can't you call your parents?" Keating asks, voice cracking.

"Because we are both working doubles starting at 7 AM, and if we are unable to work and have to call in sick, it only leaves Marisimo there on a Sunday morning and also you'll be short-handed in the afternoon. I mean, you could call in Kayak Kenny. To answer you're other question, no, we can't call our parents."

"If you saying you're sick and you're not, I could just fire you, so don't get all clever on me. Is your car drivable?"

"Yes, the wheels spin and there doesn't appear to be any damage. As for the cost of the tow, just take it out of our pay if you have to," Maloney says, to the alarm of Geyser, who needs to keep as much of his summer work money for college as he can.

"Let me get back to you. Call me back," Keating says, and hangs up.

When Maloney calls back, Keating, who before Maloney can speak, says, "Shut up, just don't move. Jimmy can get someone over there in a couple hours. You should have enough time to get to your shift by seven."

Geyser and Maloney sit on a cement curb under the lights of the gas station's office and the stupid-looking dinosaur sign. They see a pair of headlights but don't think much about it as they've just spoken to Keating. The pickup truck slows down and signals, turning into the station; *Must be some old Cooter, needing air in his tires* is the first thought Woody has, but Maloney smiles. He knows the Ford. They hear

Charlie Pride before the window rolls down, see the eyes of a young girl with blonde hair, peering back at them. When Sugar rolls down the window, they see that she's wearing a dress, not her usual denim and trucker cap look, obviously just coming home from an evening out.

Sugar turns down the radio and cranks down the window of her truck, "What you doing out here, boys? Having a rough night?"

17. Sugar: The Truck Wins Every Time

Even in a dress, Sugar looks badass in her Ford F-250. She loves this truck more than any of her belongings. When it comes between paying the rent or making a truck payment, the truck wins every time. Justifiably you need a truck to move after not paying rent, but you can't leave after an eviction if the bank takes your truck.

The boys sort of shuffle in their seats on the curb, not knowing exactly what to do. "Come on," she says, "it's getting late."

Big Bobby Maloney gets up and walks up to her window. Woody twists a paper straw wrapper from the ground between his fingers, then, without thinking, brings it up to his lips, the way one might bring a cigarette there. Disgusted, he releases it back to the ground.

"Just waiting for a tow truck," Maloney states. "You're all dressed up. Were you on a date?"

Sugar peers around the service station and doesn't see Maloney's or for that matter, any car parked in their lot. "You sure it hasn't been towed already?" she jokes.

"It's a couple miles up the road, in a ditch."

"Well, hop in. I got some chains." Sugar's voice always has more of a twang when she is behind the wheel of her truck, something she unintentionally projects, as if she had recently moved from her birthplace. Fact of the matter is, she has been here since before she could walk. Still, she acts southern, because she wants to disassociate; she hates people and she hates Massachusetts, because everything here is a struggle. There are not enough shifts in a week that could possibly pay all her bills. Food is an easy fix, as when she is working she eats, but she is also able to sneak some food home whenever Keating is working and intentionally looking away.

"Keating has Jimmy sending a tow truck," Woody says. "It may take a bit."

"Fuck, Keating," Sugar snaps with the confidence of a woman with the upper hand. "No one can blame me if he's dallying around getting a truck for y'all. He's mad at me already so I'll take the hit for this. And Bobby, I had a date with Sayid and it went really well. Nice to be taken out and not have to worry about money or anything." Then she realizes that when she's hanging with Keating, he pays for everything, but most of the time all they did was sit in the Super 8. *All I can do to stay true to myself is to be careful I'm not being physical with Keating anymore.* Still, she has to drive her truck past Jimmy at the desk, who leers in judgement whenever she leaves the Super 8, probably thinking she's doing everything.

"He said it would be a few hours," Maloney says, walking around the truck and sliding all the way across the passenger seat, pushing a discarded trucker cap against her hips. "Come on, Woodrow," he chimes. "You getting up from there?"

Sugar breaks into a wide grin.

"Don't call me that," Woody protests, slowly climbing up into the cab, careful not to slide against the right side of Maloney's legs.

"Can I still call you that?" Sugar asks.

"I don't care," he says shyly. "I'm used to it from you."

Maloney reaches up toward the dash, and Sugar grabs his hand. "Don't touch my music," she warns, as Tom T. Hall is singing about beer. He then grabs her hat, adjusts it four notches to his head size and pulls it into place.

"I think we should have stayed at Sinclair," Woody says. "Keating will be pissed. It could affect our jobs."

"Woodrow, you're such a straight edge," Sugar says. "Be careful, that could retard your brain being that way."

"I'm not so straight edged," he says.

"Study hard, get into college, work a summer job, weekends on the Cape with mommy and daddy," Sugar chimes with sarcasm.

"I don't spend weekends with my parents."

"Well, the rest of it is true."

"Nothing wrong with that, as far as I can see. I'm independent," Woody says.

"Well, I suppose," Sugar replies, releasing her left hand from the finger grooved steering wheel to make a left turn, and letting the wheel spin back to center on its own. "Some people just have those natural supports, whether they like it or not, and some, like me, are out on their own, right after high school, with their own place and their own bills." She pulls the Ford cap off Maloney's head, puts it on hers—a strange combination of urban dress up and sexy redneck country girl, but it all feels comfortable to her. She tugs the bill of the cap, still Maloney-sized as it flops over her eyes, and thinks of her parents, in their home, drinking, yelling, and possibly throwing bottles and cans at each other. She is no longer there, thank God, to play the peacemaker, the one who could take a punch or just be a big enough distraction to pull all of their angst within her inner self.

18. Maura and The Sunday Bunch

The next day Maura is on opening shift with Maloney, Geyser, Marisimo and Tribuno. The Sunday wait line at the door is about an hour long. Sunday is the busiest day of the week, with many flashes of activity: a morning rush, an after-church breakfast rush, followed by an after-church lunch rush. By 7 AM, Marisimo has fallen behind already, Maloney and Geyser are tired zombies, and Gus is acting as sinewy as the meat on Grand Slams Steak and Eggs. Plenty of Double Home Run Breakfasts are served on Sunday, and often that yields only a fifty cent tip per plate. Maura knows how to get a full dollar out of folks, but not in the sexy way Sugar does, more in the maternal, even-keeled way she delivers the food. It's food service with care and Maura is "bringing the pride" that the two Bob's constantly suggest. It helps that Maloney has taken to calling her Momma Maura, openly on the floor, which Dino Tribuno scolds him about. Dino's scoff is openly ignored and Maloney continues calling Maura whatever he wants. Dino will defend his request by citing the words of the two Bobs, like a biblical phrase, except, like the way people often misquote the bible, Dino will always get it wrong. Maloney is about the same age as Maura's daughter, so his nickname for her is something Maura is extra fond of. It's also much better than the alternative, "Salty Old Maura", which she has heard behind her back. Mamma Maura usually gets the best tip percentage in the place, because caring and eliminating outside drama is something that shows up in your job performance. If you eliminate drama, and have the right attitude, it shows up inside of your purse.

Maura overheard the story of Bobby and Woody's evening complete with the components of which involve Sugar and Keating. This is just too much drama for her liking. She hears Marisimo cursing and snorting, bitching about the same work he faces each and every shift. She thinks, *Doesn't he realize that every shift is about the same, especially on Sunday. Big rush at 7 AM, which lasts till 11 AM, then the lunch rush, then finally, less busy, the lull at 2 PM, where you have an hour of work before you go home. It's almost like clockwork.* She knows when Marisimo goes on break he will accuse the person covering the dish room of not doing anything and letting the dishes pile up on him for when he goes back. Everyone in the place observes just the opposite; the thirty-minute fill-in dishwasher works about twice as fast as Marisimo, who, in thirty minutes, barely moves fast enough to order and eat a muffin.

Maura needs a vacation. She last took one over Christmas and saw her daughter Bridget. Maura blames herself for all of Bridget's drug problems, but Bridget had free will to just say "No", Maura reasons.

On the trip, Maura helped out by buying food. Other times during the year, she sends money. She wishes her daughter would just work hard, the way she had, so Maura wouldn't feel the way she does. She wishes Bridget would make it on her own. She once told her that Grand Slams was no goldmine initially, but she was able to make a life out of it.

It's much like the life she sees Sugar attempting. Maura realizes she has never struggled in the same way Sugar does. Maura always had more focus than Sugar, whom she observes is broken, even with her own place and new truck. She doesn't have to see Sugar's missed payments or late rent to know what is going on. It's written all over her face. Maura knows there's a lot to be said about the Mamma Maura way: the simplicity and repetition of working, then going home, working, then going home, which allows you to keep it all level, etcetera... etcetera... etcetera; rinse, lather, repeat. At Grand Slams she doesn't see anyone else practicing that approach in order to get ahead. Geyser and Maloney are good kids, they will do alright when they leave here and never come back. She is distracted by all this, and it causes her to forget to bring a customer a coffee refill he requested. Drama found in anything outside the restaurant, time and time again, is costly, either of a few bucks, a forgotten refill or often much, much more.

19. The Management's Evaluation of Joe Keating

Keating has a meeting with Blond Bob in Chicopee Falls at the Grand Slams impeccably run by Dyed-haired Bob Boolay. Keating smooths the lapel down on his newly-cleaned dark suit, and dabs at the singular grease spot on his Grand Slams tie with a paper napkin moistened with his saliva. It's 11 AM on a Monday, and when he walks in, the place is dead. The same piped-in instrumental music that plays at Grand Slams in Bedford can be heard. It's the same songs, in the same order, at the same times for every Grand Slams across the country; Mike Homer strived for predictability within his product.

Keating knows them by heart, "Chariots of Fire" at 11 AM, followed by that stupid piña colada song. The arrangements are full of piano and plucked harps, with synthesized instrumentation filling in the roles of the trumpet, saxophone, and even guitar. Even when he's at home sometimes during late night, or into the wee hours of the morning, one of these Muzak hits creeps into his head. It's not the first thing that prevents him from sleeping, but rather one of the stimuli that drives him crazy, and it's the craziness that keeps him up all night. The repetitive music creates repetitive thinking about how he is wasting his life.

Today it's one of those, "this is how to be more efficient" Grand Slams meetings, with Blond Bob talking and taking Keating through a tour of the spotless kitchen, the organized walk-in refrigerator, and the overly-labeled freezer units of the Chicopee Falls store. "The shrinkage in this store is less than .2%," Blond Bob states, "which includes any mistakes or giveaways. Bedford is currently at 1%. That's not exactly bringing the pride." Keating smirks at the word, shrinkage, imagining the time, during Kayak Kenny's break, that he somehow managed to walk into The Super 8's pool.

"Less than .2% means less than two cents on $1,000."

"Well," Keating says, "this is a slow store. It's easy to not make mistakes. We generate receipts in ten days what takes a month in

67

Chicopee. Even at our 1% shrinkage, we are earning ten times as much gross income than they are."

"But you could make more. Shrinkage and professionalism go hand in hand. Besides losing out in waste, there's the potential to lose out on business: the customer's perception of a restaurant—their experience and treatment—will color their decision to return or not. It makes them generalize about how they feel they are being treated and cared for. In Bedford, you have busboys rushing around like they are trying to catch a train leaving the station. You have waitresses that are as old as the chain, and the younger ones not looking as good as they can. And as far as career development, do you have even one happy employee who works harder, more professionally, and speaks highly of their job? Who exactly do you have that can move up to a managerial role?"

"I was thinking Gus could make the jump."

"The part-time cook? He's kind of mouthy, a real wise ass." Blond Bob catches himself and looks around to see if anyone overheard. "Even back on the cook's line you need to watch your mouth."

"Maloney?"

"It's a college job for him," Blond Bob says. "He's not a lifer."

They walk past the Manager's office, where they see Dyed-haired Bob, looking more pale-faced against his jet black hair than ever.

Keating feels the need to act like a company man, something he's not comfortable with and hasn't tried in a while. "Working on the Employee Time Report?" he asks Dyed-haired Bob. "They're due today."

"I finished those last night. I'm working on an assessment for the Grand Slams task force on bringing the company into the new millennium. It's about a new computerized system, which will automatically sort the demographics of our customer base living in certain areas, and the likelihood of ordering certain menu items based on age and location. From there, we will present new items which will sell well in those areas."

"Good work," Blond Bob says to his namesake.

"Sounds complicated. I think we should sell beer in Bedford," Keating says, eyeing the Budweiser tap located in the Center Station of the Chicopee Falls Grand Slams. "We have a lot of beer drinkers in Bedford."

"It's currently under discussion," Blond Bob says. "I think we are about done here, so I hope you have heard what I had to say," he addresses Keating, while nodding at Dyed-haired Bob. "Let me walk you out, Joe."

On the way out of the near-empty restaurant, instead of holding the front door for Keating and letting him advance on his own, he shadows him out to the parking lot and stands next to the driver side door of Keating's Impala. "Joe, we need to talk about your performance."

"Yeah?"

"Your performance and attitude reflects upon the store's performance. Profits should be higher, and I'm getting bad reports about you in general. You have Hanscom Air Force Base right there— so the restaurant is always packed, and it should be doing better!"

"I'll work on that. I mean, I'm doing the best I can."

"You need to do better. You will be relocated or worse, if you don't get your fucking shit together."

Keating looks around the lot to see if Blond Bob's curses were overheard, which Keating could note as corporate hypocrisy, but to his disappointment the lot is empty. "Our parking lot is always packed," Keating says to Blond Bob.

The ninety-minute drive brings on an increasing amount of anxiety and anger to Keating. *They're fucking out to get me,* he thinks but also, *Can I change? Do I have to in order to keep my job?* He also thinks of a cold draught beer, which is not available at his place of employment. He is only on until 3 PM today, which means that after his drive on the

Mass. Pike he only has an hour left on the work day. When he arrives through the back door of the Bedford Grand Slams, Maloney and Sugar are laughing at something, while Marisimo and a few of the other staff, including Geyser, are standing around the break table. Keating applies his usual tact, shouting, "Hey, shitheads! Get some fucking work done!"

Everyone scatters the way a circle of black oil dissipates when a drop of dish soap is placed on it, except Keating represents more the greasy black spot rather than something clean like soap. Everyone knows that he is the oily scumbag.

Sugar walks by and rolls her eyes at his latest performance and it's become so quiet at the crowded Grand Slams that you can hear the theme from *M*A*S*H* playing through the round overhead speakers on the ceiling.

20. Geyser, Double Shift

Woody Geyser stands at the Center Station at Grand Slams, waiting for Keating to disappear either to his personal booth in Section 1 or into his office out back. He'd rather avoid him at all costs. He has a plan: If Keating goes to sit down in his booth, Woody will bus the two full tubs in Center Station back to the back area and remain there till Keating gets up to go home or heads to the back himself. If and when Keating heads back to his office, Woody will either move up front or move out of sight in the dish area and stare at the bus tubs.

Sugar comes from her section to join him. "Avoiding the boss?"

"It's that obvious?"

She places her mouth inches from his ear and whispers, "His meeting must not have gone well."

"Meeting?" Woody eyes her, knowing full well why she has insider information about meetings.

"Every month or so, or as needed, he has to travel to meet the two Bobs in Western Massachusetts. This one was 'as needed'." Her soft breath is on his ear.

Woody is having a difficult time concentrating, her lips being so close, "As needed?"

"They must be on to him; 'as needed' is never good," she says, but immediately is sick with the thought of everyone else at Grand Slams knowing her business with Keating.

"You going to his party?" Woody asks.

"Noooo!" her laughter is much louder into his ear than her whisper, giving him goose bumps. Now back to a normal conversational distance, she says defensively, "Why would I do that?"

"It's right next door, you know... " he pauses, his face red. "where you guys hang out sometimes. You usually don't turn down a party."

Sugar's mood has shifted suddenly from playful to annoyed, not liking what Woody knows about her. "Listen, Woodrow. If anything is

71

happening, believe me, you'd be the last to know. Besides, it's not much of a party there at any time." She looks at the clock over the cook's window. "Anyway, what the hell are you doing here this late? Didn't your shift start at 7?"

"Maloney and I are working doubles."

"You are sure you're not staying to see me? 'Cause that would be like stalking and that would be creepy."

"No, I'm not being creepy." Woody shifts uncomfortably in his work boots, rocking ever so slightly from the heels of his feet to the balls of them. "I'm hanging out here so I don't have to wash dishes."

"And if I wanted to I could inform Joe that Kayak Kenny is more helpful out here than you, and you'd be stuck washing dishes forever."

Maloney comes out from the back wearing a brown bus apron. "I think you should come tomorrow night, Sugar. Joe really wants you to go."

"He told you that?"

"No, but Joe really wants you to go."

"Well if he were talking to you about it, I'd definitely not be going. Anyway, I can make other plans just like *that*." Sugar snaps her fingers on the word "that."

Kenny appears as if in synch with the sound, also wearing a brown busboy apron. "Keating says, I'm busing today. You guys need to flip a coin to see who's in the dish room."

"Fuck, really. I don't want to be in the swill station," Geyser says. "I can't take the smell."

Maloney grins. "Keating told us the same thing. We can flip a coin."

Sugar reaches into the cup she keeps for her tips at the Center Station and pulls out a quarter. She cocks her arm to toss it, and Maloney yells, "Quick, Kenny, call it in the air. Heads, I win, tails you lose."

"Tails," Kenny yells.

"It's heads!" Sugar says while laughing too hard at the gag to properly advocate for the injustice of it all.

"Dishes!" Maloney and Geyser jeer to Kenny, as Maloney pulls at Kenny's brown apron by the leather strap and then, in another quick motion, pulls the entire thing over the head of Kayak Kenny.

21. Sugar, For The Righteous, Not The Sinner

Sugar, partly out of principle but mostly out of discomfort, will not go to a motel party hosted by Joe Keating. Again, it's the guilt by association phenomena. Plus, she has been flaunting her outside dating in front of him, because he had that period of being possessive: calling and calling and calling. He would not leave her alone, and was obviously dogging her. His messages on her answering machine never failed to make her sad though. *Who am I to make some guy feel bad. The only act he is guilty of is liking me, or less than that, just wanting to hang out with me.*

She tries to find an understanding ear in Sayid, but he is a bad choice, having limited experience with women, particularly women of American culture. Even though he has not actually been with a woman sexually, he has managed to turn the tables and asks her about her history with other men. Every time she tries to explain, he shakes his head, sometimes saying, "No, no, no," as if he is overwhelmed and disapproving of her. He's not being judgmental, he just can't believe someone he thinks of as being so pure, someone pure enough to marry, could ever be in those situations. Surely, it mustn't be true. The conversation gets very uncomfortable, so Sayid changes it to general religion and his own beliefs.

Sugar doesn't agree with much of what he says about his beliefs. She likes him, but how can he really buy into the fact that a woman's main purpose is to serve men. She argues that women have come a long way in this country during the sixties, but Sayid counters with, "It's not a belief but rather the only acceptable way to live life... so it is written."

She decides to let this one be. It would be no use trying to convince him about the modern western woman over a few hours of drinks. She's knows she will never, ever, behave in a way he would approve of, never attempt to act that way, just to please him.

"Do you believe in heaven?" she asks, moving to another concept.

"Yes."

"For all?"

"All the righteous, not the sinners. Certainly not animals."

"Animals have souls. I believe they go to heaven," Sugar says, intentionally challenging him, but when she looks at him she sees the face of someone who is trying to understand the world; much like a child might when new information comes in and blows their minds. In reality, he is just thinking about this for the first time, the ideas Sugar shares with him. Again he is feeling uncomfortable, trying to defend his beliefs, so he says, "God makes all the rules. It's a fact."

"Animals have evolved the same way humans have. You don't believe in evolution or science?"

"Only what God gives me to believe."

"And you're a scientist?"

"I'm an engineer. Sugar, you make me think. I like that you make me think. I love you."

Sugar stops. She wasn't prepared to hear that, not this quickly. He has never experienced love, so how can he say that? She's not sure, but she thinks maybe it's all out of desperation, his rush to get married so he can have sex. She thinks about how she has to push him away when he is the aggressor, and how he cries afterward out of the guilt and the shame for both of them.

Tonight when the scene repeats itself, outside in the rain, she once again has to be the one to defend his religious beliefs. He has managed to make her feel awful about herself.

"Sayid, we need to talk about this pattern we are in."

"Oh, God, oh, God," he wails and Sugar doesn't care if he is crying or if it's the rain washing down his face; she just wants to go home.

22. Kayak Kenny

Kayak Kenny is looking forward to attending Keating's motel party, even though no one has invited him. Even when he overhears his co-workers talking about it, the subject is changed, and no invitation is extended. People then scatter. He is like a fart. Word is that the small room in the Super 8 makes it too confined to be used up by the likes of Kayak Kenny when it can be used up for beer, chips, and sandwiches. Why take up space for someone who is slow, wears a dingy, yellowed, short-sleeved button down shirt, and seemingly always has a lump of oatmeal or dried egg yolk hanging off a part of his sleeve?"

Unfortunately, this is all true, and during his shifts his grungy, formerly-white shirt becomes more and more stained. Whatever food or liquid that's inside the bus tub always seems to overflow when Kenny's carrying it: coffee, syrup, orange juice, fried eggs, hash browns, breakfast, lunch and dinners, plus unidentifiable substances. The brown leather bus apron is not adequate to prevent this, and Grand Slams doesn't offer full body suits for their dish room employees.

Somehow, concentrating to the full extent he is capable of, Kenny manages to overhear vital information about the party, and asks Sugar, who is more than happy to lie that, yes, indeed there will be a party and she will see him there.

Kenny is buzzing around telling Maloney, Marisimo, Geyser, and anyone within earshot that some of the waitresses might be there and that Sugar *will see him there*. Maloney tells him how fantastic that is and how going to a party is a good move, much better than buying a kayak and asking girls to ride with him.

"You should get a room in The Super 8," Maloney says, and then with an added exaggeration to his voice adds, "Sugar, if she's going, would love that." Maura, who is now on break, gives Bobby Maloney disapproving eyes.

Kenny becomes excited and very animated, and when Kenny gets this way, his jaw swings about a mile a minute, almost as if it's unhinged. Maloney takes a good look at Kayak Kenny, his clippie drooping, attached to only one-half of his collar. "You look like a mess. You have to clean up a little if you're going."

Kenny's face drops, obviously hurt.

Maloney, now feeling bad for him, pokes him on the shoulder. "Fuck, man, don't worry, it's okay. You can clean up a little after work so that you'll be ready for action."

The interaction between Kenny and Bobby Maloney is amusing enough to cause the grumpy Marisimo to laugh loudly, as he'll never allow himself to be the butt of anyone's joke.

Kenny turns to the happy Marisimo. "Why don't you come with me?" he asks. "When is the last time you partied?"

"Man," Marisimo says, "I want to party but I'm too old and I'm blind, man. I'm blind in the one eye. You ask me this? What are you stupid? You... stupid. Look at you... you look too stupid and yellow to party. You yellow, man. You look like you going to die."

"That's enough," Maura says. "Kenny? I need some help up front. Can you help me?" Her tone, as if he's the only person in the world that she could ask, is kind; Kenny wishes his own mother was as kind.

"Okay, Momma," Kenny says, as all his worry is replaced by a goofy smile, "I will be happy to help you out."

23. Keating Makes a Date

Keating waits until eleven-thirty and then calls Sugar, who for once picks up her phone. His plan is to play it cool, as he already knows that she is not coming to the party, but perhaps there is some other plan she wants to make with him instead.

"Hi, Joe," she says.

"Hi. I'm glad you picked up. We haven't talked in a while and I wanted to see if you're okay."

"Why wouldn't I be?"

"Well, no reason, I guess."

"Listen, I know why you're calling. I don't want to hang out with all those people tomorrow with you there. It'll be uncomfortable. You understand, right?"

"Sure. Say, how are things with the A-rab?"

"Excuse me?"

"The Arab."

"Sayid is not an Arab. He's Egyptian, well... he's American now. Arab! Jesus Christ."

"Oh, I see. So it's going well with that American? Funny-looking American, I think."

"Sayid is really nice, not that it's any of your business."

"So, he's nice?" Keating says, then pauses. "Nice, huh? He's nice enough so that you don't want to come to the party. You don't like nice. Is that the best you can say about him?"

"Yes... um, no it's not. What's wrong with nice? I'm trying to not be so cynical here."

"Well me too, it's just the rest of the world that's a piece of shit, which zaps the positive out of me." He laughs but she doesn't. He knows he is being hurtful, and his cynicism, which she is trying to avoid in her life, is clearly worming in, affecting her. He knows that she has had enough cynicism in her life from living in a home full of abuse. And he knows he can manipulate this. "Listen, baby, what about the next night? I could buy some extra shit from Jimmy and we can hang

78

out. It'll be like old times." There is a silence on the other line for about five seconds, and he breaks it. "Listen, I respect where you're at. You're seeing someone. I get it."

"I don't define or label anything I'm doing with anyone anymore. I'm seeing someone, not seeing someone, it doesn't matter. I just do what I do. Joe, really, you have nothing to say, whether you understand it or not, we—me and you, were never a couple. You get that, right?"

"So what about hanging out?" Joe asks. "We have fun, don't we? I miss your tiny titties."

"Joe, ugh, don't talk about my breasts. Things with you and me can't be like that anymore. I like to be taken out, you know, dinner or a show or something. All you and I do is hang out at the Super 8. If you want to get on my good side, something that feels like an actual date would be fun for me."

"There you go. Now we *are* sounding like a couple."

"Don't kid yourself about that; a girl likes to think she's more than someone to go to a motel with. Here's what I want from you: I just want to have fun. I'm sick of having to hang out with Jimmy for the first hour until he leaves, then flipping through the television stations until the sun comes up. I'm sort of sick of getting high, Joe. I like being taken out and talking. That's what I appreciate the most about Sayid."

"You mean we don't talk now?"

"We do, but it doesn't amount to much."

"You just like his money. He has a nice car. Is that it?" Joe answers, taking a stab at what it is about Sayid that she might actually appreciate. It can't be what she says, because Joe thinks he knows Sugar. He *knows* her. "Does he have a big penis?"

"Gross! It's amazing how you don't know who I am," Sugar says.

"Okay, Okay, Okay, so you want to go to a show?"

"Yes."

"If you want to go to a show, we'll go to a show."

"Great! That's a start for me wanting to hang out with you again."

"What kind of show?" he asks.

"Joe, that's up to you to figure out. You know a show-show, a musical or something." Suddenly she feels exhausted, and the thought of having to get up for work in four hours makes her even more so. "Joe, I'm on shift in the morning. We need to cut this off for the night, okay? Goodnight, Joe."

"What kind of show?" he repeats, but Sugar doesn't hear it over her final "Goodnight." Joe hears the dial tone and wonders *What kind of show would Sugar like and if I figure it out, has she actually said yes to going?*

24. Momma Maura's Unrelenting Matriarchy

Maura doesn't know what to think about a Grand Slams party in a motel room. Not knowing what to think is her defense in dealing with things she doesn't approve of. This time she has a strong opinion on what to think about the party: it's terrible. It's terrible, because she knows what the two Bobs would think, as well as the Bobs' corporate bosses, as well as their bosses' bosses, all the way to the late Mike Homer, who, she suspects, is flipping in his grave like a pancake on a spatula.

Maura notices her Grand Slams pin has streaks on it, so in the Grand Slams bathroom, for the seventh time this morning, she polishes it with a paper towel. She knows it's shiny now, but she can get it even more so if she just buffs it one more time. At least her obsession is only polishing a pin, she thinks; *obsession in other regards tends to get a lot of people, like her daughter, in trouble.*

Maura re-attaches the pin to the front of her uniform, directly over her nametag. She flicks her tight curly hair in place with her hand, and then checks the mirror. "Mamma Maura," she says out loud to her reflection. The name rolls off her tongue like the catchy name of a menu item: Eggs Benedict Arnold (Eggs, Hollandaise Sauce, and Ham on Arnold white toast), The Bunt Burger (when you have to sacrifice being hungry), The Suicide Cheese Play (Fried mozzarella sticks you dip in melted cheese) and The Momma Maura (Employment and life advice over soft empathetic criticism).

"If only I *was* their mother," she says. She knows all the stuff happening lately, like the motel party, the blatant disregard of professional rules and poor conduct, would all be nipped in the bud. The workers would want to make a good impression. Then she thinks of her own daughter and how powerless she is over Bridget, and realizes, sadly, that there is nothing she can really do. *Let go? Give up? I've never been one to give up, not on a person, not on anything. I can always give it a shot and then whatever will happen will happen. It won't be on me.*

81

It's 6 AM, and Maura's officially on shift. Kayak Kenny, the Night Porter, is standing by the timecard rack with his punch card in his hand. The second he sees Maura, he slides it into the machine and punches out, telling her to have a good night.

"It's morning, dear," Maura says.

"Morning, night... I don't know anything this early."

"Get some sleep. I'll see you later."

On shift at the time of opening is only Maura and Gerry, the cook, who has worked for Grand Slams for nearly as long as she has. You'd hardly know he was there the way he mechanically cooks: boils bags of frozen sauces and puts up the omelets and egg scrambles. He's not very fast, but he never seems to fall behind either. *He's the type of person Grand Slams needs more of*, Maura thinks.

"Where's the rest of the crew?" he asks her.

"They'll be in soon," she says, knowing that there is no use or purpose to say bad things about any of her co-workers. All it does is blow up in her face. She can think bad thoughts, though.

Maura sees Sugar's truck pull in from Bedford Street. She's late again. When she is arriving from Bedford Street, Maura knows that, at least, she hasn't rolled in from the back parking lot where Joe Keating or actual guests of the Super 8 usually walk over from. Still, she looks exhausted.

"I'm sorry I'm late," she says in passing as she heads immediately to a customer's table. "I had a late night phone call. Kept me up."

Maura doesn't say anything, but when the initial tables are cared for by both of them and all of the order taken, there is a slight lull and Maura finds herself alone on the floor again. Maura swings out back to find Sugar, who is standing in the break area waiting to hear Gerry's bell, indicating that her order is up. "Are you alright?" Maura asks.

"Just a little tired."

"I know you're tired and it's not just this morning. Are you alright, in general—because I know when things aren't going well."

"You know that? That's funny," Sugar says. "That's hilarious."

"Well, as you know, I have a daughter about your age," Maura adds, but incorrectly, as her daughter is older. The correct comment would have been that she has a daughter who *looks* Sugar's age, but actually is nearly ten years older, and this fact isn't lost to Sugar, as she knows Maura's story. At Grand Slams everyone knows everyone else's background, and even some customers do too. "Sorry, I just wish that you would make better decisions than Bridget did. I see you struggling, and I can't help overhearing what you say about your rent and other bills, sometimes off handedly, as if none of it matters. Well, honey, it does."

"What do you know about it?"

"Well, are you going to *that* party? I'm sure Joe will have a lot of drugs there."

To hear salty old Maura mention drugs in any way makes Sugar grin. "Actually, I'm not."

"Good. I know, based on my own experience, that by working here you can make it on your own, but only as long as you cut out the other stuff, which is expensive. Don't think I don't know what I'm talking about, because when Bridget was doing exactly what you are doing, I was in denial. I think this Sayid guy is a good catch. He would be good for you. You'd be all set."

"Look, *Mamma*, if you want to help me, then don't help me," Sugar says harshly. "You're not my mother. I already had one of those, and I didn't like her very much." When she hears Gerry ring the bell she adds, "Now, if you'll excuse me, the people in Section 2 Table 7 need their breakfasts. Why don't you focus on something work related, such as how long it takes for me to bring it to them, and if you want to help you can bring more coffee over to my tables."

25. Geyser's Many Do-overs

Woody Geyser and Big Bobby Maloney have the day of the big party off. They decide to go golfing at the Leo J. Martin Memorial course, a rather lengthy public, par 72 course in Weston, just a bad slice away from the Mass Turnpike. Woody, a golf newbie, tries his best to blend in, as he does with everything in life. The foursome behind them is growing impatient as Woody's tee shots have him spending a lot of time in the woods. By the thirteenth hole, a 400 yard beauty, Woody is into his second pack of golf balls, an average of losing about one per hole. From here on out it's a given that a tee shot slicing or hooking into the woods will constitute a do-over.

If Woody thinks about the term, do-over, it's the complete revision of something, as if the original never existed. It's exactly what Woody wanted by going away to college—a do-over. There are few natural times that one can re-invent himself, and college was one of those times. If you were an awkward and shy bookworm, like Woody, college offered the chance to come out, be cool, party like there was no tomorrow. Thing is, like it or not, tomorrow always came, and Woody was still that same awkward kid.

Woody scored 1200 on his SATs, but ended up at UMass because he didn't apply himself much in the college selection process. His parents felt a liberal arts school would be best for him until he at least decided on what he wanted to become focused on. So there were November college tours to SUNY Oswego, Hope, University of Wisconsin-Milwaukee, and Lake Superior State, all for some reason located near the Great Lakes. He even applied to Kalamazoo, just because he liked the name, but never got around to seeing their campus. The ones he saw, he wasn't too impressed by, and they seemed too far away to not be enthralled. He favored Oswego, based on what he had heard about it, but during their tour on a bitter cold day the guide mentioned that ropes were set up on campus so that when the wind kicked up off Lake Ontario students wouldn't get blown off the walkways. *Fuck that*, Woody thought.

Near the bottom of his list was UMass Amherst, which is where he toured last on an unusually warm day later in that month. It was on a Saturday, and beer bottles littered the campus. Their guide, Bubbly Barb, seemed more than amused between tales of their football heroes and all the wonderful fraternities and sororities. In one area, walking toward "a typical dorm", the trees were decorated with sneakers and toilet paper. When they reached the dorm room, Barb knocked four times without an answer. "Well, then," she gushed, "they seem to be out, so let's just have a look." She opened the door slowly, and the room was pitch black; then the light from the hall began to seep in, and they could see crushed Budweiser cans on both bureaus and desks. Bubbly Barb gasped as a hairy arm reached out from under the covers of the bottom bunk bed. It was the only thing moving, just an arm, as the head was completely submerged and still. It reminded Woody of a scene out of a horror movie—the predictable camera shot of a hand moving in, about to grab the sexy B actress's leg and drag her into the cover of darkness to her death. Instead, as the entire tour stood like wooden soldiers, the arm reached out, grabbed a tall plastic bong off the floor and then retreated back under the blanket.

Bubbly Barb flashed a large fake grin, spread her arms out wide, and herded the group out of the room and back into the hallway. "And that's a typical dorm room," she said, cheerfully off the script, without missing a beat.

"Mom? Dad?" Woody said. "I'd like to go here."

26. Sugar, How Not to Dishonor

Sugar's plans have fallen through with Sayid on the night of Keating's motel party. Sayid's breaking of the date happened in a rather odd sequence. Sayid is weird sometimes. Last week there was a package delivered for Sugar from Macy's. It was a watch Sayid had bought for her, with a note that read, *For all our time together.* What guy sends a gift in the mail after a week and only a few dates, and also, why didn't he present the gift to her in person? Wouldn't that have been a more intimate thing to do? Sugar feels that Sayid, when it comes to anything intimate, is completely clueless.

Sugar put the watch on and admired it. She wasn't big on watches, but it was a gift and even though it was beautiful, there was an obligation to wear. But after a few days, when she took into consideration the little note he tucked inside the box, the watch became more a fond thought. She pictured him spending hours at the jewelry counter, trying to pick the perfect one for her, based on size, shape, band and face color. Sayid was a cerebral man, and every outcome must be meticulously reasoned. She hated to admit it but she liked being thought of in this way; with him calculating all of the variables about her. All this thoughtfulness made her like the watch; a fact she didn't want to think about at all.

That night, she went to put the watch back into its box and found the receipt Sayid had suspiciously left in the packaging. Four hundred and fifty dollars—that was more than a month's rent. She called him and said that she couldn't accept it. She was uncomfortable with gifts such as this.

"Of course, you must accept it. It is my gift to you," he said.

"No, no. It's too much. It'll make me feel... I don't know, that I owe you something, or that I'm indebted or committed in some way... It makes me feel strange."

"When a woman receives a gift, it dishonors the man if she does not accept it."

"Let me think about it."

The phone line went silent, as it often did when Sayid was on the line. Usually it was because of his shyness, but this time it felt different.

The next day, she wore it to work, and a customer wearing an officer's uniform from Hanscom Air Force Base kept eyeing it, peeking over the plastic menu at it. "That's a nice watch," he finally said.

"It's from my boyfriend."

"Well, what's a girl like you wearing a watch like that, doing at a place like this? It's a really expensive watch. He shouldn't let you work."

"Well, I have expensive taste, and I like to work," she said and smiled, not so sweetly, because in situations such as this the tips are never worth it.

Sugar was confused because first she didn't want the watch, then she defended the watch, and lastly, she stated a relationship with Sayid to a total stranger, even if she was only using that status to brush off the comer-on. She was even more confused when the phone rang that night and it was Sayid sounding distant: "I'm not sure about seeing you this week. I'm really busy at work. Perhaps on the weekend?"

Sugar tried not to connect this phone call with the lack of assurance she gave him toward accepting the watch. Still, she couldn't help thinking exactly that. *Have I insulted him? Was it a cultural thing—did I do something beyond wrong?* She pictured his face on the other side of the telephone line, blank, robotic and lacking of emotion, the opposite way it looks after he tries to eat her face with his lips, then feels that he has made a horrible error in morality.

"So, you're breaking our date?"

"No, I'm just going to be busy and tired."

"If you're so tired would you like to end the call now? Do you need to go to bed?" Sugar replied, matching his tone of indifference.

"Perhaps that would be best," he said, breathing out a sigh of relief.

"Okay, then."

Again, there was a long pause before Sayid said, "Goodnight. I love you."

"Okay, then," Sugar said again and hung up.

Sugar is disappointed because she would like to be doing something if she's not attending the party. It's awkward as she can't be herself around him. She also doesn't dare be herself around Keating or at work, where she puts on a fake personality for both of them. The only time she feels like herself is when she is alone in her apartment. Perhaps other plans can be made for tomorrow night so she can avoid that.

She has not hung out with Bobby Maloney much since last winter. He might be going to Keating's party, but Sugar thinks that she can convince him to do something else. She flips through her pink and orange flowered phone book and finds his number.

27. The Keating Show

"Something new," he thinks. He flips through the *Boston Globe* looking for a show to take Sugar to, but instead stops at the sports section. The Red Sox have lost about as many as they've won this year and have just gotten swept by the Yankees. This year featured their typical old, slow team with good power, not going anywhere: Dwight Evans, Fred Lynn, Jim Rice and Tony Perez. June had started out so promising, with a six-game winning streak, but now the team seems set in not going anywhere.

A show? What kind of show would Sugar like? He has asked around, and Maloney was the only one who could answer him specifically. Geyser had answered with a question, "A Broadway Show?" and Keating didn't really know if seeing a show in Boston was a Broadway Show, or if they had to go into New York to see a show, playing on the actual Broadway.

"*Shear Madness*," Maloney said. "It's new. I saw it with my parents, and it's a mystery that takes place in a hairstyling salon. The plot is different each time. The audience solves a murder. I think she'll like it."

"The homo hairdresser with scissors did it," Keating reacted, jerking his head back, while smiling, trying to induce laughter from Maloney, who, in turn, didn't behave in that way.

In his room, Keating is now rustling through *The Globe*, looking for the location and the phone number for tickets for *Shear Madness*. *It's new, it's a comedy, and it sounds much better than a stuffy opera or frolicking musical. These shows are fucking expensive*, he thinks, when he sees the listed price. A quick thought of barter crosses his mind. *If only I could trade with Ticketron the same way I do with Jimmy Pudlow.* He wants tickets in hand so he can present them to a grateful Sugar, but the money spent would cut into the amount of drugs he can purchase from Jimmy tonight. There are not enough meals in a day to barter with Jimmy for the amount he currently uses, and taking it all into consideration, he has traded meals for the rest of his life already.

"Deals are about going onward and upward," his father used to say. *Oh, Dad,* he thinks and grimaces in regret. *You would be so disappointed.* He remembers his father's tight sideburns, astute mustache, and the fresh smell of his cologne placed on his neck in just the perfect amount—as opposed to his greasy smell of Grand Slams, thin mustache, and cheap suit.

The late Jonathon W. Keating, Joe's father, was a hardworking, self-made businessman. People would say that his suits alone would close a deal, because clients would pick up on and want to be associated with Jonathon, based on his air of success, as if you couldn't go wrong with a man appearing as good as that. Little Joe would tag along whenever his father was around, making them close through proximity, not emotions. Jonathon's associates used to laugh and tease Joe about the "Little Joe", the character Michael Landon played on *Bonanza.* Jonathon never groomed Little Joe Keating as his successor, which Joe never understood. Perhaps his father would have taken him under his wing, in due time, if he hadn't died when Joe was twelve. Little Joe wandered around the funeral home, physically and mentally lost amongst the rooms overflowing with people who loved and respected his father. Little Joe felt so small that day, and also so short that he felt he disappeared under the height of the adult world. His mother kept telling him not to wander off, thinking he was escaping into the funeral home's other rooms, but he was right there the entire time, but invisible.

Keating anxiously dials the number for The Charles Playhouse and fishes through the inner pocket of his wrinkled suit for his wallet. He hopes he'll be able to get through the transaction without his credit card telling him that he can't.

28. Kayak Kenny

Today is the day. It's party day. Kayak Kenny knows it and there is no denying him. He will be getting off work at 10 PM, walking back, past the pool, past the Manager's Office and into the crazy, party room, packed with beautiful waitresses. Many of them, he's been told by Maloney, are from Grand Slams across the country—a virtual beauty contest of servers. Maloney even stretched the lie, telling him some of them posed for the Grand Slams bikini calendar, which Kenny had no clue existed. The thought excites Kenny. There's always a chance with women who do not know him. If the party goes well, maybe he'll get that extra room Maloney was talking about, and maybe, just maybe, Jimmy Pudlow will give it to him free of charge. Maybe Keating's credit would be good for it, and if not, Kenny thinks he can lend Jimmy his kayak for the day, as a trade, once it's bought, of course.

Kenny has been saving money. At ten dollars a paycheck, he only needs twenty more dollars to buy the kayak he wants. Just a few more shifts as a busboy and he will have enough cash to go to Eastern Mountain Sports and become a first-time kayak owner. He's been looking at their catalog as if it were a bikini calendar, except the provocation is not derived from beautiful waitresses in bathing suits, but from the gorgeous red, blue or yellow kayaks. *Once it is in the water, the waitresses could wear anything they wanted*, Kenny thought.

Tonight, Kenny is taking out the trash more often than necessary, so he can peek at the motel parking lot to see if cars are arriving. He is eager, anticipating the good time to be had. He even brings out old empty boxes from storage that have been lying around for months, so he can compact them. It's a slow night and he's working the dish area by himself. Gerry is on the cook's line and he works well with Kenny. When they are out of a certain type of plate, Gerry does not refer to the plate by number, but will bring Kenny an actual plate of that size, so that Kenny knows exactly what is needed.

On the contrary, when Gus works, he'll shout out, "We need number 6 inch plates!" but Kenny doesn't know a size number 6 from a size number 7, and when Kenny's working with Maloney and Gus shouts out, "I need six inches!" Kenny doesn't understand why Maloney laughs, so he laughs too.

Tribuno is up front pouring coffee for the counter's only two customers. Maura and Sugar are covering the front, mostly standing around waiting for new customers to walk in. Kenny tries to bring up the party with Sugar, but every attempt at conversation about it is interrupted by her saying, "See you there!" and then winking at someone else. Maura narrows her eyes at this teasing and scolds her, but Kenny doesn't comprehend where Maura's contempt toward Sugar stems from, and wonders if it could be directed toward him.

"Why is Momma telling you to stop it?" he asks Sugar, while bringing silverware up to the holders behind the counter.

"I think it's because she is feeling left out and too old to go to the party. It's all different when you're old."

"Hey, Maura, you can come!" he shouts across the restaurant and then notices Dino Tribuno. "Hey, Dino!" he shouts. "Are you going to the party?"

"You're fucking kidding me," Tribuno answers.

"Are you too old too?" Kenny asks.

"No, because I can't believe you are talking about the party because I guess you didn't hear yet. Maloney just called in sick, so I need you to cover the Night Porter job tonight."

"No way!" Kenny shouts. "I'm not doing it."

"Oh yes, you are. No one else can come in, so you are mandated to stay."

Kenny feels like he's going to have what his mother refers to as a tantrum. He walks aggressively around the corner of the counter, making the turn like an offensive guard leading the Green Bay Packers on a power sweep, and accidently knocks down Maura, who is pouring a gallon bottle of ranch salad dressing back into a ten gallon container for overnight storage. Maura drops the bottle, and it spins in mid-air and spills the same way, in a circle, on the ground. Momentarily it looks like a circular lawn sprinkler, watering the grass.

"Are you okay? Are you okay?" Tribuno runs over, knowing that a Workman's Comp form would need to be filled out and sent to a pissed off Blond Bob.

"I'm fine, maybe a little ankle twist," she answers. "I knew the party was going to be a bad idea. It puts everyone's feelings on edge."

Sugar pulls her to her feet, as Tribuno heads out back to address the loud slamming of pots and pans by Kayak Kenny. "Yeah, a terrible idea," Sugar responds. "Makes people want to call in sick, don't you think?" Sugar smirks, knowing she's the one that has caused Maloney's illness.

29. Geyser: Hanging With Shadowy Figures

Geyser's Toyota Corolla sputters into the Grand Slams lot and parks in the back by the dumpster. Maloney has changed the plan, saying he might only be able to stay at the party for a few minutes. Woody was hoping it would be longer, since he still believed there would be some people there he hadn't really spoken to that much, and there would be Kayak Kenny, and Woody needed a buffer. Woody assumed Maloney changed the plan because he is working tonight as Night Porter, and before punching in he'd have a beer and maybe a line with Keating before getting started in the restaurant with the vacuum and steam machine. Woody runs his palm over his short spiked hair. He doesn't see Maloney or his car in the lot, and it's now 10:35.

Out of the darkness, behind the dumpster, Big Bobby Maloney appears, wearing dress pants and a polo shirt, carrying a six pack of Lowenbrau. The beamed light of the parking lot catches his large head and prominent forehead, making him look pale and washed out, before he twists and ducks to avoid being seen. Woody looks again for Maloney's car, the Dodge 440 Monaco, which looks like a police car, but it seems to be hidden somewhere in the lot. Maloney crouches next to the driver's side of Woody's car, out of sight, in case the back door of the restaurant opens and he's spotted.

"What the hell?" Geyser says.

"Shhhh. I'm not supposed to be here. I called out sick."

"Oh, no. And that's okay with Keating? Wait. You're not sick... and why are you dressed like that to hang out over there?"

"Um, duh-uh," Maloney's grin breaks open widely, not answering the question. "I called in to Dino. He was all confused because it's the third of July and at midnight it will be the fourth. He doesn't understand the holidays all that well. You know, it's big trouble if you call out during a holiday."

"So, who's working the overnight?"

"Kenny has to because he's there right now."

"Oh, no!" Geyser laughs. "He must be pissed."

"I'm sure, but in the long term, he'll earn more money toward his kayak, and then *the women will all like me*," Maloney says mimicking Kenny's voice.

Maloney reaches for the back door handle of Woody's Corolla, and Woody unlocks it, and as the door opens the rusting-out section creaks. "I hope someone explains that to Kenny in the exact same way that you just did. Why aren't you sitting in the front? Why are we driving over anyway?"

"Don't want to be seen. Come on, just drive." Woody starts the beat-up Corolla, and Maloney lies down in the back seat. Woody parks next to Maloney's huge Dodge Monaco outside of Room 133, on the far end of the row of rooms.

Maloney's behavior, hiding from his place of employment in order to party with the boss, is something which would ring odd to most people, but Woody isn't fazed, since the scenarios which present themselves through his job are neither very black and white nor are they normal. Woody and Maloney stand outside Room 133, looking at each other. Maloney is holding the six pack by its built-in cardboard handle, but Woody, always socially clueless, is empty handed. It's been ten seconds and neither initiates knocking on the door. Finally, Maloney bangs three times with his free hand, and Keating yells, "Who is it?" loudly through the motel's painted wood door.

It is silent for a few seconds, before Geyser responds, "Um, Woody Geyser and Bobby Maloney." Keating disengages the bolt, slides the chain, and opens the door only halfway, so that Maloney has to push it wide enough open for them to walk in. Woody notices immediately that it's just the three of them, a bag of chips, a container of dip, and a small pile of cocaine on the table in front of the television. There are two small, black plastic motel trash cans full of ice and beer. Maloney places his six pack on the table, offering it up to any of the three of them, before trying to arrange his bottles in the pile of ice Keating has made inside a black plastic trash can.

"So, boys, what's the word?" Keating asks. Maloney is clanking his bottles to shift things around and open up space in the trashcan. Woody remains standing, noticeably shifting his weight from one foot to another. He could sit on the bed, but doesn't want to because he can't get the image of Keating and Sugar rolling around in it out of his head. Keating turns to Maloney. "Aren't you on shift in a few minutes?"

Maloney doesn't answer, and puts his Lowenbrau bottles back into the six pack holder and places them directly on top of the pile of bottles and ice. Woody explains that Maloney called in sick tonight, which elicits a look from Bobby Maloney, indicating, *Shut your fucking mouth. I wasn't going to tell him that.*

"Sick, huh? Did you call Tribuno?"

Maloney nods and Keating indicates it's no big deal, as he hands Maloney a white plastic straw. "Dressed kind of nice tonight," he says to Maloney in an accusatory manner. Keating has figured tonight out to be one of those small nuances in life, putting two and two together about an absent Sugar and a well-dressed Bobby Maloney. It's the type of thing Woody never seems to notice, as it never occurs to him that Maloney is dressed very nicely for a motel party.

"Oh, I have a family gathering. Can't stay too long," Maloney says.

Woody runs his right hand through his bristly crop. *Shit, a family gathering,* he thinks. *I'm about to be trapped here with Keating.* Woody takes a step toward the iced-down beer, grabs one, and returns to the exact spot where he was standing. Again, by not noticing Maloney's attire, he has missed an obvious piece of information, and now he is left to stress about being one-on-one, alone with Keating very shortly.

"A family gathering?" Keating asks. "Whose family gathers at eleven o'clock at night?"

"Oh, mine does. They've been at it all day. I told them I had to work earlier, so now I need to make an appearance."

"You'll be back, won't you?" Woody asks.

"Well, if I'm not lucky," Maloney says. Woody laughs, thinking Maloney is making a sarcastic joke at the expense of Keating's party, but Keating knows exactly what Maloney is inferring, so he smiles his evil crocodile smile and jerks his head back. "Well, come back when you're all done; otherwise, I'll write you up for calling out for tonight."

Maloney grabs the straw to sniff another line on his way out, snf closes the door, which reminds Woody of the bars of a jail cell slamming shut. Then he hears a few Fourth of July bottle rockets being set off early.

"Well, college boy, it looks like it's just us for a while."

30. Sugar's Plutonic Time

Sugar is glad she has a friend like Bobby Maloney on a night like this, and thank God he's just a friend. In the Grand Slams bathroom after her shift, Sugar arranges her blonde hair into a French braid, applies blush, and pulls her Dwight Yoakam concert t-shirt tight over her chest. She decides not to go with the trucker hat, having left it on the front bench seat of her Ford, in favor of wearing an outfit versatile enough to blend into any location Maloney might suggest. Even though her hair is glazed with grease from work, she looks pretty good. She is supposed to meet him out back, in the dark area of the rear parking lot. Any date that would ask to meet in a dark parking area, besides being a bad date is also not acting very much like a friend—but Maloney gets a pass being that he has to be in hiding in order to do this.

Sugar walks out with Maura, who's favoring a tender ankle and has a plastic bag full of ice tied to it with a Handi-Wipe. There is a dollop of ranch dressing on her uniform from her earlier accident.

"You know, I never wanted to be that waitress who had to prop her swollen feet up when she got home from a shift, but tonight I may be forced to."

Sugar holds the door for her and they are both surprised to see Bobby Maloney, looking sharp and clean, not in hiding, standing next to Sugar's truck. Sugar checks for suspicion on Maura's face, but she is looking determined and uncomfortable just to be walking as she waves to Maloney.

"Momma, what happened?" he says then sniffs hard for any leftovers from his nostrils.

"Oh nothing, just knocked over by an angry Kenny."

Maura sees Maloney's face turn with retaliatory anger, and adds quickly, "Oh, no, it wasn't intentional." Then she changes the subject: "Boy, don't you look nice for someone too sick to come to work."

Sugar sees Maura wanting to ask the next question, probably something about her and Maloney, but Maura stops herself. *Good,*

Sugar thinks. *Our previous interaction surrounding her maternal instincts must have sunk in.*

"Well, you kids have fun," she says, limping away.

Sugar starts to walk with Maloney, back to the far corner where his sedan is parked, and grabs his hand. "Do you mind if we take the truck? I don't feel comfortable leaving my truck visible here."

"I kind of like to drive," Maloney objects. "You look good, by the way."

"Fine, and thanks for the compliment, but let me remind you that this is not a date. You know that, right, that this is not a date?"

Maloney looks a little sheepish and then says with a put-on confidence, "Of course I know that this is not a date. You know, I'm out of your league."

Sugar waits so there is no possibility she is seen from room 133 while Maloney walks to his car. She notices the headlights are off as Maloney drives to face her.

"Your lights," she says.

"Oh, yeah. I just didn't want them to be noticed by anyone in the motel. I don't like to disturb people who are trying to sleep."

"Oh, I don't think the people in Room 133 are trying to sleep. Not... one... bit." She laughs. "I'm sorry I sounded bitchy earlier. Thank you for the compliment."

"It's fine. Don't worry about it."

"So, anyway, what do you want to do?"

"There's a band over at the Web Brook."

"Country music night?"

"No, I don't think so. Tonight is a rock cover band."

"Oh."

"We don't have to go there. What about Chi-Chi's in Cambridge," Maloney suggests, "next to the Orson Welles? We could get a drink and talk. Want to do that?" His windows are down in an attempt to cool him, to dry the light mist of sweat forming on his face.

"Sure," Sugar says. "It's open late and a margarita sounds pretty good."

"Done."

As they head to Cambridge, Sugar starts in with some small talk, while Maloney, not listening, tells her that he is relieved that at this late hour it'll be easy to find parking near Chi-Chi's on Mass Avenue. Sugar wonders why guys think so far in advance about such things, agonizing over finding spaces and parallel parking.

She grimaces through his radio choice which has given them, for their enjoyment, Toto, REO Speedwagon, and Billy Squier, rather than her beloved country songs. Music usually helps her pass the time, and is needed on this drive, which is longer than it should be, since Bobby Maloney has taken Mass Avenue through Lexington, all the way to Central Square. Sugar is glad they didn't go to the Web Brook where everyone knows her because she was going there nearly every night about six months ago. Maloney looks over, trying to catch a peek at her pretty face, but instead sees a scowl and hits the radio's span button to a Billy Ocean love song.

"No, not that," Sugar says, which forces him to instead shove a Billy Idol cassette into the deck. Idol is not her style, but at least she's not heard it enough to despise it.

Maloney easily parks, as Central Square as well as Chi-Chi's is pretty deserted. The waitress in a farfetched, overly colorful, Mexican getup is on them right away. Sugar thinks it's a good sign so she orders drinks which arrive lickety-split.

"Sorry to miss the party?" Sugar asks Maloney.

"Party? It was just Woody and Keating in there when I left."

Sugar gets a sad image of an old Keating sitting alone in a dank house, later in his life. Who throws a party where the only person to attend is someone you've known only a month or so? She immediately feels guilty. "I'm glad I didn't go, but I still feel bad."

"Well, what's the deal with you two?"

"We're just friends, but of course he wants more. They all seem to want more... whatever that is. I mean, I don't feel that I have much to offer."

100

"I don't see how the two of you can be even friends. You don't seem to have that much in common."

"Oh, Joe's okay. If you knew him, you'd think so. He says you are one of the few people that he likes there. He called you a decent human being."

"Yeah, don't get me wrong. Joe's okay. I feel bad for him and I do think he's an interesting character, but I can't see myself hanging out with him unless I lost a bet or something."

Sugar feels she knows where this is going. Maloney is going to ask her or imply that she is using him or hanging out with him for drugs. While this might have been slightly true a month ago, Sugar sees Joe Keating as somewhat of a wounded animal needing compassion, rather than someone she is using for drugs.

"I feel bad for him too," she says. "That's most of it. Even tonight, I feel bad that it's just him and Woodrow Geyser. I'm feeling a little guilty."

"Do you want to go back to The Super 8?"

"No. I don't want to in the least, but I still feel bad, mostly not being there, even if it is no fun." She finishes her drink and points to the empty glass as their waitress walks past. Maloney doesn't order another. "Did you know that Woody and I graduated high school together, but I hardly know him? I can't see Woody saying much around him," Sugar continues. "I bet there's a lot of dead air."

"Oh, Woody is alright. We've hung out a lot this summer. He's a good guy and actually pretty funny. I just think he doesn't know how to act around people."

"He shouldn't be so shy."

"Why? Would you find him attractive if he were more confident?"

"Kind of. His personality, as it is, not so much, as there isn't much there when he is shy and timid, but I can see that he's a sweet guy."

"Maybe the two of you should hang out… but word is, you don't have too much extra time because you're getting pretty serious with what's his name."

"Who? Sayid? Pretty serious? No."

"No?"

"Oh, he's okay, but he's like all the rest, he wants something from me. Get this… he wants to marry me. I understand why, but it still feels funny for him to expect such a huge commitment without even knowing me."

"He proposed?"

"Well, not really, but in his religion you can only have sex after marriage. I don't know, he seems to have some experience in that department that he shouldn't. He shouldn't know how to kiss the way he kisses. I'm sure he really only wants to get married because he desperately wants to have sex with me or with *somebody*. If his religion didn't fuck with his head so much he probably could go through with it. But now, the way he is, he'd completely become hysterical and I'd have to console him. Anyway, I'd consider marriage with someone like that, just to be taken care of, if he had his shit together. I don't think I'd be able to convert to his beliefs, though. I think that's another expectation I just couldn't meet."

"He seems to be about as clueless with his ways of courting as Kenny is with his way of wooing women with his kayak," Maloney says, which makes Sugar chuckle. "So, Sugar," he adds with a devilish smile, "Will you marry me? How about it? We could get married in a kayak."

"Ummm, let me think about it," she says playfully. "I'd hate to fuck up our friendship." The waitress, who is done serving Maloney, has plopped the check in front of him. "Excuse me," Sugar says. "Before we settle, I'd like another."

31. Joe Keating Spills Some Secrets

Discomfort with people can all be overcome by a few lines of cocaine. In just a couple of minutes, it will be the Fourth of July, and that might be something to talk about if they want to keep it shallow. He and Woody are passing the straw back and forth regularly and often.

Joe Keating has been very secretive about his upbringing. He has told Sugar about his father but hasn't mentioned his mother to anyone. It is a difficult subject to talk about, or even reference, because it would make it too real, remind him of what he is doing now to deal, or not deal, with his upbringing.

"It's not a very upbeat story," Joe inhales and starts. "My father, Jonathon was abusive to my mother, Annabelle, who was thought of as an attractive woman but personally, very dark and depressed. The abuse was mostly verbal, but occasionally dad became physical. Alcohol played a role. Annabelle was more of a heavy drinker between the two of them, and some said that was what eventually killed her. Some say it was the pills, the large amount she took daily, until the last day when she took even more." Joe hasn't returned the straw to Woody for four snorts. "Thing is, Jonathon Keating was insanely jealous, and it was an accepted fact of their marriage, but ironically, they accepted that Jonathon had nothing to be jealous about. Annabelle fell in line and did nothing Jonathon could be suspicious of."

Woody wonders about the use of their first names rather than just plain "mom and dad". Then he thinks, Psych 101, UMass Amherst. *Emotion detachment is the inability to connect to others emotionally, as well as a means of dealing with anxiety by preventing certain situations that trigger it. There is a deeper layer of Joe Keating.*

Keating continues, "Jonathon would react to other things, how men at the market, at bars or in town looked at her, or greeted her. This was something she had to discourage. Jonathon with his fine suits and expensive colognes had no problems with women. Around the office, it was known that Jonathon would take in a few strays. At home, Annabelle was aware of this fact, but she never said anything, only fell deeper and deeper into her isolation."

Woody reaches out to take the straw away from Keating, but he jerks his hand away and readies himself to pull in the largest line of cocaine yet.

Keating's eyes twitch as his head begins to bobble around, his neck as a fulcrum. His speech is quick, more excited than the way this story should be told. "Once, Jonathon had no idea where she was and believed she had run off with someone else. I was the only one calm enough to search the house. My father was way too angry to function at the moment, but I found her, curled up inside the dryer with a bottle of Jack Daniels lying next to her."

"She passed out in there?"

"No, she passed away, and I got to be one of her pallbearers. Although there were many other men, much stronger carrying the coffin, I felt the full weight of the moment—that she be seen in a certain way in order to send her off into a better place. It never happened. The stories of Annabelle continued to be told and retold through the poisoned, stubborn point of view of Jonathon Keating, and it was all bullshit."

Woody doesn't know what to do. "Hey, Mr. Keating. Could I have another line?"

"Sure," he says. "Forget I even said any of that."

32. Geyser: Remaining Silent

When he's left there stuck with Joe Keating's tragic story, Woody Geyser wants to do every grain of coke that Keating has because, what else is there to do after hearing that story? Already, he has done more coke than he ever has in his life, and the pounding of his heart, he hopes, will eventually stop before it rips out his chest and through his t-shirt and is left pulsing erratically on the thin motel carpet.

For crying out loud, Keating is telling him about his mother and father, who he refers to as Jonathon and Annabelle, a conversation which has passed the time, but when the rush from the high is on a downward spike, Woody becomes irritable until the next line is set out.

What is there to say when someone you hardly know is spilling their guts out about their childhood and it's not pretty? Woody thinks to bring up his own basic parents. His father worked hard while his mother stayed at home. During the '60s, Woody concluded that they were pretty square, not discontents or hippies, but they voted liberal Democrat, so they had *that* going for them. Woody always leaned toward liberal, and didn't even know a hippie, until he met some old ones protesting on campus. Hippies. What did that even mean? Did it mean people that shoot from the hip?

When he was a kid, his classmates wore Levis and fashion that reflected the style of counter-culture. Kids wore psychedelic shirts or ones with rock bands pictured on them, while Woody's clothes, bought by his liberal mother, reflected a more conservative way. Woody unfortunately wore button-down shirts and JC Penny blue jeans that were 100% blue but not 100% cotton. He was tall and awkward, in bad clothes, and was bullied. Going to high school was absolute misery but he wasn't going to tell Keating that.

When he went to college, all of that changed. Woody wanted to act pretty normal and to get that way, he did what normal kids in college did; he drank a lot. He did that so well that he developed the strange sense of pride in how he could drink for longer and consume more than any of his former classmates in high school could. With a chip on his shoulder and an "I'll show them" attitude, Woody progressed to the extent that he was exactly where he was supposed to be right now, in a motel room, snorting lines with a boss who shouldn't talk so much.

The police could be here, he thinks, but isn't sure why he even thinks it. He isn't sure whether he has said it out loud or not. Then he says it out loud. *What am I even saying?* he asks himself. *Why am I even saying it?*

Woody looks over and sees the heavily sweating Keating pull the curtain back from the window and sees the flashing blue lights in the parking lot. Keating reaches over and flips on the air-conditioner full blast. It must have been what Woody was subconsciously picking up on, maybe the blue lights were in the corner of his eye. If dawn hadn't edged its way into the darkness, their troubling lights would have been even more prevalent. Cocaine makes him think too much. Then, his thought is broken by a loud knock on the door.

33. Marisimo The Muffin Man

Marisimo arrives early that morning for his 6 AM shift. The light from the waking sun is painting the clouds. He grabs ten muffins, ditches nine of them in his tied-off jacket sleeve, and knocks on Tribuno's office door. It's this misdemeanor of muffins that Marisimo needs to cover up. "Don't worry," he yells. "I put my one muffin on my timesheet. Wanna see my one muffin?"

Tribuno opens the door and waves him away. "How do I know that you only had one muffin? You may have had more earlier."

"You asshole!" Marisimo shouts and walks toward Kenny, who is sitting in the break area, his work complete, nodding off with a big smile on his face. "Hey, Sleeping Beauty! Shouldn't you be at the big party?" he asks in his thick accent, the word "big" sounding like "beeg," as every "i" adds an "e" and every "e" adds another "e," to create a longer phonic.

Kayak Kenny scowls at the missed party reminder and points toward the office door. "I'm all done, and he won't let me off." He adjusts his pointing hand into a fist and pounds the table. "He says I'm paid till 6 AM."

Marisimo can feel his temper rising, which often gets him sent home from work. The place is full of landmines today, but he has his own stuff to be angry about and can't worry about being a champion for Kenny. "I'm going to go for a walk," he adds. "I'll be back."

"If you're not, I'll be asked to stay. I've already been stuck once," Kenny laments.

"You not too smart," Marisimo says. "I'm early. I'll be back at six. Don't worry, it's the Fourth of July, so I have to be back. I make double money."

Marisimo walks to the back, carrying his jacket, the sleeve full of muffins, his hand bent like a coat hook to cradle the load. If the party is still going on, there are enough muffins for nine people to enjoy a muffin if they are hungry. Marisimo used to be a generous man back in his country; he would cook for everyone in the neighborhood every night.

Outside, Marisimo sees the blue, flashing lights and thinks there might be trouble. Maybe "Beeg Headed Bobby," or Keating, is under arrest. He pictures the people in the room next door who have blown the whistle on the party. "It's too loud. I can't sleep," they're saying to the police.

Instead, he hears someone yelling in the parking lot close to the Super 8 office. As he gets closer, he recognizes Keating's friend and hears him yelling at him. "Why the hell are you yelling at me, Mack?" Marisimo yells back to Jimmy Pudlow, who is walking ahead of two cops, toward the police cruiser, hands cuffed behind his back.

"Someone was out to get me! Some son of a bitch from the restaurant ratted on me! Was it you?"

"No, no, no." Marisimo says. "Are you in trouble, Mack? Trouble? I think you're in trouble, Mack. I think so. No more free breakfasts for you, you cheap bastard!" Marisimo laughs.

"It was you?" Jimmy yells and turns his back to him, so he can give him the middle finger, while still in handcuffs.

The burly officer spins him back to forward position. "Sir, you have the right to remain silent... "

34. Keating's Cloud Of Dust

"Oh fuck, oh fuck, oh fuck!" Keating cries at the knocking, then realizing how loud he is screaming, turns to Woody and says, "Shhhhh!" as if he is the one creating the frantic noise. Woody is frozen, but Keating is a circus, a parade in motion, managing to panic and stay calm all at the same time, while running in circles, then North to South across the motel room. "Don't open that door," he whispers harshly.

There is another loud rap, but this time Keating says nothing. He pushes the pile of coke off the table surface, into his cupped hand, runs to the bathroom, and shakes it over the toilet. He claps his hands together, causing a small, temporary, white cloud of dust. He then reaches into his trousers for the rectangular paper, throws that in too, and flushes. Before the third series of knocks, Keating prepares a wet washcloth in the sink, wipes his face with it, then uses it on the table to wash off the rest of the remaining white powder. He then throws the washcloth into the toilet, flushes and tells Woody to get the door, as the water rises, then sloshes over the top. Woody doesn't move. He remains frozen.

Too much potential to be in this type of trouble, is what runs through the accelerating mind of Joe Keating. Keating sprints past Woody, lifts the door handle, smiles, and smoothly says, as if he's dealing with an irate Grand Slams customer, "Can I help you with something?" As the door opens completely, Keating's phony smile sags back to reality, as he sees that it's Marisimo. With his thick accent and his arms full of muffins, he announces, "Hey, boss. You want one?" A large bead of sweat falls off Keating's chin and onto a shoe-worn area of the green carpet.

35. Geyser: Another Trap

Woody Geyser looks past Keating and catches the sight of Marisimo holding out an armful of muffins, looking as if it is some sort of majestic offering. At first, in confusion, Woody thinks it's a trade for the hundreds of dollars flushed down the toilet, as if Marisimo knew what had transpired during the knocking. Keating and Marisimo stand and stare at each other, like two cats about to brawl, neither of them moving for almost ten seconds, both of them now offering each other an angry face.

Marisimo shouts, "I didn't steal them!" and Geyser wants to laugh at the ridiculousness of the situation, but he knows he could possibly get fired for such an offense. He sees Keating rush to get past Marisimo and head outside. Marisimo haunches into defensive position, then shoots his right arm up to guard against a possible punch, then cocks his left and throws it weakly over Keating's right shoulder, grazing his ear. The muffins cascade to the ground, like a blueberry avalanche. Keating is unfazed by the weak punch and continues past Marisimo, who cries, "Don't hit me, I'm blind, man. I'm blind!" but Keating has bigger fish to fry.

"Hey, what the hell?" Keating shouts, now outside the door, his head checking left and right for the police. The blue lights are still flashing, but they are still half a parking lot away.

Woody carefully walks past Marisimo who is shaking the pain out of his left hand. "What the hell is right," Woody says, as they see, in the distance, Jimmy Pudlow being shoved into the patrol car, his head pushed down, as they thrust him into the back seat. "Good thing you got rid of all the shit," Woody says to Keating, when he re-enters Room #133.

"What?" Keating says, rubbing his right ear.

"Good thing…" Woody sees Keating's right ear has turned a rosy red.

"I can't hear you, my ears are ringing," Keating says. "I'm glad we got rid of that stuff. Jimmy might talk."

"Jimmy was yelling," Marisimo says. "He said some son of a bitch from the restaurant called the police on him."

"I think it's time for me to go home," Woody Geyser concludes.

Woody sits in the driver's seat of his Corolla and jerks his tired head down, then rests it slowly against the steering wheel, careful not to set off the horn. This was a near miss, as he thinks about the events of the night. The sun is starting to heat things up, and it's going to be a hot Fourth of July. Woody is so exhausted, he thinks that he may sleep through the entire holiday, perhaps, if lucky, wake up that evening to his parents watching the Boston Pops playing the 1812 Overture on television. *Yeah, how lucky*, he thinks with self-degradation. He hears his mother's *"Don't think we don't know what you are doing, because we do."* in his head and wonders if he, himself, knows what he is doing?

It doesn't have to go that way; in fact, none of it has to go that way Woody thinks about what's been going on recently in his life and how he needs to stop it. All this got out of control fast. There's six more semesters of college, before he... before he what? In all actuality, he has no idea what he'll end up doing. Maybe he'll end up like Sugar, not doing anything productive with his brain and working permanently at a place like Grand Slams—he sees how easy this would be. Even the sun rising slowly this morning, and ever so slightly, reminds him that time is going by.

At home, his mother is scrambling eggs when he opens the door. Looking through one room and into the kitchen, Woody can see the plastic spatula stop and his mother twisting the knob of the gas grill to off. Woody thinks that there are a few ways to play this. He could bolt, to his left, sprint up the stairs, basically running away from this problem, thus making his avoidance obvious. His other option is to nonchalantly and casually turn left and head up the stairs, la de-dah, like taking a stroll in the park. He could also nonchalantly walk straight into the kitchen and greet his mother, which is not preferable since his legs and arms seem to be twitching from the effects of his all-nighter; but also, it might be a bad idea because his voice often sounds strange

111

to him when he's high, which would cause enough personal discomfort to arouse suspicion in his mother. Casually he tries to veer left, the nonchalant stairs choice, but his mother seems to be set on her own first option, which is bolting in from the kitchen and confronting him—the impossible for her son to use avoidance move.

"Are you just getting in?"

"Yup," he croaks.

"Are you on something? Your speech sounds a little off."

Woody stands there, limbs locked in a restraint and tries to think fast. The best thing that just came out of his mouth was a hollow sounding, "Yup." This is not good enough. Woody decides to go more dramatic, "I met someone tonight, mom. I think I'm in love." He's immediately sorry he has said anything.

Woody's mother is shocked at this revelation, and combined with how Woody is looking, it is all rather ludicrous. She is stuck on what to do or say, so during her confused pause Woody activates the first plan: sprint left, up the steps, but saying, "good night" over his shoulder.

When Woody gets upstairs, two flights, to his attic bedroom, he lies down and thinks about Sugar and imagines how easy it might be to hang out with her, if he too were out of school. That would be so low pressure, if only, he felt, she could stand him. Then he thinks, *Who the hell is she, to think she's better than me?* He then thinks how she didn't come to the party tonight and wonders if it really is a step down for her to hang out with him; is she holding him in the same regard as Keating? Is that why she was absent? Then suddenly, he gets the image of Bobby Maloney's polo shirt and puts it together. That preppy outfit Maloney was wearing at 10:30 at night wasn't for any family get together. Both Maloney and Sugar were free last night and chances were that they got together for something else. It's a thought that causes him a sudden rush of adrenaline, a side-effect of his sudden anger followed by the other side-effect: feeling sorry for himself at the same time. *It's always someone else*, he thinks. *It's never me. Life needs to change. Life's about to change—today.* And with that Woodrow Wilson

Geyser resolved that he was about to make a conscious effort to change things...starting tomorrow.

36. Maura: The Franchise is Limping

Maura hobbles in with an ace bandage wrapped around her leg. She can limp around without it, but wearing a visible bandage will increase her tips by at least 25%. Lucky for her, she may not have to walk as much today because she is training a new waitress.

Kayak Kenny's head is resting on the table, eyes closed with a pool of saliva on the table's surface, dreaming of the spray from a river on his kayak-loving face. At rest, his skin looks the color of a bad embalment.

He has been asleep since Marisimo left, but now he has returned with the crime-scene facts. Kayak Kenny finds it's always difficult to understand fact from fiction, especially with Marisimo, who isn't a reliable reporter. The two of them together process information like the telephone game everyone played as children, where a sentence is whispered at one end of the line and it changes completely when you get to the end. Here, the line is only two, but the results are the same. Marisimo shuffles back to the dishwashing station.

"Rough night, Kenny?" Maura says with genuine concern. Kenny, with visible effort, remains with his head up, like a zombie, slurping in any excess saliva from the inside of his mouth. Maura pulls a napkin out of the holder, pulls her Grand Slams pin off, sprays it with orange solution, and polishes. Slippery, it drops onto the red cement floor with a muted ring. Maura grimaces in advance, as a bending movement would cause pain in her ankle.

"The guy at the motel was arrested. Someone called the police and spilled the beans," Kenny, leaning down to pick up Maura's gold-colored pin, repeats.

"Is that all? Was anyone here arrested at the party?" Maura asks.

"I don't think I know who was arrested," Kenny says, forgetting the information he had reported.

"Oh, my," she said. "That shouldn't have happened. I hope everyone shows up for shift today."

Debbie, the new employee, walks in twiddling her long, auburn hair into a ponytail.

"I don't care. I'm leaving right now no matter what," Kenny says. "No one is going to make me stay. Not today. Not on the Fourth of July! My parents are taking me to Lexington Green. I love the fireworks. There are balloons, hats, and sparklers. Plus, I have now earned enough, so that I can go and get my kayak! I like that!"

"You have a kayak?" Debbie asks with honest enthusiasm.

"I will in a few days," he answers proudly.

"Sounds like fun. I'm sure you can't wait to be out in the water," Debbie says.

"You look awful, Kenny," Maura adds, taking on her gentle, maternal tone. "Fill me in on all of your July 4th tomorrow, okay, and get some rest."

"Okay." Kenny says, putting his face back down against his arm and immediately falling back into the heavy abyss of sleep.

Part Two:

Re-trained
Re-programed
Re-educated
Happy Birthday America

37. Sugar: Pawed on The Fourth of July

On the Fourth of July, Sugar thinks about doing something patriotic with Sayid as a kind of cultural education lesson, but Sayid knows all about Independence Day.

"I've studied your country. Do you think I haven't learned about it?" he says as they are walking on the Lexington Green. "I had to pass a test for my citizenship." Sugar also notices Sayid studying her neckline, not that she's showing much, but just a little, under her yellow, cotton, V-neck t-shirt.

"Well, then, this is just a field of grass then. No new information to be picked up here," she says sarcastically.

"Oh, there's plenty," he says, completely missing the sarcasm of her last comment. "Did you know that in the Battle of Lexington, John Harrington had a musket ball rip through his body and he fell forward to the ground. He rose, fell again and tried to crawl home. He stretched his hand out to his family—and then collapsed on the front step of his home. Ruth, his wife, and the young Harrington child rushed to him as he died in her arms. The house is right over there." Sayid points across the green at a white house.

"Oh that's awful."

"No, it's romantic. I'd do that for you, if I were shot," Sayid says without a hint of emotion.

"I didn't know that fact."

"You didn't know that? Do you doubt my love for you?"

Sugar feels her stomach jump and her nerves racing at the mention of the word love. "I meant, I didn't know about the war story."

Sugar wants this to go to a subject Sayid doesn't like to talk about, the wars in Egypt where he saw horrible things. In the past, during attempts at such conversation, Sayid became detached and emotionally withdrawn, when she had hoped he would open up. "Tell me about the war."

"Well the first shot of The Revolutionary War was fired on what you celebrate as Patriots' Day in Massachusetts... "

"No, not that war, but the one in your country."

Sayid stops and looks down. Sugar, feels something is about to happen with him, but is not sure if he's going to cry or become angry. She reaches for his hand and he slides up toward her wrist.

"You're not wearing my watch," he says.

"I'm having trouble with that. I mean, I love it, but it's too expensive to wear around." Sayid looks at her with dejection, so she adds, "You'll see it on me, the next time I see you."

Sugar knows this conversation is going nowhere, as far as getting to know him. It's most likely going to stay in boring lecture territory, about the Revolutionary War, so she glances over across Worthen Road at a crowd gathering at Hastings Park. "A carnival!" she yells with excitement, and grabs his arm. "Let's go!"

As it becomes early evening, and after riding on every rusty old carnival ride, Sugar and Sayid sit on a bench, slightly away from people.

"Ouch, I'm sore," Sugar says. "It feels like I've been in a car accident and that one you stand in, held in by centrifugal force, I thought I was going to vomit on the person across from me."

"Wouldn't the force of the ride have made the vomit end up on you?" Sugar then puts on a pretend pout, "I wanted a bear," she says, lamenting Sayid's lack of skill at the rigged games.

"Those games were impossible," he says.

"I've never seen someone so bad at the basketball shoot. They should have given out the prize for six straight air balls." Sugar laughs and then feels the front neck of her soft shirt being tugged, and Sayid's face and mouth covering one of her small breasts. She feels him applying his warm tongue directly over her suddenly exposed and cold nipple. He starts to moan, loudly, as his lips and tongue suck at her erect nipple.

Maybe because it is so unexpected and maybe because she is a little hung-over, Sugar is frozen in place, unable to move. She feels she is watching it unfold from outside her body. She doesn't know if she should slap him away, move his head away gently, or say something to make him stop, which will unintentionally shame both of them. Usually the thought of sex in the great outdoors appeals to her, but she instead feels she has no say in any of this. Physically his mouth feels good, but it's still light out and the thought of families and children, being able to see them, even from a distance or walking toward them, leaves her feeling violated more than anything else. She wonders how she can be even slightly turned on and yet completely mortified.

"Sayid, we're in public! Stop!" she commands, a few nearby people forcing her out of her confused state and into one of total embarrassment.

"Oh," he retracts, leaving her breast out in all its glory. "I'm sorry, I'm sorry, I'm sorry… " Then aggressively he reaches to pull the shirt back to cover her.

Sugar retracts so she can tuck everything back in herself, and thinking of a way to save face says, "Let's go somewhere more private."

When they get back to Sayid's place, Sugar is immediately led to the sofa, her pants ripped down, and she is brought to orgasm by his perfectly soft and directed lips and tongue.

38. Sayid Can't Stop Anything

Sayid has no time to feel guilt or remorse because, once he has finished, Sugar is happy to return the favor. She is like the American girls that he has heard about but never been able to go far with. He has always stopped before anything like this has happened to him. Her mouth on his cock must feel too good to be bad.

Sayid hears loud fireworks from the celebration outside. Colors flash in her hair, as her head moves back and forth quickly. Then it happens. It seems to arrive from a place deep inside him that he's never experienced. And there's a sound coming from him that he doesn't recognize, as she removes her mouth and tugs him quickly with her hand. He knows what has happened and he knows it is wrong, but it's something that feels amazing. He has done something dangerous, provocative, even erroneous with someone he loves. He's never been into it this deep, but it's her fault that the orgasm felt so good, and it's her fault that there was an orgasm at all. He has no idea what to do. Sayid thinks she has set off fireworks from inside his body. What a silly thought to have after something so weighty has just happened.

Then he begins to laugh. Sayid laughs long and hard, with a high pitched squeal. He doesn't seem to have any control over that either. He feels his now soft penis shake with each gasp. Sugar asks him if he is okay and tries to hold him, but he is shaking too much, rolling around the floor. Sayid can't stop laughing. He sees Sugar's face, in a confused strange expression, which makes him laugh even more. Sugar grabs her pants off the floor, and he thinks about her cleaning him up, which causes his laugh to turn into a battle of getting enough air into his lungs.

He is coughing, laughing, and gasping at the same time.

Sugar asks him again if he's okay, but he can barely hear her through all the stimuli he is throwing out there. It seems to Sayid that Sugar is mouthing the words to him, so he closes his eyes, feeling a slight bit of control coming back. "No, no, no, no, no, no, no, no, no," he says regimentally, between gasps. "Oh, no, no, no, no, no, no," he repeats. The series of "no" continues, and Sayid feels that he can't stop those either. "Oh, no, no, no, no. What have I done?"

When he opens his eyes, the world seems to be back in order, and Sugar is standing over him, fully dressed now, her arms folded across the front of her yellow shirt. "I need you to take me back to my truck as soon as possible," she says. Sayid stares at her blankly. "I mean, right now!" she states.

39. Maura: Homer Where The Heart Is

Young Maura grabbed Mike Homer a coffee as he pulled out papers from his briefcase. "I miss you at the Lakewood store," he said. "You were one of the originals."

Maura hoped the words, "missed you" were pretty indicative. She knew Mike was no longer married. "Well, it is good to be out from under my parents' roof."

"Well, you look good, tired but good… then again you always did."

Maura smoothed down the front of her uniform, preening like a proud peacock. "I see you have a new car. You still traveling a lot? I hardly see you this far out."

"Well, this store in Colorado is the furthest reach of our chain, but I needed a new car anyway. You always seem to be the furthest possible point away. This is why I specifically came out to see you."

Two thoughts jumped into Maura's head, as she touched her five-year pin. The first one, the one of a managerial position, an idea she rejected nearly six years ago. It was something she had recently considered and now was dancing in her brain once again. Maybe, just maybe, if the hours could be flexible she could bring her daughter out to Colorado. And then there was the second thought, will Mike Homer finally ask her out?

"Come on, sit down," he said.

Whatever store she worked, she would sit at Mike's table, the manager's table, even if it were only for a few minutes. Mike represented the familiarity of her roots, her past, and within the day-to-day Grand Slams shifts, the only sentimentality she could accept

"I've decided to sell my ownership of Grand Slams. I have a pretty good offer," he said. "All this traveling has gotten to be difficult—overseeing, all one-hundred fifteen stores. The Board of Directors wants to expand further out to Michigan, Ohio and into the Northeast. Lord knows, it's exhausting as it is, and it is taking its toll. It destroyed my marriage, and I've just started a new relationship, which I don't want to make the same mistakes with."

"I knew about your marriage," she said, quietly hurt by his admission of a new relationship. Maura hoped her face didn't give her away.

"The new owners have franchises and general managers all lined up. They'll be doubling Grand Slams store numbers in two years, so I have something to request of you."

Maura felt her usually tough interior melting and noticed a strange look of embarrassment in Mike's face. She knew she was not going to be getting any offers of any kind.

"Maura, even though you never picked up a franchise or region here at Grand Slams, I'm counting on you, as a career person, to promote the integrity and pride of the Grand Slams Corporation. Think of the two of us: We think, act, and promote the corporation with the sense of pride and respect that I wish for you to continue. Maura, without Grand Slams you may not have had the wonderful opportunity to turn your life around and do what was best for your child. You think of the Grand Slams way, each and every time you wake to a new day and proudly zip up your freshly pressed, brown uniform. Others will never learn to love the Grand Slams way, the way we have, unless people like you step up. Maura, you are a power of example. You need to continue to make the customers think seriously about their breakfast and dinner choices, inspiring within them the desire to pick Grand Slams every time. It's up to you to take the employees, lateral to you in your job, under your wing. You must be a one-person pep rally, but do so in a reserved and prideful way, that quietly inspires others to follow your lead. Maura, you are the one I've chosen, same as out in California, to continue the mission of Grand Slams family restaurant."

"Okay, Mike. I'll always do whatever it takes to promote the company and to keep it good. You'll always be proud of it." Maura said and immediately after that, she decided that in the next two years, she would move as far east as possible.

40. Woody: Not Popped

Woody rolls out of bed and walks one flight down to the living room. His parents are engrossed watching John Williams conduct the Boston Pops Fourth of July Concert on the Esplanade. Woody has missed the entire day. When he was a few years younger, he saw the first Fourth of July concert Williams ever conducted with the Pops, which was full of old movie themes and over-arranged *Star Wars* tunes. When the popular main theme was played, Woody's disdainful "I hate *Star Wars*," caused his father to snap, "I don't know why we do anything with you anymore." Woody had been sour that night, because he had been offered an invitation to attend the fireworks with his friends, which would have meant drinking beer and having smokes with a kid named Reefer, who was previously known as John who was two years older than Woody.

Three years later, today's cocaine hangover, throbbing from his temples down to his sour stomach, made him want to scream loud enough to drown out the Boston Pops on television. His father was silent and his mother was just beginning to ask him questions. God, he felt terrible.

"I just want an honest answer. All I want to know is what exactly have you have been doing with your time?"

"Mom, be quiet," Woody says.

Of course, she knows what he has been doing because she has even told him herself. Still, he wants to eliminate the burden by confessing it all to her; wants to say that he is getting sick and tired of it. He wants to stop partying, but how can he feel comfortable with that conversation with his mother's accusatory questions, openly interrogating him, like a good crime detective. It would not be about honesty it would be about winning. *This is why and what I need to escape from*, he thinks.

"Be quiet? Don't tell us to be quiet. Your father and I are concerned, Woodrow," she says. "Aren't we, Herbert?" Woody's father lets out a grunt and waves his hand at the two of them in an attempt to quiet them himself and somehow to wish them away.

"Well, don't be. I have things under control," Woody says.

"Well, you know what I think?" his mother says.

"No, I don't, but please tell me."

"Enough of the sarcasm," his father says. "Please stop before "The Stars and Stripes Forever" begins. I'm trying to listen. I'd rather you not ruin this evening for me."

Woody is ready to blow up at his parents, but his mother notices the steam coming out of his ears, so she changes the subject. "Woody, why don't you find a nice girl—someone that might be good for you?"

"Shhh!" Woody's father scolds.

Woody considers the words *good for you*. Usually, good for Woody, by his mother's standard indicates not much fun. She'd be a dull, yet pretty girl, who would study with him and afterwards watch The Boston Pops on television.

"Mom, I told you I met someone," he says, running with his previous lie. "But it's not a top priority, but I'm going with it."

"Maybe someone you won't stay up all night with, huh? A normal girl, with normal hours," his mother says with additional judgment. "Didn't you graduate with one of the waitresses you work with? Her name is Sugar, right? She's a nice girl," she adds, almost beaming.

"Sure, Mom, a nice girl," he says. "Do you mind if I go back to bed, I'm pretty beat."

"Go ahead. Love you," she says. His father turns and shushes her as fireworks begin to erupt on the Magnavox.

41. Sugar Goes To The Show

"Sugar, why don't you find a nice guy—someone that might be good for you," Joe Keating tells Sugar, as Red Sox right fielder, Dwight Evans, camps under a fly ball directly in front of them. Sugar, pulling on her Red Sox cap, has just shared her strange Sayid encounter, on the Fourth of July, with Joe. He, on the flip side, revealed the strange happenings at his party.

"Hmm, a nice guy, you say," she replies. "Do you mean one that knows what tickets to a show mean? The Red Sox are not a show. *Cats* is a show. Fuck, anything in a theater is a show! What the hell happened to *Shear Madness*?"

Keating back peddles, because he spent $10 on these bleacher seats versus $100 for something at The Wang. "Oh, Dwight Evans is a nice guy and I thought you liked the Red Sox. And speaking of nice guys, isn't it pretty nice of me to buy these for you, even if the Sox are doing horribly this year?"

"Are we?"

"Not we, the Sox," Keating corrects.

"That's what I meant. I can barely see anyway, way out here in the bleachers," she says.

Even though Sugar, like the rest of the spectators in Section 37, can hardly see the players, many of the fans have noticed Sugar, who drew some cat calls from the Bleacher Bums when she got up to get a beer and run to the bathroom.

"So, back to the Middle Eastern guy. Tell me something. After he did that in the park, you ended up going home with him?"

"Yes, it's hard to explain, but that's the last time that's going to happen. Obviously, Sayid blew it."

"You mean, you're no longer going to see him?" Keating says almost with glee, until he sees the sadness in her face. "You didn't actually like him, did you?"

"There was a lot to like about him… I mean, his looks, his job, his money and even though he was naïve, he was nice. What I didn't like was his lack of acceptance with women and his other warped views," she said. "I don't want to be in the business of having more experience than my partner, even if he physically seems to know what he is doing. Mentally it's a whole other story." Some of their neighbors in Section 37 have quieted, eavesdropping in on their conversation. "I wish it would have played out differently. I don't want to feel badly about myself."

"Well, look. We can still hang out and do some different things now that Pudlow is gone and the motel option is off the table. If we want to buy anything, it'll have to be directly from the Convoy driver on Wednesday. I think that will be pretty easy."

"That sounds okay and I just want you to know that after everything that has happened, I feel pretty safe with you Joe, unless those times you're acting like a lunatic, which you sometimes do. It's comfortable, and I need comfort right now," she pauses. "So what happened? Jimmy was arrested?"

"Yeah. Thing is, Jimmy swore that someone from Grand Slams called in to report him. That's what he was yelling when they were taking him away. I think it was that moron, Kayak Kenny."

"Why would he do that?"

"Because he didn't get to go… "

"Do you think he's smart enough to do something like that?"

"He's smart enough to dial a phone, yes, but his ultimate plan? What I think is that he was so pissed that he had to work and was just trying to break the party up, not target anyone. He's dumb enough to send the police to a non-specific place and that's why they ended up in the office and not in my room. He's dumb enough to not have a job anymore. In fact I dialed his parents' house and left a few messages telling him not to bother coming in anymore."

"Are you sure about that, Joe?"

"In terms of motive, no one else would seem to have any. The only one I can't account for would be Maloney. Maybe he was just disgusted because he said he had a family get together and I didn't believe him. Who has a family get together at 11 PM?"

129

"I can account for him. He was with me," Sugar says.

"You were with that wise ass!"

"Oh, he's nice… not that I want to date him, but he is a nice guy. We're friends."

"Isn't that what we are talking about? A nice guy for you, who, by the way, looks really damn cute in a baseball cap. You, I mean, wearing the hat, not him."

"Thanks, but I initially thought Sayid was nice," Sugar says, "almost too nice, if you don't take into account his molestation. Honestly, I just don't see me with a nice guy. There needs to be a little darkness within him, but that's just me."

Keating is screwing up his face in a sudden attempt to look dark. He concentrates, narrows his eyes, and attempts to crease his forehead. He wants to look like the nice Red-Sox-ticket-buying guy, with a dark side.

"Are you feeling alright?" Sugar says. "It looks like the hotdog did not agree with you."

42. Kayak Kenny

Kayak Kenny, even after mishandling the clutch of his mother's station wagon and stalling several times, is early for his Saturday morning shift. Usually, one of his parents gives him a ride, but today he drove to work since his parents were away at a Beano convention in Bangor, Maine. Kenny is beaming because tied to the top racks of the car is a brand new, brilliant red kayak. He remembers the only time in his life that he's been this excited: the time his mother bought him a parrot, when he was eight, to help him have a social outlet. She thought that by having the bird as a model Kenny would learn to speak as clearly as the bird and allow him to become better at communication. The plan was for the parrot to pick up what Kenny said to it, which would help Kenny learn how to speak properly and directly. Frenchie, the parrot, had ideas of her own. She was unable to bond with Kenny, and to make matters worse, she could not understand what Kenny was saying. The phrases Frenchie learned came from Kenny's mother, yelling at Kenny:

"SPIT IT OUT, STUPID."

"YOU MORON!"

"YOU'LL NEVER AMOUNT TO ANYTHING."

Kenny tried to teach it to say, "My name is Frenchie," but the bird seemed to know that it had better speaking skills than Kenny and no matter what Kenny did, Frenchie wouldn't pick up on anything Kenny tried. Frenchie was a constant reminder of his mother's taunting. Even today, a day which should be a glorious one, Kenny can still hear the mantra of not being up to snuff. It's always in the back of his mind, some criticism of his job, his shifting of the station wagon and even the spending of his money on the kayak anchored to the roof.

One day, Kenny roughly grabbed the bird, opened the window, and gave Frenchie a toss.

"I got it, I got it!" Kenny shouts at the staff with enthusiasm far too intense for the 7 AM shift. "I want everyone to see my new kayak! Come on outside, everyone!"

Everyone does not include Keating and Sugar, both late. The restaurant runs well in their absence, as Tribuno has agreed to stay on until Keating shows up, and Maura is certainly able to cover all the tables in Sugar's section.

"Come see! Come see!"

Marisimo shakes his head, no. "Sorr-eee, Kenny. I don't wanna fall behind in my work by looking at your boat!"

It seems odd that Marisimo is here with him, as usually they are not on-shift together, but this means that Kenny's probably bussing, so he's happy. "On your break, man. Take a look!" Kenny yells to Marisimo, who is too busy spraying the dishes with the Giant Snake to hear him.

The next person he encounters, to request to take a look, is a limping Maura, who is stunned to see him. "Oh, no, Kenny, I can't right now. I have to cover some extra tables out front. Maybe in a bit, when it calms down, if you're still here. Why are you here? You just wanted to show us your kayak, right?"

Kenny is a little dejected. Certainly, someone wants to see his new prized possession, which he's been saving for all summer and certainly someone would love to go kayaking with him, today, after work.

"No, I don't want to see it," Bobby Maloney says, who has come in, hearing Kenny had some big kayak news.

"I didn't even ask you."

Kayak Kenny starts to head up front to see which waitresses are on, but he doesn't make it. As he turns the corner, he is nearly run over by Mr. Tribuno, who has heard that Kenny is here after being scratched off the schedule. "What are you doing?" Tribuno asks.

"It's Saturday. I'm on the schedule," Kenny says.

Dino Tribuno realizes he has not seen the obvious thick dark line etched on the schedule over his name, Kenny Slatts, something which wasn't easy to miss.

"You're not. Didn't you talk to Mr. Keating?" Tribuno asks.

"Is it because I picked up extra hours over the holiday? It's okay, I can leave and go to the pond. I'm all tied up and ready to go."

"Joe said he called you," Tribuno says.

"Well, if he did, my parents went away, and I don't know how to work the answering machine. I had my neighbor help me tie my kayak to the roof of the car, so if I'm off. Maybe I can come back and see if anyone wants to go kayaking with me after 3 o'clock... maybe one of the waitresses."

"You need to talk to Mr. Keating before you come in again," Tribuno says.

Just then, Keating and Sugar enter together through the back door, overhearing the last words of Kenny and Tribuno's conversation.

"Sorry, Kenny, I think I'm busy at three," Sugar says.

"That's right, you need to talk to me," Keating says sternly.

"What about at four?" Kenny asks Sugar.

"I'm busy then too," Sugar says.

"What are you doing here, Kenny?" Keating asks. "I left you messages to not come in."

"I'm always busy," Kenny says, getting confused within the trio's conversation.

"In fact, I left you two messages yesterday, to not come in until after you called me back," Keating says.

"If I'm off today, maybe I can stick around and see if anyone wants to go kayaking with me after 3 o'clock... maybe someone besides Sugar. She's busy."

"Kenny, not only are you off today but you should have known you're fired," Keating says very directly and not in the usual smile and jerk of the head way he does when he is joking about firing someone for fucking off.

"I'm what?"

"You're fired. You should have talked to me before you came in. You know what you did."

Kayak Kenny doesn't know what he did, only feels a sudden rage, which is obvious to Keating, who hurries into his office and locks the door behind him. Grand Slams is not an establishment with security officers on site to escort the terminated employees out of their place of work.

Kenny runs toward the office and begins to bang on the door with both his fists. "What did I do? What did I do? What did I do?" he repeatedly screams.

Sugar, Maura, Maloney, Geyser, and Tribuno all are watching Kenny loudly pound on the door, until finally Tribuno yells, "What should we do, guys?" Marisimo too, is yelling, but he's giving boxing direction to Kenny as he punches. "Left jab, then a right, now throw the cross... that's it, that's it, Kenny. Now you got it! You going to kill that door."

43. Bobby Maloney: Empathetic Man

Bobby Maloney walks behind Kayak Kenny, who's still striking the office door, now at a slower pace, wraps his arms around his shoulders and tugs him away. He then slowly pulls him down to the floor. Kenny is in sitting position, twitching around and moving his head in an attempt to butt it against Maloney. Kayak Kenny has no idea it is Maloney, and no idea who or what he is fighting.

Maloney uses a soothing tone, calls his name repeatedly, until Kenny becomes docile, like a little Kenny Kayak no longer on the stormy ocean, just paddling around an early morning glass-like lake. When they've been sitting calmly for five minutes, Bobby is able to talk to Kenny and know that Kenny is listening. The way they are sitting, they look like two rowers competing at the Head of the Charles Regatta.

"Hey, Kenny… buddy, I'm off today at three, so what do you say if we go kayaking later, me and you?" Maloney says softly into his ear.

Kenny breathes out, the air slowly floats from his lungs, and he is calm, his face changing color from agitated red to his usual unhealthy jaundice. He has totally forgotten about what has happened. It is almost as if he has blacked out. "Really?" he asks. "Do you think anyone else will want to come? Maybe that new girl, Debbie."

"Debbie?" Maloney asks.

"Debbie Johnson. She did a training shift with me," Maura says. "Tall, dark, and pretty. Almost too pretty, I think. Isn't scheduled until tomorrow."

"Debbie Johnson? She's at UMass in some of my psych classes."

"She likes kayaks," Kenny says, a little too excited to come off normally.

"Keating must have hired her," Maloney says. "Look, I can ask her, but if she says no, don't get all bent out of shape."

"But if she says, yes, that means… "

"Yes, maybe she likes you, Kenny. Maybe she likes you."

Keating pushes the door hard against their two bodies, forcing it open. "Is it safe to come out now?" he asks. "Bobby, let this be an example on how Grand Slams handles snitches."

This morning is a prime example of the way everyone seems to get along with Bobby Maloney. Even Keating gets along with him much better than the usual supervisor/employee forced work relationship. Maloney has the ability to make the awkward, like Woody, comfortable; the comfortable, like Sugar, humble; and the blow-hards, like Keating, human. Maybe he learned this skill by being the new guy, son of an Air Force man, with all the moving around he had done in his life. Maloney had to fit in at every new location. It was something Maloney didn't speak much of. His father made sure he learned to box, so that his classmates wouldn't have an initial edge; the chance to beat him up, which earned him instant respect. It also earned him a little luck too, as boxing became a topic which helped form a friendly relationship with someone like Marisimo. That's how things worked with Bobby Maloney.

He also learned to work hard because of his upbringing. Air Force men are taught to work for everything that they have, to focus and fine tune, so things in life can be worked to your advantage. Maloney resented having to come home from school on the weekends to Grand Slams during the semester, but he knew why it had to be that way. Bobby Maloney had to work and earn extra money so that he could help pay his own way and be the best person he could be. Mostly, he was already that person, he just didn't consider himself in that way.

44. Sugar Knows Where Not To Go

The shift seems to last twice as long for Sugar because of her hangover and the Kayak Kenny drama. Maloney is standing by the time-clock at 3:05, waiting for her, as she reaches for her card.

"You want to come with me?" he asks.

"Didn't we just hang out a few days ago?"

"No, not that. Remember, I told Kenny that I'd go kayaking with him today, to help him test it out? He's going to be here any minute."

Sugar laughs. "Just don't smile at him, okay? That might give him the wrong idea."

"So, you're not going? I think Woody said he'd go."

"No, I'm going home. I feel horrible."

"Yeah, you look a little disheveled."

Sugar suddenly feels even more tired than she did a few minutes ago. She doesn't like looking out of sorts, and it being pointed out hurts her feelings. Her parents were always so good at picking out things like that.

"It's okay," Maloney says, noticing. "You're still the best looking gal, I know."

"Thanks. Why don't you try to give that new girl a call. What's her name? Debbie?"

"Yeah, Debbie Johnson. I know her."

"Then give her a call. She sounds nice and she might want to go today. You would come off looking pretty good if your competition was Kayak Kenny. Unless you think he might have the chance to bag her." Sugar says. Even Maloney, who knows her well, doesn't pick up on the fact she is not joking but rather being disingenuous about Debbie. Sugar's immediate default is that people as attractive as Debbie are to be cut down.

"Do you think she's nice? Fine that you're pushing her off on me though, I mean I'd rather go with you," he jokes.

Sugar smiles in appreciation of his comment and watches Maloney exit through the swinging doors and walk toward the pay phone on the side of Section 1. She leaves through the back to where her truck is, to be sure she's not waiting around when he comes back. She also wants to avoid Keating who wants to grouse to her how his job sucks and about an emergency meeting here tomorrow with the two Bobs. She's already heard all about it.

The truck turns over smoothly and Ricky Skaggs starts wailing his *Highway 40 Blues*, clear as a bell, through its speakers. As the truck's air-conditioner overtakes the vent's hot air, she glances at herself in the rear view mirror and agrees with Maloney's assessment from minutes ago. *Maybe he wasn't just teasing, but why would he point out how terrible I look,* she thinks. *Men never get it.* She guns it out of the parking lot and shoots a left onto Bedford Street, without stopping, and heads toward her apartment.

Nine months ago she would have not have been headed to Billerica but rather to her parents' home in Lexington. She looks down at her right leg that presses on the accelerator, and presses with her hand on her brown stockings, which match her uniform, and are dark enough to cover up the red, inch-long scar from her father's thrown ashtray. It was a usual scene at her parents' house, them drunk and fighting, with her inserting cutting remarks which anyone would find funny, except her parents, who were caught up in the heat of the moment. Anything that could be done to keep them from killing each other was urgent, and Sugar was willing to put herself in the line of fire in order to be the peacemaker. Usually an ashtray would be thrown against the wall, for dramatic effect, but his intent changed after a better than usual zinger from Sugar. Maybe it was because he was a terrible shot, and maybe it was because it was so big and heavy, but the ashtray solidly struck her shin, instead of his intended target, her head.

Last night, Keating saw the scar, and placed his lips on it, his hand tenderly squeezing the meat of her calf in an intimate moment that Sugar incorrectly internalized as him noticing her flab, and probing at what she saw as her pudgy legs. She never allowed Sayid to see her legs, because he would stay focused on them in an over the top lustful way which also made her feel very uncomfortable. She felt Sayid would overheat, as if her legs were the most erotic object in the world to him, which wasn't too far from the truth. Maybe everyone's perception of her legs was not based in reality.

The cab of the truck is cool and felt like sitting in the restaurant's walk-in freezer, but now the walk from the truck to her apartment is so hot, in comparison, she feels dizzy. Inside would be hot too, but the wall unit air-conditioner will cool the place down in no time. She walks across the dark room, sunlight kept out by her shades, and pushes the unit to "HIGH." It's the first thing she does, every time, then stands in place, letting the initial blast of cold air hit her upper body. The red light of her answering machine blinks like a neon sign in a bar room window. She knows it's not Keating, because they hung out last night and he'd be happy about that. When she hits the play button, at first she thinks the tape has worn out, the message sounding so distorted. Then she realizes it's a long and high pitched wailing of Sayid, crying and trying to say something. The message plays until it times out, and then she forces herself to listen to the next three, all equally filling her with revulsion, all equally indecipherable, until she clearly hears the very last nauseating line where he says, "You can keep the watch to remember me by. I don't want it back."

45. Geyser: On Algae Pond

Woody Geyser has changed from his Grand Slams uniform to a pair of cut-off denim shorts and a t-shirt. He wants to take his own car; thus, he'll have an out, so he follows Bobby Maloney's Dodge Monaco, the lead car, and Kayak Kenny's parents' purple Crown Victoria station wagon to Spy Pond in Arlington. How Woody got roped into this doesn't surprise him as he realizes his modus operandi: Feel uncomfortable when you say "yes," uncomfortable when you say "no"—always feel uncomfortable. Woody tries to opt out early by intentionally missing a yellow light in Lexington, but their fearless captain, Kenny Kayak, stalls the station wagon trying to shift, on his way through, leaving the two lead cars waiting for Woody on the other side of the intersection.

Earlier, Maloney told Kenny that Debbie may meet them there, immediately causing Kenny to have what Maloney would say was an out of body experience. Geyser also notes that there was a different Kenny present this afternoon, not the one without a job banging on the office door, in protest, or the one who had held his head firmly against the cement after the misunderstanding surrounding his birthday meal. Geyser knows, through all his discomfort, that his presence would be appreciated, and that it was a good idea, according to Maloney, to have a few people present as a buffer for Debbie.

After snaking through Massachusetts Avenue from Lexington through Arlington, the three cars make a right at Linwood Street before The Capitol Theater and navigate on it until they can't go anymore. On the grass there are various sunbathers, and past them is Spy Pond, a pea-soup colored body of water, totally empty of swimmers. Even the two golden retrievers in attendance weren't going for a swim. The color of the pond is dynamic, a brilliant puke color, much more vibrant in green than the dull tone of Kenny's face. A few younger teenagers sit cross-legged on a long wooden dock, but dare not to stick their feet in the water.

"Here we are!" Kenny shouts.

"It looks kind of gross," Woody says. "It's full of algae."

"It's okay," Kenny says. "Just help me untie the kayak!"

"Gerry makes soup like that from a bag and boil," Maloney cracks. "Maybe, if we're lucky we'll find chunks of ham in the water."

"I don't think I want to go in there," Geyser announces. "The last thing I need is some bacteria to swim into my dick hole."

"Me either," Maloney says. "But we can help Kenny get the kayak into the water."

Geyser and Maloney start untying the close to two hundred knots which hold the red kayak flush against the roof. Geyser breaks out a pocket knife, but Kenny shakes his head and tells him that if he cuts the rope, he doesn't have any extra in the car for the kayak to be re-tied later.

"Great," Geyser says, the pre-launch activity of untying of knots causing him to sweat abundantly in the hot sun. "With that shit water, there's no relief from this heat," he says.

When the kayak is ready to be placed down into the water, Kayak Kenny slips a tiny child-size orange life vest over his head, giving him a bobble-head look. Kenny wades into the pond, along with Woody and Maloney, who stay as close to the edge of the land as possible. Kenny tries to mount, but the kayak slips out from under him, like a wet bar of soap held in a shower, and he falls into the shallow green water, which parts around him.

"Ha!" they hear from the shore, and the three of them turn to look. Debbie's smooth long legs are walking toward them, along with those of another girl, a shorter squat woman with dark stubbly hair on hers. Maloney recognizes her as Debbie's college roommate. Debbie has on a white, terrycloth beach robe and a large sun hat. She is looking at the unlimited sheet of algae on the water and is frowning. Kenny sloshes out of the slime and gets about two inches from Debbie's face to ask her the magical question, "Do you want to go out in my kayak?"

"Oh, you go," she says, obviously skeeved. "I'm just going to get some sun." Her roommate, too, makes a disgusted face at the water and at the boys.

"It's okay. It's my kayak and I can make the first trip all by myself."

"Have you ever been on one of these? You kind of fell on your ass," Woody says quietly to him.

"No, but I've seen pictures in magazines," Kenny counters.

"Fine, then, that's legitimate. Let's try this." Woody drags the kayak back up to the grass, so that the pointed front is in the water and slaps the back of the plastic seat, motioning for Kenny to sit. The girls join him, to help drag the kayak back up, rolling their eyes at their obligation. On land, Kenny is more comfortable boarding, and he looks as happy as a man can once the two-sided paddle in placed in his hands. Staying on the grass, the other four give the vessel a shove, Maloney and Debbie on one side, Woody and the stronger girl on the other. After the big shove, Maloney's arm brushes against Debbie's, and she blushes the same color as Kenny's kayak.

In the water, Kenny's kayak is cutting the algae like butter. He paddles as fast as he can, building up speed, as he distances himself one hundred yards away in just a few seconds. He then turns back to head back to shore, thinking that after such an impressive display, there is no way Debbie would say no to him a second time. As he picks up speed, the four landlubbers become alarmed: Kenny's kayak is on a direct path toward the extended wooden dock.

"Slow down, Kenny!" Maloney yells. "Stop!"

Kenny hears him and begins to paddle even faster, falsely believing this to be the solution. "I don't know how to stop!" he yells repeatedly in some sort of panicked mantra.

Debbie and her roommate begin to yell too, along with the teenagers on the dock. Kenny's face has become less yellowy-green from the exertion, and also more like that of a confused elderly person, who mistakes the gas pedal for the brake. He is almost at full speed when he shouts his final shout. The kayak strikes the dock at alarming speed, cracking the bow and leaving the thrown Kenny, in his life preserver, bobbing like an apple, in the green slimy water.

46. Joe Keating's Do-over

Joe Keating holds a pot of coffee in his left hand and two Double Home Run Breakfasts in his right. He feels well rested, his suit is clean, and his sandy hair is soft and shiny, not stringy like the slivers of greasy hash browns Gerry has slung over each plate with his spatula.

Even Keating's mustache is straight and manicured today. Sugar told him he looked handsome and wished him luck. He was hoping he wouldn't need luck as he knew this presentation was the best he could do for himself.

Joe always wished the stringy hash browns were different. If he had a vote, they would be made with chunks of potatoes, peppers and onions, which also could be in frozen form. Frozen, like most of Grand Slams items, the soups, the gravies, the burger patties, etcetera, make things very easy for the chefs to work with.

At Grand Slams, Keating has learned to work with what he was given, but he did ask Gerry to straighten the items on each of the plates, and add minced ham in the scrambled eggs, just for that added special touch before delivering the food to the two Bobs.

"Let me fill that coffee up for you," Keating says to Blond Bob. "Bob? Your hair looks good, really natural today" he says to the other one. "More coffee for you?" Seeing his dead looking black hair makes Keating's skin squirm.

"No thanks, Joe," Dyed-haired Bob responds, at Keating, but rather off to the side, at Blond Bob.

"Joe, sit down," the blond Regional Manager says.

Keating places the coffee urn down on the table and slides into the booth. His fills his own cup and plants a smile on his face. Sugar heads on over, but Blond Bob waves her off with a polite gesture from ten yards away, which makes Keating nervous, as the Bobs always encourage Sugar to come over to their table.

Dyed-haired Bob Boolay sits with his elbows on the table, hands folded high in front of him, ready to play the role of listener. His gaze is now centered directly on a silent Joe Keating, who is surprised that the big man hasn't started eating, after all, he's a big boy; his tie jutting out at an angle at the crest of his large stomach. Dyed-haired Bob and Keating look at each other, then back to Blond Bob, waiting for him to begin the meeting.

"Let's not mince words," Blond Bob says finally, causing Keating to think of the symbolic extra but untouched minced ham he's served on his plate. "I've received two phone calls, whose sources I cannot reveal, but they are very concerning to me. Both of them reflect upon your job performance and leadership role here at Grand Slams. Your ability to lead a crew is not at all within the vision of Mike Homer, who I knew personally and whose vision I was reminded of by the caller during one of those phone conversations. Do you know what I'm talking about?"

"Yes, and let me say that I promote the Grand Slams brand the best I can."

"Really?" Blond Bob says. "Perhaps you need some re-training, to re-learn how to *Bring the Pride.*"

"I'm willing to do whatever it takes," Keating says, omitting the part of his thought process which tempts him to end his sentence with 'to keep my job.'

"Good, Joe, good," Blond Bob says. "So starting now, I've assigned Bob Boolay to take over store #509, here in Bedford, and after a paid week off, you will come back and train for your new role."

"New role? Are you taking my store from me?" Keating states with an incredulous tone.

"No, we are taking control of *our* store from you, maybe only temporarily, depending on how your training goes. The key will be how you respond to this, but you will start from scratch as if you are a new employee. Let's call it a fresh start."

"Like a new employee," Keating repeats flatly.

"It's better than like a former employee," Blond Bob says and adds, "and speaking of former employees, based on the information we received, Kenny Slatts will be reinstated and paid for his missed shifts and you will have no vote on this. Joe, enjoy your week off—do something fun and relaxing for yourself."

47. Maura, Two Bobs Don't Make A Mike

Maura sees the two Bobs slide out of the booth, and stand up to shake Joe Keating's hand. Keating then walks behind the counter area to return the coffee pot before pushing through the swinging doors out back. By the time Maura has the chance to go to the back herself, she has taken an order and Joe Keating is gone—thank God for that. The Bobs are sitting down enjoying their breakfast hauls. Maura hopes Blond Bob didn't get too specific about her phone call to him.

Maura feels relieved. Keating has been punished, but still, she can't help feeling bad in spite of knowing it was the right thing to do. Maura is full of over-empathy, to the extent of, if the "Killer Clown" serial murderer, John Wayne Gacy, was observed to be suffering with the flu, or stuck writhing in a bear trap, it would stir Maura's empathy pot—even if it were an angry stir, it would still stir it.

Maura restrained herself from approaching the table while the meeting was going on. It would be like an arsonist, standing at the scene of the crime, watching firefighters extinguish the fire they set. Now after Keating has left, it's a good time to check on the Bobs' table to see if there was anything they needed. Before reaching for the fresh pot of coffee, she shoves a few packets of orange marmalade into her apron before strolling over, as she knows it's Blond Bob's favorite.

When Maura asks if everything is okay, they continue their conversation, which is surprisingly not about Joe Keating, but about renovating their buildings across the region. Gone will be the orange and purple donut shop look and replaced by more homey wood grain. More comfortable and attractive looking uniforms is in the plan, and also a larger, more open kitchen area. Currently, the customers can only see Gerry and Gus, behind a three-foot by two-foot opening, which, in their white chef hats, has the look and feel of one or two popes in a puppet show. Dyed-haired Bob is speaking with enthusiasm, but Blond Bob feels that Mike Homer's vision should be honored in some way. After all, Mike was the first to bring in loaves of bread and meats to the original donut shop, to offer lunchtime sandwiches and create what is now Grand Slams Restaurants from the original Homer's Donuts.

Ironic, she thought, *Honoring Mike Homer was about the store's interior, not about the managerial move they just made. Mike Homer would have had none of that, known for cutting and trimming the dead wood of employees and their attitudes, instead of building counter areas with only the look of wood. What's more important is what's inside each employee, rather than what's on the outside, such as, the generic buildings, the uniformed employees, the look of the menus.*

"You made the right decision to call me," Blond hair Bob says to Maura after finishing up his thought about the color of the rubber mats in the restaurant's entrance. "So, this is your new boss in Bedford." Blond Bob points to Dyed-haired Bob with his palm up.

"Well, temporarily," Dyed-haired Bob adds, "until Keating gets re-trained."

"Temporarily?" Maura asks.

"I'm sorry," Blond Bob clarifies. "But I spoke to corporate and they didn't want any chance of a lawsuit. Keating is gone, but he'll be back, all re-trained, re-programed, re-educated in the Mike Homer way. He'll be starting from scratch. Mike would have loved to have been around to see him change to a decent company man."

Maura lets the coffee pot weigh in her hand and rest at a slight angle against the tabletop. "Mike would have fired him and found a decent man to replace him," she responds sharply, then realizing her tongue slip, looks at Dyed-haired Bob. "No offense, Bob, but I didn't mean you. You're going to be a Band-Aid, not the replacement I would have liked to have seen. I know that Dino Tribuno would have wanted and appreciated a promotion as well."

"You know, Maura," Blond Bob says. "Mike Homer was right about you. You are more tough than tender, certainly tough enough to run a Grand Slams, but your toughness and tenderness need to be more balanced. I appreciate your feedback."

Maura walks away, shaken that things didn't go exactly as she had planned. In fact, a lot of things don't go in that way. A quick thought flashes in her mind about her daughter Bridget and about how she had left her, making her more tough than tender from that point on. It draws her thoughts away from the two Bobs and when the regrets about her daughter fade, she sees the Bobs shut their briefcases and get up, but without leaving any money or tip whatsoever.

48. Sugar Hanging By The Telephone

Perhaps Sugar should have gone kayaking because it's one of those boring sit and wait by the phone days, where afternoons quickly become evenings. The only person calling is one of the people she is avoiding, Joe Keating, because even though they just hung out, meeting with him would not be a light or fun time. It would be dealing with him, needy and difficult.

Staying in wouldn't be that bad, if that's what it came down to. *At least I would be taking care of myself, getting some sleep and looking refreshed,* she thinks. Looking good has never been a problem for Sugar, but recent comments have put her head in a place that, in no time, makes her doubt everything.

Joe Keating has called twelve times, the messages ranging from the implication of making the best of it, to a straight anger of his situation; from bewilderment of her not answering or being there for him, to straight anger of her not answering or being there for him. Fact is, she was neither physically nor mentally there and certainly didn't want to be.

As painfully inappropriate as her time spent with Sayid was, she missed filling some of her time with him. Their cultural differences were interesting subject matter, but their other times, when it was physical, were really bad for her mental state. Why would anyone want sex immediately followed by guilt and shame? It's like a woman on a diet, giving in and enjoying an ice cream sundae, then wanting to kill herself—just don't have the sundae. Sugar wanted the option to be able to avoid Sayid, to be in charge of the end of that relationship, but he grabbed it first. She also wants to be in charge of many more elements in her life.

When the phone rings again she sees in the caller ID box that it's Keating and this time she grips the receiver, almost answering it. Before she pulls it off the cradle, she opens her hand and releases the receiver. "Not today, Joe. Not today."

It's a damn shame that Kenny was the one heading to the lake, having all the fun. Kayaking would have been much more pleasurable if anyone else initiated, but he owned the kayak, and he was in control. If it were Bobby Maloney, Woody Geyser, and the new girly only, then the IQ of the group in total would have been tolerable to hang with.

Even the awkward Woody Geyser seemed less awkward recently. In the beginning of the summer she thought he was quiet, quirky and weird, someone who was uncomfortable having people around him, but now, more than a month later, she understands he's just shy. She also knows he can be humorous around the select few people he lets into his life. When Geyser and Maloney are together the interactions seem pretty normal. She wonders why in the world she never had gotten to know Woody Geyser when they were classmates. Perhaps she should stop calling him Woodrow—that might bring his guard down a little. Maybe tone it down with others too. Maybe she shouldn't immediately think of Debbie as "dark haired bitches on wheels" before having the chance to know her. Sugar knows the way she views others needs to change. She misses having parents but is not yet ready to forgive them enough in order to add them to the list.

The watch Sayid gave her sits by itself on her dresser, which is rare, that it is sitting there, because she wears it all the time. The jeweled hands read 8:15, which means that if there's a call, and an opportunity for a night out tonight, it would end much later than she wants—but there's no way to prevent that, nothing she can control, once the watch's hands and the wheels start spinning. She picks the watch up, admires it, and slips it over her wrist.

The rent was last paid in June, the truck payment is late, but one more shift and she will be up to date on that, only a few weeks behind schedule. She thinks being late makes an independent gal like her seem fashionable. She once thought Keating intentionally gave her weekday evening shifts so that she couldn't pay the bills, causing her to be dependent and stay with him. She even stole the schedules from the past six months and researched that theory; counted every shift given to everyone, and to her disappointment, she found out things seemed equitable. *Damn him*, she thinks as the phone rings and this time, instead of ignoring it, rips the handset off the cradle without looking at the number.

"What the fuck do you want, Joe?" she asks, annoyed.

Instead she is greeted with Bobby Maloney's laugh. "Hey, Sugar, do you really think I sound like Joe Keating?"

49. Keating's Hot-Dog Haven

Joe Keating will give up trying to reach Sugar via telephone by 8 PM. It's 7 PM now, and that means a calculated four more phone calls, spaced 15 minutes apart. If Sugar won't pick up maybe he'll go to bed early, a bit funny since when he was working he hardly ever went to bed, but now, with nothing to do, he thinks sleep is the best option. First, he'll eat, but as he contemplates what, he rests his hands on the sticky, crusty, yellow counter top of his kitchen. He tugs at a knife, semi-cemented there by marmalade and tosses it into the sink. Then, he thinks over the possibilities: *Circle the Bases Burger, Super Chicken, Slamming Steak* and his mind goes sour. *I need to not think of food in terms of menu items.* He walks to the pantry and pulls out a can of Franco-American Turkey Gravy. *Mmm, The Nursing Home Special,* then he becomes angry. *I can't even go a minute without using the slang of Grand Slams.*

Back at the refrigerator, Keating pulls the freezer door open. It's not been defrosted in over six months and the hanging element has grown a thick, solid, fuzzy, white chunk of ice over it. Equally frozen is a pack of wieners, which he yanks out of their enclosed ice block. *This is fine,* he thinks. *Grand Slams only offers hotdogs on the children's menu, or by special request from hungry adults who can't boil water themselves, at home.*

The stove top is covered with various burnt remains of quick meals of long ago, some of which had boiled over, pasta sauce which had been sloshed out of the pot by a sloppily handled spoon, bacon grease, and soup which wasn't poured successfully from pot to bowl. All of these have settled and found a home here on the top of the previously white metal stove. Keating fills the aluminum sauce pan with water and clicks on the gas stove.

Turning to face the living room of the basement apartment, where he's lived for the past five years, he can't help but notice the truth, and the truth is, his place is lit by low wattage bulbs and the old couch is lumpy and upholstered in scratchy material. The bed visible, two rooms away, is covered by sheets and blankets that look like they've

153

been randomly tossed around. Last time he laid on them, they felt heavy, damp, and stale.

The water starts to boil; he dials the number and Sugar still won't answer. Keating decides to fuck today and that tomorrow something good will happen. His car has a full tank and a suspension with pay can well be considered a vacation. The greyhounds are running at Seabrook tomorrow at one o'clock, and he thinks with all of his bad luck lately, he is due for some of the other variety. He thinks that is true, if there is a God who believes in the probability of illogical overcorrection, then tails have been flipped all week, so heads are pretty much guaranteed.

The hotdogs hop and spin in the boiling water, and when Keating frees them from their dance, he notices they have gray spots on them; far too disgusting, even if covered with mustard, for human consumption.

50. Geyser: Dancing With Himself

Woody is getting ready for work. He has the afternoon shift, 3-11, today. He wishes he had this shift all the time, until it hits around 8 PM, then he wishes he were home. He takes a comb and pushes his short hair back, as it lifts up then falls like dominoes. He squeezes out some yellow Dippity Do from a tube, rubs it onto and between his fingers, and then fans his entire hand through his hair, the gel making the spikes hold. He then slips on his brown work pants, along with his favorite t-shirt, The Clash-Sandinista, which will be visible through his thin, white, button down shirt.

Thank God all the black bow ties have been thrown behind the ice machine, so he won't have to deal with that clip-on embarrassment today. It's bad enough being a busboy in a place like this, but to also look like the Good Humor man is just too much. He sprints down the two flights of stairs from his bedroom and his mom is waiting at the bottom of them, standing in the living room.

"Maybe we can talk at some point," she says. Woody reads her face as concerned rather than disciplinary, so he responds that he'll be back later, knowing that the talk most likely won't happen by the time he gets home from Grand Slams.

"Maybe tomorrow?" she says.

"It would have to be after work. Tomorrow is Saturday and I'm on 7-3," Woody tells her.

"Are you okay? Feeling alright?" his mother asks. "You seem quiet.

"I'm fine. I'm fine. You're going to make me late."

"Well, you can always talk to me, okay?" Her tone is full semi-conviction.

"Yeah, I know."

"Have a nice day at work," his mother says, as the front door of their house swings to a close.

Woody starts the Toyota, its engine complaining, but Woody turns up the radio when "Dancing With Myself" comes on, to drown

155

out the rough firings. He's relieved to be out of the house because the conversation his mother wanted to start with him is one that they'd had before. She is never direct and only hints at what she is concerned about. In fact, after he was released from the hospital at fifteen, she has never specifically mentioned the words pills, depression, or suicide in any conversation, yet she is his mood monitor, as if there were some way of her knowing that today might be the day that Woody might try it again. If she thinks he's too moody and there is a concern that he can't talk about then she wants him to acknowledge what's behind it. Even if what had happened was a cry for help, a cry for help often doesn't produce help, rather it produces elephants in the rooms of a house.

"You seem quiet," she had said to him on the Fourth of July. Of course he'd been quiet. Quiet is the condition when you had done a lot of cocaine and there was none left or available to do. It's the condition why you'd been yakking away all night about nothing and honestly, you just don't have a single word left in you anymore. Woody had felt tired, in fact he pictured his own energy level like the downward graph of a failed stock market, except his hadn't been selling stocks... only his soul.

Since Keating and Jimmy have been disciplined, in different ways, there haven't been any drugs of any kind at Grand Slams. It's been two whole days and Woody is obsessed. It was rumored that Keating had been arrested too, until Sugar mentioned to everyone at the break table that Keating was at home, suspended with pay. When the food truck came on Wednesday, the Convoy driver hung around an extra hour not doing anything. No one seemed to care or found it odd that the driver was asking relentlessly about Jimmy or that Joe Keating wasn't at work watching the driver's every move. That's when Sugar told everyone what the story was.

When Woody pulls in the back, Bob Boolay, with the most recent and darkest dye job ever, is standing a step outside the open back door, looking at his watch. "You're five minutes late," he says to Woody.

"Sorry, Bob," Woody says, trying to get past Dyed-haired Bob, but finding his path blocked.

"It's Mr. Boolay. No more Dino, Joe, or referring to people by their last name only. It's Mr. Boolay, Mr. Tribuno, Mr. Keating to start. Then we will refer to each other by job title while on shift, such as Busboy Kenny or Dishwasher Marisimo. The guys on the line in white with the hats are Chef Gus or Chef Gerry from now on. No Pope this or Ayatollah that. Got it?"

"Yes," Woody responds. Out of the corner of his eye he sees Kayak Kenny, wearing a crisp new bowtie, zooming past with a brown bus tub and slamming it on the stainless steel dish area.

"I want you to wait three minutes before you punch in, so your time will be rounded up to 3:15. We're all in need of some refocusing around here. And from now on bow ties will be required," Dyed-haired Bob Boolay says. "Here's yours." Bob Boolay pulls out a sealed cellophane bag, with a black bow tie inside. The bag is labeled with a number 27 on it.

"This is your assigned bowtie. Plus sign the clipboard next to the proper number, to indicate that you've received it. If for any reason you don't have it with you, you will not be able to work in the front of the restaurant. Am I clear?"

Woody confirms and walks past Dyed-haired Bob, after he allows him entrance. "I think you're going to like the new professional approach," he tells Woody. "Now you can start with your new attitude here." Dyed-haired Bob motions Woody toward the dish area, which has ten to twelve full bus tubs with dirty dishes ready to be loaded onto a rack, and hands him a green apron. When Kenny speeds past, Woody sees that Kenny is like an older sibling who is about to steal his favorite toy and then, break it like a vindictive prick.

"I was here first!" Kenny yells to Woody. "I was here first. I am working up front!" Kayak Kenny is almost laughing.

Woody is halfway through his shift as a dishwasher, something he absolutely hates. He gets through dishwashing shifts a couple of ways.

One way is thinking about celebrities he's read about in rehab performing menial cleaning tasks such as scrubbing toilets with a toothbrush as part of their recovery. With Kenny working up front, the normal rhythm of dishwashing is out of synch, as Kenny tends to forget about bringing back the dirty dishes till every bus tub is full of them, then they all arrive at once. He hears Dyed-haired Bob try to explain to Kenny how "it is done," but Woody in the course of two months has heard Keating, Tribuno, Maloney, and even Maura go over the same issues with Kenny before each of them finally gives up. It's only a matter of time before Dyed-haired Bob starts bringing back tubs, slapping on a brown apron, over his suit and tie. By the time Dyed-haired Bob has cleared all the full bus tubs to the back, there are five more up front that have been filled.

When the dishwasher falls behind for any reason, this is when the demands come:

"We need more seven-inch plates."

"We're out of silverware."

"No glasses in Section 1."

"No ice cream boats."

Dyed-haired Bob is red in the face and straining while carrying more bus tubs back, obviously not used to the heavier work load of the busy Bedford store. He gives a look of disgust as he passes Kenny, gulping a Coke through a straw.

On top of the tall, side glass racks, Marisimo has left a small radio on which he plays the music from his homeland during his shift. Woody is sure that the new regime will not allow anyone to use the radio, but feels that he should get the first try, because he's stuck back here with dirty plates of dried up fried eggs and the stainless steel inserts of toasted on brown cheese sauce, to be soaked and so they can be scrubbed more easily later. When he clicks the on-off/volume dial, no sound comes out; the batteries are dead. Woody then begins to hum softly to himself, the Billy Idol song stuck in his head, until he has broken out in full song. Usually it's only Marisimo that sings back there, singing along with his radio, the slow romantic songs from The Dominican Republic.

The wait staff passing by takes notice as Woody has a pretty decent voice and the tile surrounding him has added some deeper resonant reverb to it. Of course, everyone is a critic. Maura doesn't like the song, and Debbie would like to hear the Stones. Dyed-haired Bob has a request too. His request is for the radio to be kept "the hell" down and that "work, and not the radio, happen during work time." He tells Woody this after he yells at Kenny to get back in the dish area. Woody thinks that Dyed-haired Bob is putting in for reinforcements, to help him catch up, which Woody doesn't need, as he can catch up on his own; he's the fastest dishwasher they have. Then, Dyed-haired Bob sees the dead radio, grabs it, and yells, "Turn this the hell off!" He clicks it in the off direction, then the on direction and back to off. Then he rips the green apron off Woody, who before he can fully process the thought that he might be fired, is told to put on bowtie 27 and get to the front.

Sugar is stealing clean silverware at Section 3, for her emptied Section number 5, and heads back over in Woody's direction, staring at him all the way.

"Could you clear off some of my tables?" she asks, adding a sigh and a smile. "Kenny has left them there for thirty minutes."

Woody runs his right hand through his hair and it is still crusty, not from the Dippity Do, but rather from some old Cream of Wheat which jumped out of a bowl and into his hair, propelled from the high pressure force of The Giant Snake, the extra-large hanging hose in the dish area. He also has a large sticky spot from one of the single-serving, mini syrup carafes emptying on his bare arm. He feels pretty gross, but then fears Sugar might see it that way too and stops pulling at the crust in his hair.

Sugar smiles, and says. "I heard you singing out back. You have a sweet voice. It's not country, but it would sound good on a Ronnie Milsap song."

"A who?"

159

"Not The Who. Oh, never mind. I was just telling you, you have a nice voice."

Sugar and Woody look at each other, until she notices something, and she takes her hand and runs it through his hair, tugging and crunching away the Cream of Wheat crust, looking a little sad as she asks, "Do you want to help me get organized around looking at colleges?" Rather, he wants to kiss her.

"Sure," he says. "And thanks for taking the cereal out of my hair."

"No problem. You're kind of a mess, do you know that? In the south that would have been grits in there," she adds.

Woody doesn't know what to do, unsure if he should stay at the station or should he leave, so he just stands there until Sugar walks away. Woody lowers his head and wants to kick himself. This could have been a huge moment, an opportunity for him to leave a good impression with Sugar or at least set up a meeting with her outside of the restaurant. Instead, he felt the lasting impression was that he was just a pig, a slob, a partially eaten stuck-on glob of Cream of Wheat haired kid, a singing, sweet as syrup piece of shit without conversational skills...

Sugar turns back to look at him, notes his awkwardness and slightly withdrawn look. "Hey!" she says, causing him to look up. "If you don't know by now, I kind of like people that are messes."

51. Maura Wonders, Wendy What Went Wrong

Maura, strong on her feet and hardly hobbling today, delivers food to Sayid's table with her usual play-by-play. "One Super Chicken and one Circle the Bases Burger," she says. The girl in his booth, with too much makeup and hair as dark as Bob Boolay's, asks Sayid what a Circle the Bases Burger is.

He picks up a menu and reads from it. "This burger scores the winning run on your plate, with a big hit of beef topped with a round onion ring and a walk-off splash of barbeque sauce." He then turns to his date and speaks deliberately, "That, Wendy, is what you call redundancy, because all rings are round." He then looks at Maura and asks, "Is Sugar on today?"

"No," she says curtly, mostly because the girl Sayid is with is looking suspiciously happy with him.

"Not all rings are round," the girl says. "... like a telephone ring. Isn't that right, honey?"

Maura is not sure if she is calling her honey, or if that nickname was intended for Sayid, but either way, it makes her feel a little ill.

"A Super Chicken is like a person who is fearful of returning a few phone calls," Sayid throws out there, assuming everyone here knows the full story about him and Sugar.

"I don't know what you're talking about," the painted-faced girl replies, "Oh, you mean... "

"Yes, Wendy," he says. "We are talking about Sugar, the girl my father thought was not good enough to welcome into the family. Remember? She works here. I told you that."

"Oh... her," Wendy harrumphs, sliding out of the booth and walking through Maura's personal space. "Excuse me, I need to use the little girl's room."

"Sure thing," Maura says, with the smile that kept her bills paid all these years. "Would you like your cup of Decaf after you eat?" she asks him. Sayid shakes his head, because Wendy interrupts his answer with, "Why is it called de calf? Coffee doesn't come from a cow."

161

After Wendy walks away, Maura notices Sayid emotionally sag, his body droop and his eyes grow gloomy. She reaches down and gently rests her hand on his shoulder, in an attempt to reassure him.

When they leave, Maura notices that his tip is not as generous as it normally is. She slides the eight quarters into her Styrofoam cup and shakes it out of habit. Woody approaches the table with a cleaning rag. "Hey, wasn't that... ?"

"Yes."

"Should I tell Sugar he was here?"

"You know," Maura says. "I'm going to stay out of it. He seems a little hung up on her and if you ask me, a little too hung up."

"Hung up in a dangerous way?"

"No, but I wouldn't want my daughter to be dating him. I think Sayid's biggest danger is of embarrassing himself, and that's going to happen, real soon. I don't know that for a fact, but it's a feeling I'm getting because he's rebounding with a girl who's about as smart as that cleaning rag," Maura says pointing to the droopy Handi-Wipe Woody was working with. "You would think a smart guy like that would want to stay with a woman as smart as Sugar."

"Well, you can never tell what the story is."

Woody walks away with a full brown tub of dishes and Maura follows him to the back, past nodding and approving Dyed-haired Bob Boolay sitting at the counter.

"What do you think of that guy?" Bobby Maloney asks Maura, jerking his thumb back over his shoulder in the direction of Bob Boolay, after seeing her and Woody enter the back area.

"I like him. He reminds me of someone Mike Homer would like. He's as professional as, but not as hard-working as Mike, but no one could work as hard as him."

Dino Tribuno enters, about to start his afternoon shift. "What do you think of that guy?" Tribuno asks and jerks his hand in the direction of the front.

"What do you think? Maura replies.

"I think I could run this place. This whole place, I don't know… jeez."

"Don't worry Dino. It's kind of a screw job. Keating will be back next week anyway," Maloney replies.

"Yeah, but who knows what capacity they'll put him in? I hear he has to do all the trainings again, even the most basic ones."

"Maybe he'll be a busboy so he can work next to Kayak Kenny. I mean, shit, after his kayak incident, what should we call him now?" Maloney cracks.

"Maybe, Shipwreck Slatts" Dino says, his eyebrows shooting up in surprise that he made a joke like that. "Maybe Keating will wash dishes next to Marisimo."

"Whatever he does, it had better be better than what he was doing before he left. I don't think I could take any more of that," Maura adds.

52. Big Bobby's Boat Ride

Bobby Maloney, an over-sized nineteen year old, shuts off the engine of his oversized car, a mid-seventies Dodge Monaco, and places his hand out, asking Woody Geyser for some money. Maloney is left hanging, as Geyser and the car sit without moving.

"Hey, we just got paid," Maloney says. "Toss in some money for beer."

"No, that's okay. Not tonight. I have the early shift tomorrow."

"Are you sure? You're not one to turn down an exciting evening of drinking, listening to the radio, and talking in Big Bobby's boat. It begins right here at Lucky's Packy, Burlington, Massachusetts."

"I'm trying to cut down, I mean, after Keating's party. I was totally fucked."

"But that was the drugs, right? You should cut down on those." Now it is Maloney's turn to sit without moving, but what he is doing is waiting for Geyser to change his mind toward putting five dollars into his hand. "Suit yourself," Maloney says, still hanging.

"I will."

Maloney comes back with a brown bag housing a twelve-pack of Budweiser, some snacks, and slides the package between them. He stomps on the gas and guns his way onto Route 3A, turning right without looking. "Slim Jim?"

Woody reaches for the snack, wishing he would have bought some extra for himself or something else to chew on while Maloney is downing Budweiser.

"So, Shipwreck Slatts was kind of pissed off today."

"Who?"

"Kayak Kenny. Since he crashed his Kayak, I like to call him Shipwreck Slatts. Dino coined that."

"You think that nickname will catch on?"

"Well, whatever, but when Shipwreck heard Keating was coming in for re-training, his entire body did a little shake, almost a full body spasm, then he barged into the office to yell at Tribuno. Of course, Dino admitted he had nothing to do with it."

"Of course. Dino has nothing to do with anything—mostly he has nothing to do with anything."

"Well," Maloney adds. "if you listen to Dino, he's primed to run the entire corporation."

Geyser runs his hand upward through his spiked hair. "Hey, can I run something by you? The other day I was talking to Sugar… "

"Wait, you were able to talk to her?"

"At work. I was talking to her, at work, and things got weird. She said she likes messes."

"Was she cleaning?" Maloney cracks.

"No, she said, I was a mess, but she kind of liked messes."

"Do you want me to ask her about that? I could find out if she likes you or not."

"No," Woody pleads. "Definitely not! Please don't say anything to her."

"I may ask her."

Woody hates when Maloney does this. It was kind of a lose-lose, but in the case of either loss, Woody will mentally lose his shit. Maloney notices him quietly seething, so he adds that he's only messing around. "Look, if she put it like that, either she was flirting, or she was reflecting about guys in general that are messes, who are not you—but who she kind of ends up with."

"Huh?"

"Was she smiling?"

"Yeah, yeah, she was smiling. Is she with anyone now?"

Maloney wonders how much information he should give Woody. He knows Keating has been bugging the hell out of her and Sayid, after what he did, is so out of the picture, he is like an empty frame on Sugar's dresser. "What do you think of Debbie?" Maloney asks, to avoid the subject.

"Does Debbie like me?"

"No, I was talking about me." Maloney says. "I think she's nice and all and we seem to have a lot in common, school and work… "

"So ask her out," Woody says.

"Advice given like a dating pro."

Woody snaps the last piece of Slim Jim in-half with his front teeth and chews it for a while. "Hey," he says, "how about one of those Budweisers?"

"Also spoken like a true pro," Maloney says, passing him a can with one hand while pulling up the "Sta-Tab" with the other.

53. Kayak Kenny

Kayak Kenny can be overheard yelling about Joe Keating from the dish station, but Keating doesn't care. Joe Keating is too busy with his training. He is focusing on, *Diner Amongst Friends,* the Grand Slams training film which teaches employees to be nice at all times. There's even a section in which the customers are being abusive to a waiter and the waiter responds with a smile and greater effort in providing good service. Normally, Keating would be obviously rolling his eyes, or thinking about the recent spaghetti incident, but today he is poised and attentive. Kayak Kenny keeps yelling, even though he's being ignored. Kayak Kenny is trying very hard to be noticed.

"He tried to get me fired and now he sits there and watches TV!" Kenny complains to Debbie, the first person walking by, "and how could I buy a new kayak without a job."

Debbie, after the Spy Pound adventure, knows that Kenny's brain works kind of slow and is not at full capacity. She had previously thought he was a stoner or just perpetually tired from working so much instead of the slightly deprived, mentally sluggish man complaining to her. She passes by Keating who is preparing for the quiz covering the *Hot, Hot, Hot* pamphlet.

"Debbie," he says. "This pamphlet was written about you." This time, it is Debbie who rolls her eyes.

All of this is seen by Kayak Kenny. Kayak Kenny looks at things the way a dog might; eyes open, getting credit for understanding more than he does, actually not grasping much of it.

Kenny sees that Debbie, after ignoring him, is now talking to Maloney. He also has observed Keating trying to talk to Sugar, who is spending her time talking to either Woody or Maloney. Tribuno, he notes, talks to the two Bobs, and sometimes Maura, unless he is bossing employees around. Kenny notes these interactions but doesn't know what they might mean. Kenny would like to talk to Keating, but Keating isn't talking to him which pisses him off, because he would like to fight with him. Kenny, left to his own devices, ends up yelling about Keating to the dirty dishes.

Dyed-haired Bob taps Kenny on the shoulder and Kenny jumps as if he's leaping on a trampoline. "Can I have a word with you?"

"No, no, not again," Kenny cries, thinking that this is the end. "I'll never be able to afford another kayak."

"No, it's just things have been loud today. I want to talk about that."

"I'm mad," he says.

"Just come with me," Dyed-haired Bob prompts him.

Kenny follows Dyed-haired Bob into the office and the door shuts behind them. Dyed-haired Bob pulls the desk chair out enough so that his large stomach can fit behind the desk. "Let's start with this. The most important thing that a Grand Slams employee can have is pride and job satisfaction, because it *"Brings the Pride"* and leads to professional A+ work. You seem to be displaying a lack of satisfaction today, without any gratitude, even after you were reinstated. What can we do to make that better?"

"You can fire Mr. Keating..." Kenny says.

"Well we can't—"

"... that asshole," Kenny concludes.

"Well, we can't, and also we can't have that language around here. Professional standards are being violated. You will see that Mr. Keating will be a changed man after his training. He will be a prime example of increased professional standards around here—someone to emulate. Expect it! Speaking of which, have people been referring to you as Busboy or Dishwasher Kenny while on shift?"

"Maloney has been calling me a swill pig today," he says.

"Well, he should not do that. What about the professional designation."

"I'm called Kayak Kenny, but today Bobby Maloney also called me Shipwreck Slatts. I don't like that."

"Well, that's not a professional designation." Dyed-haired Bob says, sweeping the bangs of his brittle black hair to the side. "From

168

now on I'm hanging a clipboard up on my door and every time someone calls another employee anything else but their designated name, that person should place a mark next to the offending party."

"Who is Mark?"

"A mark is a line. They should place a line next to the offending party."

"I didn't get to go to the offending party. I had to work."

"Look, Kenneth," Dyed-haired Bob says, placing the clipboard in front of Kenny. "When someone calls you anything but your designated name, you can place a line next to their name. Do you understand?"

"I think so," Kenny says stroking his chin. "If someone calls me Shipwreck Slatts, instead of Kayak Kenny, then I draw a line and cross out their name. If their name is crossed out will they be fired?" Kenny is suddenly worried that Maloney might be fired, so he doesn't attempt to draw a line through his name.

"No, like this," Dyed-haired Bob says, pulling the clipboard away from Kenny, in order to demonstrate how this will be done. "If you are not called Busboy Kenny, you can draw a small line here, next to whomever." Dyed-haired Bob places a mark next to Marisimo's name, as an example, even though Marisimo is not on shift today.

"Oh, anyone I want. Today Maloney called me Shipwreck Slatts, so I'm going to put a line next to Keating's name."

Dyed-haired Bob is frantically scrubbing with his palm the hair over his forehead in frustration. "No, you have to... damn, you're stupid! " He looks at his hand and is surprised that no black has rubbed off onto it.

Kayak Kenny makes an angry face, because Dyed-haired Bob Boolay has called him by a name he is deeply familiar with, a name he has been bullied with ever since he was smacked in the head by a canoe oar. Holding the pencil tightly in his closed right hand, like a knife, he snatches the clipboard away from Dyed-haired Bob with his left hand, and places a long loud slash through the name of Bob Boolay.

54. Keating, The Insider vs. The Outsider

What people think of Joe Keating is not what Joe Keating thinks of himself. People think Keating is shady. Keating is an addict, who is always holding. Keating is no fun. Keating's relationship with a girl the age of Sugar is creepy. Keating will never rise up the company ladder. Keating lives for the attention from women. Keating is lazy. Keating is a "cocaine monkey." Keating does not care what others think about him.

These are all true, except he is not always holding, but used to be able to get some anytime he wanted from Jimmy Pudlow. Now he has to wait for the truck to arrive, once a week.

When Keating pals around with his friend Sugar, it makes him feel pretty good. The reality of the situation is that, often, it is out of convenience for her as Sugar does not have to drive thirty minutes to her house. Also, she conveniently likes drugs and she likes hotel rooms. Even motel rooms are a stretch she is willing to take. Even hanging out with Joe Keating is a stretch she's willing to take, but this stretch is getting larger and larger now that the deal he had with The Super 8 is off the table.

Joe and Sugar feel that sometimes their conversations can be interesting. They also feel that sometimes they can get completely halted. How things go is completely based on the amount of, or lack of, cocaine in their systems. Without the drugs to stimulate him, Keating falls into boss/employee/work subject matter, followed by the misogynistic repetitive objectification of Sugar's petite body parts. Joe finds it funny, but Sugar, either high or not, never pretends to be amused anymore.

Joe Keating has been scoring 100% on the quizzes, but all of the work is now being done in the break area, in plain view of everyone, and not inside his former place of status, the closed door of his office. Now, completely visible and with no place to hide, Joe Keating is stuck with boss/employee/work conversations in regard to his role as the

170

trainee. He is stuck watching the same films, taking the same tests that Woody Geyser, Debbie Callaghan, and Christ, even Kayak Kenny have taken. He hears the same dumb jokes in his head that Maloney makes at the same points of the same videos. When he passes the break area today, Maloney says every time, "It may not be your way, but it's the Grand Slams way and you always want to hit a Grand Slam with your customers." Keating must fake laugh, to show he is now a team player. He must also trim his mustache so it is no longer droopy. After the fake laugh he's sure everyone can hear, he tells Big Bobby Maloney to *go fuck himself* at a volume only loud enough for the two of them to catch.

Dyed-haired Bob now sits at Keating's old desk, which is cleaner than ever before, completely detailed and organized. Dyed-haired Bob has used some of the Grand Slams special cleaning products and soft sponges to *"Bring the Pride"* back to the manager's office. The door is open, an unusual occurrence as recently as a week ago. Under Keating's rule, the only time he kept it open was to overhear conversations. Today the only thing Keating is trying to hear is the food delivery truck, the Convoy, due in to supply all products.

Dyed-haired Bob is preparing the Manager's B Training Packet, the training for days two and three, which covers helping others during rushes and other busy times. Thursday and Friday, Blond Bob will give him the Manager's C Training Packet, which covers everything he used to do, which includes preparing and organizing Manager's A and B Training Packets for days one through five and the quizzes to be taken after every completed section.

When Sugar comes by to take her break, Keating keeps the video running but locks his attention on her. "How's it going, my pirate's dream?"

"Huh?"

"You know, sunken chest and valuable hidden booty."

Sugar looks at him, drops her fork into her plate of fried eggs, and clomps off. Dyed-haired Bob, with door open, overhears the interaction and dials corporate, asking for Blond Bob.

Dino Tribuno walks in and camps himself directly over the seated Keating. Nine months ago, Keating had given Dino the exact same packet and quizzed him on this exact same film, except that a part of Dino's training involved the caveat of, "we don't do it that way here". Now Dino throws that quote back to Keating, who replies, "but we will now."

Dyed-haired Bob, who had planned on a positive report today to give Blond Bob, is now saying that there may be more training needed. Chicopee may need to take care of itself without him for a bit more.

At 2 PM, Keating is called to his old office by Dyed-haired Bob who hands him an 8 ½ by 11 inch white envelope and a VHS tape, both decorated with the bright red and yellow Grand Slams logo on the front. "You will have three quizzes today, which I'll take a look at, but the Manager's C Packet will be reviewed by Blond Bob, who will interview you on Friday.

"Does this mean that next week, I'll be back at my old position?"

"Based on how you do, along with your attitude and approach, there is a chance of that, but I'm not going to make any promises. Blond Bob's final interview is to make sure you will be *Bringing the Pride*" from now on."

The beeping from the Convoy's backup warning alarm can be heard outside, over Keating's conversation with Dyed-haired Bob, so Keating excuses himself and heads out the back door. He waits for the parking lot traffic to pass as he crosses, locating the exact spot near the Super 8 Office of where the cab of the food delivery truck will stop moving. He stands there waiting at attention.

55. Geyser's Overwhelming Awkwardness

Sometimes, Woody Geyser feels so innocuous he fears that he may disappear. He may as well be invisible, but inside there's a simmering of angst and discomfort that very few have been able to peel back and then see him for the actual person he is. This hardly bodes well, in general, for interpersonal relationships and dating.

For example, Woody knows that this is typical of his behavior: He has worked several shifts with Debbie, but perhaps, to overestimate, he has said no more than one hundred words to her and of those 95% have been work related. When he and Maloney are by themselves, they talk about her much more freely and in the same way they used to and sometimes still do, talk about Sugar. Maloney says that Sugar once told him that his faux confidence was difficult to read, that at first Maloney was strong and appealing, but as a short time went by, the confidence faded and then, the friend-zone window flew open. Woody replies that he doesn't believe in that concept because he's content if he is considered within any zone at all, which, of course, is another symptom of feeling he's invisible.

Woody tells Maloney that with Sugar it's not what she says but the tone in which she says it. When she is sweet her words are relaxed and sing-song, but when she doesn't want much to do with you she is pointed and direct. Lately, Woody has noticed that when she calls him Woodrow, even spoken when she has been sad, the name is caroled like one of the parts of a perfect two-part harmony. Ironically, the only time Woody feels he is in tune is when he is by himself, doing such things as singing songs from the Grand Slams Top 40 in the dish station.

When Woody is back home, he'd like to seep into the thick carpet of his parents' house and not be seen. When his mother vacuums, there is a risk he can get sucked in and disappear forever. He knows, even in metaphor, there is a problem with that, yet he continues. Eventually, his will be dumped with the dirt from the vacuum bag, into the trash and then, worse for wear, he will be discovered.

Woody knows, as much as he tries, he can't disappear. He is always found out. He thinks his mother and father *do* actually know what he is doing, so even when he's not doing anything, they now think he is lying. Of course the, "I think I'm in love" lie when he was coming home from an all-nighter didn't help his integrity one bit.

A few nights ago, when he was trying not to drink, he came home to his waiting mother and, to overcompensate for his lack of credibility, told her that he was trying to cut back. Initially, he thought it was a good idea, but tonight he knew he would be coming back with the smell of quite a few Budweisers on his breath after being out with Maloney. Oh, to disappear, to disappear, to disappear.

The first time he drank in high school, it was just the opposite. He went from being invisible to being visible, but in a way which was accepted. He drank a six-pack during his free period, and then threw up inside the school. He was immediately notorious, and if popularity was to be measured on a scale of 0-100, he had gone up about 50 points.

His father's "boys will be boys" approach to this had been alright at first, but since he has been to college and his drinking has become more noticeable, this approach by his father has faded. Boys could be boys, but preferably be boys that handle their alcohol, without having a problem. That was the message conveyed by his father through his strong silence as his dad often communicated best in that way.

His mother, on the other hand, was a talker, looking to verbally resolve every situation. If it were only that easy, if things could be tidied up neatly in a box with a great big bow. His mother wanted the family to function like happy little television plots everyone watched on shows such as, *Family, Highway to Heaven, The Brady Bunch* and *Leave It To Beaver*. If only the Beaver's usual angst and anxiety was more realistic and couldn't be wrapped up with love and understanding in thirty minutes. What if it were left untreated? What kind of show would that be? It would be real, that's for sure, something you could tune into to watch people suffer.

56. Maloney: In The Friend Zone

While driving to work, Maloney is considering Sugar's theory about his faux confidence. Not to second guess himself about his status with her, because he is grateful for Sugar's friendship and only her friendship. Maloney knows there is no way the two of them would ever become involved. They both know it. She would have to be the one to make a strong play toward him in order to change. The ball is in her court, but the ball has been lost. It's just a court. At one point she might have liked him romantically, then there was a delay on that, and now he's been relegated to a really good friend in the friend zone. *Could have been worse*, he thinks. *Sugar is a pretty cool chick to hang out with and have on my side.*

He plays it out in his mind—the friend-zone thing, how he ends up there, using various Grand Slams related metaphors. Friend-zoning is kind of like a 3-11 shift. At the beginning of it, you are all happy and full of energy, exactly like the potential of starting a relationship. At the middle of the shift, you work as a team, and it gets late and you get tired of the game, but perhaps it can still happen. Then, just when you think you could still make it, a tour bus coming back from the Lexington Green stops by, and 100 people all enter the restaurant at the same time and you're fucked. You never had a chance.

Friend-zoning, Maloney thinks, is also like a boxing match that ends in a draw. At one point you may even have the girl on the ropes and you're confidently going in for the knockout. Maloney goes with this thought, even though he's against anything having to do with punching a girl. Anyway, he thinks, you go in for the knockout, but it takes too long as you don't have a knockout punch and then, when she comes out of the corner swinging, keeping herself in the match, it's been long enough for you both to realize that you cannot finish. Thus, the match results in a draw or in this case, the potential lover, winding up in the friend-zone. Either way, the ending is cordial, as it should be, two boxers hugging after an even match.

175

Maloney, now on the clock, sees that Debbie is working tonight and is no longer shadowing another waitress; her training is now over and she is flying alone for the first time. Maloney pulls a comb out of his back pocket and runs it through his straight, dark hair. Then he takes a quick assessment on Debbie's work performance and observes her customers trying to flag her down, some of them so vigorously that they could be hailing a cab in New York City during rush hour. There are many plates of food sitting under the heat lamp, waiting for her to deliver, and Gerry continuously rings the bell for her to come and grab them. Tribuno has to pick up some of her orders and get them out to the hungry jack-offs, who just want their burgers or eggs and don't care if Debbie is behind or not. Tribuno has to answer the same two questions again and again: "Where did our waitress go?" and "Is she new?" Also, there is a line at the door because the tables aren't turning over as quickly as they should be, causing a domino effect. Since the tables aren't turning over, there are no dirty plates for Maloney to bring back to Kayak Kenny to wash.

Maloney heads to the back so he can avoid the customers asking him where Debbie is and then he finds out exactly where she is. Debbie is standing a few feet outside, puffing on a cigarette, hair scattered, and a couple of runs in her stockings.

"I don't think I can do this," she says, eyes angry and on fire.

"Oh, yes you can. You'll get used to it. How do you think Sugar started and for that matter, Maura, years ago?"

"Fuck that. I don't want to be like Sugar or Maura. How long do you think I want to stay here?" she responds.

Dino Tribuno runs into the back, sweat dripping from his face, dampening his mustache. "What the fuck are you doing?"

"I'm on break," Debbie says.

"Break? I should get all those tips. I'm basically earning those."

"Keating lets me smoke," Debbie fires back.

"That's while you were in training and now because of his shit, he's in training too. You're on your own now, so put that butt out and head up front—break's over!"

"Yeah, yeah, break's over," she says, firing the cigarette off the concrete, so that a plume of sparks pops off the cigarette.

"This won't do," Tribuno says in a harsh tone. "Things will no longer fly the way they used to. There's a new Keating coming soon."

"Well if that's the case, he can cover my tables and probably do better than you are doing, Mr. Tribuno. Look at you huffing and puffing."

"Careful of the irony," Tribuno says.

Kayak Kenny overhears the commotion and Keating's name and walks out from behind the dish station, more yellow than ever. Maloney, Debbie, and Tribuno are scurrying in motion, in three different directions, but Kenny zeroes in on the strong-willed waitress.

"Hey, Debbie," he says jogging after her. "When I get my new kayak, do you want to go out with me again? It'll be better than the last time and I can give you a ride…"

"Suck it, Shipwreck Slatts," she responds quickly.

Kayak Kenny remembers Dyed-haired Bob wants him to do something when this happens, but he has no idea what it is.

When the rush finally dies down, Maloney finds Debbie outside, smoking another cigarette. Even though it's busy, he found the shift to be pretty boring, as the more the professional attitude the new regime has brought, the less the fun. This is his overall conclusion.

"Debbie, did you *"Bring the Pride"* today?" Maloney asks sarcastically.

"Yeah, right," she says. "I'm thinking about why I didn't bring my prideful ass back to retail. I think I made a mistake thinking that this was a good idea."

"Tough night?"

"You saw what happened and on top of that, I made less than 15% on my tips. The Double Home Run Breakfast is set at $2.99 for the month, so do the math. This shit ain't paying for college."

"Want to get drunk?" Maloney asks.

177

"Yes, the thought had crossed my mind, but I was just waiting for someone to ask me. Hmmm, it was either you, Kayak Kenny, or Mr. Tribuno. Tough decision as your competition tonight is either stupid or married, which makes them both stupid, I guess."

"I think we should go for margaritas."

"Umm... no. I think we should go for beer in a dive that has darts and pool."

"The Web Brook?"

"Perfect."

57. Maura: A Momma, To Almost All

Maura often feels that she is good at all things related to Grand Slams but bad at everything else relating to life. She and Grand Slams Restaurants are joined at the hip, a long term relationship. Her relationship with her own daughter isn't this cut and dry. That relationship fills Maura with regret. Wasn't Bridget just toddling around, her curly blonde locks, almost white in color, bleached out by the California sun. It doesn't matter if Maura is now everyone's mother here at Grand Slams, when her own daughter is far, far away.

Visiting last Christmas wasn't quite enough and it almost didn't happen. Keating asked her to stay and work because she was needed, but it was only when some of the college girls came back to work during their Christmas break that she was given the green light to go. Although she is proud of her twenty-year pin, it doesn't grant her the respect that she definitely deserves as a Grand Slams lifer.

She had called Bridget a few weeks earlier on her birthday. Her daughter hadn't called in a while, which wasn't unusual, but the lack of a call caused Maura to worry that she might have relapsed. Afterward, she wondered if Bridget sounded right. During the birthday call, Maura asked if Bridget wanted to come to Massachusetts and visit. Maura would pay for her plane and expenses, but Bridget had balked, mentioning some interview for a job that would never be mentioned again.

Did I fail? Maura wonders. She and her daughter lived on two sides of the country, and barely spoke. It's the reason she does what she does, giving a mother's opinion to Sugar, Maloney, Kenny, and sometimes Woody Geyser. *That kid is one tough nut to crack,* she thinks. Maura can't understand him, much like the way a person can't see a rock under the surface of the water until their boat or kayak hits it. Often you paddle into a dock, as obvious or visible as it may be. Woody's own mother, Maura reasoned, seemed nice enough. A bit overbearing but, still very nice. Perhaps there was something else going on?

If only things had been easier. Maura never thought she would grow old, her self-image wrapped up in the goals and appearances of a restaurant. Of course, it made sense that she made the call to bust Keating, but she was sorry that it netted Jimmy Pudlow. About that, she felt awful, but there was nothing that she could do about that prideful act, nothing that wouldn't have left her job and her life totally exposed for what it was.

58. Sugar: Watch Out For Your Tables

Sugar fields an apology from Maura for seating Sayid and his date in Sugar's section. They wouldn't take no for an answer about an alternate placement, so they are there, sitting in front of the big window of Section Five. Sugar sees Sayid and his heavily painted with make-up date taking a sip of their soft drinks. Sayid stares intensely but forlornly at Sugar. The morning's ominous, dark sky could erupt into a thunderstorm at any moment. Wendy's stare, in comparison, could only be described as a similar dark cloud with an umbrella of supreme smugness.

"Fuck, I don't believe it!" Sugar says, causing the customers in Maura's section to look at her. "Tell them to wait a minute," Sugar says and retreats to the back.

Sugar is breathing heavy, her tea kettle about to blow. *What the fuck am I getting upset over?* she thinks. She reaches up to sweep the hair off her face, and her expensive watch momentarily scrapes her cheek. Quickly, she pulls the watch off and tucks it into her apron, next to her order pad.

"What's wrong?" Joe Keating asks.

"He's here in my section."

"Who?"

"Sayid and some bimbo are sitting in MY section."

"I'd assign another waitress there, if I were permitted to, or I'd move them for you, but I'm also not allowed on the floor."

Woody and Marisimo hear what is happening and walk over. "You, okay?" Woody asks.

Sugar nods. "I'll be okay, Woody... and Joe," she says. "Thanks."

"Hay No Se Que Hacer," Marisimo starts to sing. It's the slowed beginning of a sweet merengue song, "*Hay No Se Que Hacer*," voiced over the sound of a large thunder clap. "You should dance," he says, temporarily stopping his warble, moving his hands in a slow circle, a prompt for Sugar and Woody.

Woody takes her in his arms, inhales her scent as they sway for several seconds, and Sugar feels herself relax in his embrace, until the tempo in Marisimo's song quickens, forcing her into a laugh and to disembark from him, the rhythm completely off. She is grateful that Woody didn't grind against her like some boy might at a middle school dance. Something like that wouldn't be so difficult to believe. "You smell better than anyone here," Woody says. "Not at all like the eggs and syrup everyone else smells of."

Sugar thinks he is joking, but notices his reddening face and his shy demeanor makes her smile. At one time she would have made fun of that, but after what she has been through recently, she honestly feels a bit different. "Thanks guys for cheering me up," as she reaches out to squeeze Woody's arm.

Coming out of the back Sugar heads over to Sayid's table. Wendy is staring her down while Sayid is looking both devastated and disgusted at the same time, refusing eye-contact with Sugar.

Why did he even bother to come here, if he looks like that, Sugar marvels. "Well, what can I get you?" Sugar says, trying to sound as nonchalant as possible.

Sayid tries to speak, but all he can do is swallow hard, so Wendy pipes up in her thick Somerville accent. "I'll have a Circle the Bases Burger. You know what that is, don't you honey?" she says to Sugar.

"Yes, I know what it is. I've been serving it for over a year."

"It's a redundancy burger. Isn't that right, honey? The Onion Ring makes it a redundancy."

Sugar turns to Sayid. "And for you?" Sayid can only shake his head slowly.

"Baby, are you alright?" Wendy says to him. When she gets no response, she pushes her water over to his side of the table and tells him to drink it. Wendy looks up at Sugar. "You know, you're an asshole for hurting him like that. Do you know what he told me? He told me that you forced him to do things he wasn't comfortable with—sins against his religion. You made him a sinner."

182

"He started the sinning on his own."

"Well, whatever! When things happen with him and me, it's all my fault, and when he says 'no', I listen. So listen, honey, no means no! Got it?" Wendy snarls.

"Yep," Sugar responds bluntly. "and is that everything?" Sugar spins to turn away, and when her back is toward them, she hears Sayid say the word that he usually ends his meal with, "Coffee."

Coffee, Sugar thinks, upset that she could have been affected a few minutes earlier by the sight of them. *And only one word. Usually he says, 'It's time for coffee' but I guess I've hurt him so much by being that slut that I am, he can only say one word. I must have slutted the other three out of him. Plus, that bitch treating me like she's above me—she can suck a big dick.*

When the Circle the Bases Burger is up, Sugar brings the plate to Center Station and rests it there. She grabs a cup and fills it with Sayid's coffee. Pulling the watch out of her apron, she drops it in the full cup and delivers it to their table.

59. Keating's Interview

It's Friday and Joe Keating sits in a booth in Section 1 across from Blond Bob, fielding a sequence of interview questions, some he'd originally heard years ago.

Blond Bob: Tell me Joe, how do you reinforce, in a non-monetary way, a behavior by an employee that you want repeated?

Keating's First Thought: *Become a rah-rah fucking cheerleader.*

Keating's Answer: Verbal encouragement during the task is very important. It's important that other employees hear what you are reinforcing too. Saying things like, "Bobby, I like how carefully you are carrying that bus tub." or "Marisimo, you are working much faster than your usual snail pace today." Really keep the employees on task in the way Grand Slams would like to curve their positive work behavior.

Blond Bob: Okay, good. Now how do you build and maintain morale with your staff (in a non-monetary way)?

Keating's First Thought: *Why build morale as this place will suck the morale right out of you. They respond better with teasing and sarcasm, trying to avoid it, and of course, they respond to money. What the fuck is all this non-monetary way language?*

Keating's Answer: Encourage them to spend time with each other outside of work. For example, recently some of the staff went on a kayak trip together. It was a load of fun that didn't involve money.

Blond Bob: How do you demonstrate that you value people for who they are, rather than for what they accomplish?

Keating's First Thought: *You kiss their ass, give them your drugs, and pretend you are into what they are into.*

Keating's Answer: Getting to know the employees for who they are and taking a real interest in the things that are important to them in their lives is important. *Quit saying "important".* For example, we have a lot of college students working here, so talking about their studies and

184

where they think they will land at a job is important. We also have people like Maura, who has been here for over twenty years, and for people like her. It's important you build up the fact that they are loyal to the company and that they have no outside life. This is the Grand Slams way.

Blond Bob: What are the primary management styles? Describe each. Which is your predominant style?

Keating's First Thought: *Iron fist, my way or the highway. Hmm, do I remember yesterday's training video—I'm about to nail this.*

Keating's Answer: Well, there's the autocratic management style, where the manager makes decisions without much regard for subordinates. As a result, decisions will reflect the opinions and personality of the manager, which in turn can project an image of a confident, well managed business even if the subordinates feel powerless. The second is a democratic style, where the manager allows the employees to take part in decision-making: therefore everything is agreed upon by a majority vote. That's a good style if you want to go out of business. Lastly, the Grand Slams preferred method is the consultative form, which is also essentially management ruled. However, decisions do take into account the best interests of the employees as well as the business. Communication is again generally downward, but feedback to the management is encouraged to maintain morale, as employees feel they have a say, even if they don't. As far as my style, I'd say it's autocratic, but if I want the employees to falsely feel they are a part of the process, I can pretend it's consultative—which is what you and Bob Boolay practice.

Blond Bob: What successes and shortcomings have you experienced with your management style?

Keating's First Thought: *I've had success with being the all powerful, but because of that, people hate me.*

Keating's Answer: I would say success wise, this Grand Slams will live and die with my decisions, but the numbers we have here, in pure economic terms, makes my work here successful. The shortcomings are that I become the fall guy and scapegoat. I think what happened recently, my suspension and re-training was an example of that. Perhaps, this time around, I'll do it the Grand Slams way.

Blond Bob: Describe a challenging situation and the method you used to meet the challenge.

Keating's First Thought: *When Jimmy was arrested I had to go directly to the Convoy to score.*

Keating's Answer: When the staff gets busy and behind in their work, stepping into their job to help out, trying to meet the goals of employees and also maintaining the goal of customer satisfaction. On the employee end, like what I watched yesterday, the feeling that we're all in this together is a good motivator. On the customer end, they see the main man, me, the guy in the suit, who is humble enough to give great service in the face of less capable employees.

Blond Bob: Describe an assignment you were given that you knew would be unpopular, but you completed successfully.

Keating's First Thought: *This week's fucking training.*

Keating's Answer: I complete a lot of unpopular tasks successfully. Nearly everything here is unpopular to some or all of the employees and certainly unpopular for me. Increasing the ice cream menu and training the wait staff to make the desserts affected their timing and their tips, but I told them that they didn't have a choice and they needed to suck my... I mean, suck it up. Turned out that the new ice cream desserts were a big hit.

Blond Bob: Describe a situation when you went above and beyond to complete a task you were proud of.

Keating's First Thought: *Getting into Sugar's pants!*

Keating's Answer: Helping out with the delivery truck is something that most managers do not do. What usually happens is that

186

extra employees are called in from home, for a few hours, to complete that task, which brings up payroll numbers. For me, it means working more than my usual hours, so that we, as a company have less outward cash flow. Cash flow is very important in helping us move in the right direction, certainly it shouldn't be used on the delivery truck, not if I can help it—I can save money that way, plus establishing a positive relationship with the driver makes it a great big happy world at Grand Slams.

When they're finished, Joe Keating thinks he has nailed it. His answers had just enough swagger and confidence, mixed in with the company ideals. Keating cannot wait to regain his position, so that the first thing he can do is make up something horrible Kenny did on the job and fire his ass.

Blond Bob takes the answers to the written test back to the office and scores them, leaving Keating at the table. Then he fills out an "Impression Sheet" based on the interview to fax to the corporate office after he speaks to Dyed-haired Bob. Kayak Kenny walks into Section 1 to grab the dirty plates from lunch which have been left on the table behind Keating for over an hour. Keating has an urge to trip him, even imagines the sound of all the dishes shattering. Instead, he looks away, but only until Kenny opens his mouth.

"I didn't snitch," Kenny says, "and I still work here."

"You're the only one that could have made the call."

Kenny's voice grows suddenly loud. "I didn't make any call."

Keating needs to quiet him down quickly, otherwise his entire week of being an exemplary corporate man will be tossed out the window. "Hey, Kenny, let me give you some work advice."

"I don't want to hear it."

"Well, I'm going tell you anyway. If you want to get that replacement kayak bought and launched before a few summers have passed, don't fuck with the management, because no job means no money, which means no kayak," Keating warns, as a flash of lightning from the storm illuminates Kenny's face like a Frankenstein monster in an old-time horror movie.

"It's raining anyway," Kenny says. "So there."

Blond Bob and Dyed-haired Bob Boolay are wobbling and walking through the back swinging doors to rejoin Keating. Kenny sees them coming; worries that something bad might happen; and scurries away like a rat grabbing a piece of moldy bread and burrowing back into his rat hole home.

60. Marisimo Speaks A Romance Language

Marisimo does not care if Keating gets reinstated or not; the dishes will still arrive just as quickly, and he will be just as overwhelmed. It doesn't matter who's the boss, as long as there is temporary breathing room and also a plan to bail him out when he can't compete with the work load. At night, when Marisimo sleeps, he dreams he sees bus tubs of dirty dishes approaching him, like he's in a boxing ring and each series of tubs is a lightning fast combination of punches. Then in the morning, he slips on his vinyl pants, a threadbare button-down shirt over a black t-shirt; it's the same thing again and again.

Temporary breathing room for an old man like Marisimo is represented by taking an unscheduled break, when he can eat a muffin with no one giving him shit about it. Today, when he crooned his song for Sugar, when she and Woody danced, he felt like a real person rather than an old dirty man, washing dirty old dishes. The two of them dancing reminded him of his own wedding, he and his wife with nothing except themselves to live for. The most important thing was not how poor they were, but how rich they were in each other's arms.

"You a good dancer," Marisimo tells Woody, as Woody slides a brown tub full of filthy plates and breakfast remains across the stainless steel station to Marisimo. "You should take her out to the club. I think she will like salsa and merengue. She's a good girl." He pushes his hand down upon his deep wrinkles, causing the skin under his eyes to pull away from his eyeballs, exposing a gully of red.

"She likes Country-Western," Woody replies.

"Well, teach her. Salsa and merengue are country music… in MY country. It's very romantic, and before you know it—Uhn, Uhn, Uhn!"

Sugar and Maloney turn the corner together as Marisimo is still grunting. "Hey, what's going on back here?" Maloney asks. "Sounds like you're doing the corned beef hash."

"I'm just telling the kid that he… "

Woody Geyser doesn't want to hear the rest of it with Sugar present, so he rushes away before his face turns red from the thought

189

of he and Sugar together. Woody also wants to distance himself from Marisimo's awful animalistic grunts.

"... that he needs to go dancing with you."

Bobby Maloney raises his eyebrows upward on his large forehead, and Sugar swats Maloney's arm playfully. "So, I hear you and Debbie went out?"

"Yes. It was a strange evening but it worked out okay."

"So are you guys a couple?"

"Maybe."

"Uhn, Uhn, Uhn?" she jokes.

"We might have messed around. I'll tell you all about it later. Are you free?"

Sugar pushes her blonde bangs out of her face. "Oh, for this? Sure I am. Margaritas at Chi-Chi's?"

"Sure, but don't get all jealous when I tell you. It might make you wish you hadn't rejected me."

"Oh, I wouldn't worry about it."

Marisimo, hearing everything, claps his hands, hops around a little, and gleefully cheers, "Beeg head Bobby, Beeg head Bobby! Way to go, Beeg Bobby." Marisimo is all about love and romance, even as a listener, as it brings the generalized hope of love into his dreary dishwashing day—living vicariously is much better than not living at all.

61. Maloney's Plutonic Time

When the 7-3 PM shift ends, Bobby Maloney needs a few minutes to go home and get a fresh shirt, but it takes Sugar much more time, two hours to get dressed and ready for their trip into Cambridge. Her apartment in Billerica is in the opposite direction, so when Sugar is ready, she parks her truck at Maloney's house so that he can drive into Central Square. Maloney again worries about parking near Chi-Chi's, on the 1000 block of Massachusetts Avenue, as it's now dinner time, The Orson Welles Theater is next door, and his car is the size of a killer whale. At least the music crowd for Jack's is still a few hours away.

After the long drive all the way up Massachusetts Avenue, he luckily arrives right when a car pulls away from Uncle Bunny's. Incredible Edibles, an ice cream joint with a quick customer turnover. Chi-Chi's is directly across the street, so they avoid getting soaked from the rainy deluge. The dirt and grime of Central Square, Cambridge has turned to side of the road gunk, and rivers of thin, silky mud with gum wrappers and napkins are dancing down the rapids into the street drains. Maloney has been avoiding Sugar's direct questions about Debbie, so far, because he says he needs to concentrate on driving, the weather, or his other excuse, "I'll tell you after a few margaritas." There is about a twenty-minute wait at the door, so Maloney and Sugar head to the bar where they end up standing by the crockpot of queso and the baskets of chips, their drinks in their hands.

"So?" Sugar asks.

"Let's wait till we sit," he evades. "Hey! Joe Keating should have the news by now, whether he'll be at his old job or not."

Right when Maloney says that, two seats open at the bar and Sugar darts between two waiting men in suits, sits on one of the stools and throws her pocketbook on the other. Maloney walks through the businessmen and shrugs his shoulders, making the peace, because many a lesser intention often will lead to fisticuffs.

"What the hell?" Maloney laughs. "That move you just pulled is something close to what happened last night, except the guys we ran into were metal heads looking for trouble. Wanna hear?"

"Well, I'm dying for details."

"Well, let me tell you about our night. The Web Brook was packed and the band was pretty good. Did we ever see Three Colors, you and I?"

"I don't know, I really don't remember."

"Anyway. It didn't seem like their usual crowd, but Debbie was into them... she'd seen them before. So, we're standing by the pole, to the right of the stage, and these two guys were close by, making her feel uncomfortable, you know, standing close and looking at her, so I asked her if she wants to go up to the bar for a drink. We head to the bar, but when we get back, the two guys are standing exactly where we had been. Debbie muscles her way in front of them, and I'm right there, as an innocent bystander, but of course, because I don't want anything to happen to her, one of the guys pokes at her."

"Pokes at her?"

"Yeah, he gives her boob a little poke, just enough so it bobbles a bit. So, she was like, 'hey' and I step toward them, but then the second guy takes a swing at me—which I ducked of course, I've been trained to evade... and his attempt showed me he had no boxing skills. So, when his miss took him off balance, I clocked him with a right, and he goes down. Then, I go after the other guy."

"I'm surprised you didn't get kicked out."

"Well, I grabbed Debbie's arm and ducked into the crowd. The bouncers passed us heading in the direction of the fight. We took off into the parking lot to get the hell out of there. Parking lots can be dangerous places, places where guys want to kill you. Pretty exciting so far, huh?"

Sugar looks at Maloney as if she's never seen him before, while trying to give him an unimpressed look. "And then what? What happened next?"

"We bought some beer and went to the back of that shopping center in Bedford, drank and made out. She really had a lot of energy."

"So you actually went for it? Energy?"

"Yeah, she had the sex drive of a man. It was all arms and legs and body parts in the back seat of the car. It was pretty good."

"Bobby Maloney! Who knew you were such an animal?"

"She said she had some sort of a crush on me at school. Hey! Are you jealous?"

"No, of course not—I'm happy for you. Are you and her, like a couple now?"

"She called me this morning, but I don't know what we are."

"Do you want to be a couple?"

"Oh, sure. I mean, I think Debbie's really cool and I can see her at school. We have a lot in common, our studies... lots of stuff. I think you'd like her too if you gave her a chance. I was thinking, maybe we can all go out sometime after work."

"I don't want to be a third wheel."

"Well, I could ask Woody to come," Maloney adds. Sugar perks up and notices out the window of the restaurant that the rain has stopped. Large beads of water have settled in formation on the hoods of several parked cars, the big droplets colored and bathed by the neon lights of Massachusetts Avenue. She thinks of her affiliation with Joe Keating for the past few months, and Sugar wishes she could get in any of the cars and go somewhere. It doesn't even matter where.

62. Keating Gets Congratulated

At 4PM Friday afternoon after his interview with Blond Bob, Joe Keating has a progress meeting with both Bobs, in the usual meeting booth in Section 1.

"Congratulations," Dyed-haired Bob says, as they head over to their seats.

"Congratulations," Blond Bob says a few seconds later.

"Thank you. I'm glad to be coming back as Manager of Grand Slams #509, Bedford," Keating states, puffing out his chest.

"We are congratulating you on successfully completing your training. Joe, sit down. There's are a few things we need to go over first."

The Bobs plop their big butts in the seats across from Joe, their weight producing a whoosh of air from the vinyl benches, almost like an exhale. Simultaneously, they take time to flatten their ties, adjust their positioning. Keating is stuck, freezing a smile on his face longer than he wants to.

Usually the smile wouldn't last that long but today Keating feels proud of his accomplishments and ready to rejoin The Grand Slams community, something he hasn't felt in years. He has even stashed his drugs and not gotten high at the restaurant this week in order to look and be sharp, to make the impression that he is a changed man.

"Joe, we're keeping you on, but only as an assistant manager at this point. This won't be forever, but you'll be under the direct supervision of Bob Boolay, who is staying on. We feel that it's an essential part of your continued training to transition in this way. Dino Tribuno has accepted the top Managerial Position in Chicopee, on a trial or intern basis, with the added responsibility of overseeing the Holyoke store. In fact, he's already staying at The Rodeway Inn, behind the Chicopee restaurant."

Keating knows what this means and that it's a screw job. The assistant managerial position is the one which receives the shifts that the manager didn't want or that are found undesirable. It involves more nights, weekends, and also there is a requirement of working at least one graveyard overnight shift every week. There is more contact with the fuck-ups of the employment spectrum, more of The Kayak Kennys, less of the Mamma Mauras. The fuck-ups in the customer sector, the crazies and the drunks at 2 AM. At the same time, he would have to be impeccable in his work, which would be scrutinized by Dyed-haired Bob weekly. Keating shifts uncomfortably in his seat.

"Now, we want you to succeed and to succeed you must hit the ground running, so since Dino Tribuno isn't here anymore, we need you to start and take over his shifts this weekend, as well as covering your own, which means tonight from 11PM to 7AM, and then covering 7AM to 3 PM, Saturday. That being said, after this meeting, we want you to go home and get some sleep."

When Keating gets home he calls and leaves a reserved message on Sugar's machine. A few hours later she returns it, after coming back from Chi-Chi's, figuring there's nothing committal about returning a call from a friend. "You sounded strange on the machine," she says. "Are you alright?" Keating has been through 4 or 5 lines of cocaine already, hoping what he has squirreled away will last till the end of all his shifts, but knowing at this rate he is going to be in trouble.

"Well things are kind of difficult. Bob Boolay is in my job until further notice. How about you?"

"I'm drunk. I was out with Bobby." She hears Keating sniffing and taking a snort.

"How's that going?" he asks.

"Going? As in, how are me and Bobby? We are friends, just like me and you, Joe... friends."

"Well, my friend, I'm supposed to be up for the next day or so, but do you want to hang out Saturday after shift? You are working 7-3, right, and I'm heading back in a few hours and work till 3 also... I don't know for sure what's going on, as that shoe-polish-headed asshole makes the schedule now."

"Bob is not that bad of a guy. He's kind of laid back and if you don't cross any lines and stay corporate, he's really by the book, which is predictable. No surprises, unlike someone else."

"So you don't mind working weekend mornings?"

"Since we've not been hanging out so much, and I've been clear headed, mornings are okay. The tips are better those shifts too. I don't think Bob is doing this to punish me, but rather, to give me what he considers the best money shifts I may want."

"Man, who made you so boring," Keating cracks, knowing his basic innocent comment would hurt Sugar's feelings. "And you don't seem so clear headed at the moment."

"I'm not boring," she says, falling to the challenge. "Fine, then, let's hang on Saturday, if you can keep up with boring little me."

"See you in the morning," Keating says. "I'm going to try to get some sleep."

"Sure, you are," Sugar responds and snorts into the phone. "Sure, you are... wait, in the morning? Are you and Dino on together? I thought he had the shift?"

"Dino's on shift, but in Chicopee. They promoted him. I guess they needed a manager with a strange accent out in Western, Mass."

"I'm happy for him. He has family to take care of... you on the other hand, the way you spend your money and how you comment about accents or other shit like this, is why you had your recent job problem. We can talk about all this tomorrow," Sugar slurs.

"Sure. Boring, boring, boring."

"I'm NOT boring. I'm just feeling a bit out of it. Your butt is boring," she says with resentment.

"There you go, Sugar. We'll get you fired up and back on track. See you tomorrow."

Sugar hangs up without any further acknowledgment and wonders what the hell just happened. Keating, again has anticipated her self-loathing and manipulated her into hanging out, but this time, it is accompanied by the silence a simple hanging up on him produces.

63. Geyser: The Same Rain Falls In Lexington

Woody Geyser sees the rain droplets implanted into the window screen of his bedroom window and larger beads on the pane forming a miniature pattern of lights. It's 11 PM and he's bored, wishes he had a drink, but also, he cannot sleep. If he had his druthers about him he wouldn't even be trying to sleep until much later, but those 7 AM shifts seem to creep up on him. Druthers? Who says druthers? Even Woody's inner-voice finds his thought pattern to be odd.

Who would he be on shift with tomorrow? He runs through the Grand Slams roster of Bedford employees and makes his shift forecast. *Rainy with a chance of Keating*, he thinks, but not quite sure what role or capacity Keating will be at now that he's finished his training. He knows Dyed-haired Bob won't be there because it's the weekend, which means he'll be on with Dino Tribuno. Maybe both Keating and Tribuno. As for non-management, definitely Maloney and Mamma Maura, and most likely Debbie, as the new people always get the early morning weekend shifts. Marisimo would be in back washing dishes, which meant Woody would work up front. Since it was Marisimo, he would be spending time in the back too. Will Sugar be on with him or will she be on the evening shift? It's Friday night and Woody is thinking about all of these things. It's 11 PM, and he's bored.

Downstairs in the refrigerator his father has a twelve-pack of Bud Light. There are exactly eight left. He could have one, only one and he might not know. Woody carefully tiptoes down from his attic room, his feet on the edges of the stairs so that there is not any loud creaking. *Ugh*, he thinks. *I can justify the loud creaking. I have to use these same stairs to go downstairs to the bathroom, don't I?*

Just as he thinks that, the fourth stair from the bottom makes a loud groan under his 155 pound frame.

"Woodrow, is that you?" his mother calls from his parents' bedroom.

"Yes, Mom. Just getting a drink... of water. A drink of water," he repeats.

"Are you coming in or going out?"

"Neither. I've been in all night." For someone that is always keeping track of him, why does his mother often not know where he is. "I think I might be going out tomorrow after work. Just telling you that."

Woody does not have any plans, but the announcement he makes is for the benefit of him perhaps making some. He would talk to Maloney in the morning, and if that works, he will go out and only have a few beers. He could have a few, only a few, couldn't he?

64. Maura: The Shifting Around

"Hello Joe," Maura says, obviously disappointed. "I thought I'd be working with Mr. T today."

"I pity the fool," Maloney says, while scooting past with a stack of clean dishes to restock.

Keating smiles, but Maura notes his face is a bit plastic and pasty looking. If Hasbro made a restaurant manager action figure, Joe Keating would be the G.I. Joe of restauranteurs.

"Dino is running Chicopee and overseeing Holyoke," Keating says. "And I'm taking Dino's position, but only temporarily."

We'll see about that, Maura thinks, not wanting him to be the main man in charge ever again. Maura has been around long enough to know that the assistant manager is just a lame duck and when push comes to shove, the people above him, Dyed-haired Bob Boolay and Blond Bob make all the decisions. Maura knows she has failed at removing Keating completely, but to have emasculated him, just this little bit, gives her some slight satisfaction. Maura quickly checks to see if Dyed-haired Bob is on, overseeing this transition, but she grows displeased to learn that this morning it's only Joe Keating running the show. "Where's Debbie and Sugar?" Maura asks. "They should be here already."

A good thirty minutes later Debbie walks in, forty-five minutes late. Then Keating does what is unthinkable for him; he sends her home. "You will come in tomorrow and we will discuss this and develop a plan of action to fix your tardiness," he tells her in the office. Then after she visibly storms out for the others to see, Keating comments, "I learned that in Friday's training. People will be held accountable. Is Kenny here?"

Sugar arrives now, later than Debbie for the same shift and is told by Keating to hurry up and get out on the floor. In Center Station, Sugar asks Maura what is going on and she tells her, "Debbie was told to go home." Maura then asks Sugar why she is here, and Sugar just smiles her sweet smile. "I guess I'm just too important."

200

Maura is furious about Joe Keating's decision making process. She has tried removing him; she has tried reasoning with him; and for far too much time of her life, she has tried working with him. Joe Keating is the type of person that makes good people like her daughter go bad, encouraging them to not give a shit, to discount any potentially damaging situations.

Maura notices Keating sticking his head through the line-cook's window from their work area, either to observe the shift or to see if anyone is in the position to see him and he can get away with something else. Maura is never quite sure of the intentions of a slime-ball like Keating. Maura, on her way to one of her tables, detours to the back, toward Keating and immediately walks straight at him. "What's going on, Joe?" she asks.

"Hi, Wait Staff Maura. I told Wait Staff Debbie to go home, what's the big deal?" Keating says. "You can cover, I know you can handle the extra tables."

"Why was Debbie told to go home and not her," Maura adds, pointing to Sugar, who is handling a complaint regarding forgotten toast at a table which Debbie should have been on.

"Wait Staff Sugar can handle the extra work, and if I send her home after I've already sent Wait Staff Debbie home, we'd be really short. If I called someone in, it could be hours before they get here, and the breakfast rush would be over. Are we really doing this, Wait Staff Maura?" Keating grins sardonically, a new automatic response every time he does something from his training in "The Grand Slams Way."

"You were not particularly fair when you were manager, and I don't want to see it continue. I have Manager Boolay to report to, so you'd better be careful or I'll come after you again."

"Again? What do you mean again?"

"I didn't mean to say again… just take this as a warning, Joe, I mean, Assistant Manager Keating."

"Just do your job, Wait Staff Maura, and I'll worry about my own."

Keating takes two quick steps toward the cook's window and continues past but not before saying. "Hey, Chef Gus. Put up some goddamn rye toast, will you!" Keating then grabs a coffee pot and fills his cup.

65. Sugar: The Good Customer

At the end of her shift, Sugar rides with Keating to have drinks and appetizers at the Bel Canto Restaurant in Lexington. She has not changed out of her brown waitress uniform, which is obvious as the Bel Canto is brightly lit.

"So this is where you take a boring girl?" she asks. "It seems pretty boring."

"Well, I thought we could talk," Keating says. "I'd like to tell you that I miss hanging out with you, besides that other stuff. I really miss your company." Joe takes a few gulps of his Bloody Mary and smacks his lips. Sugar has seen him do that with his lips in his sleep after being up a few nights.

"That's nice of you to say," she responds, "but after what you said last night on the phone, I have a tough time being into it. I mean, who wants to hang out with someone that cuts you down?"

Keating scrunches his nose, which makes his mustache twitch, then he jerks his head upward a few times and whispers, "I'm going to the men's room, if you want a blast follow me and I'll leave you something on the sink."

"Well, I'm going to have to say no, because once I start, it becomes an all-night kind of thing and I don't want to be up all night."

"Don't worry. I wasn't even sure if I had enough left to leave you even a tiny line, plus with you being different and all."

Sugar sits and waits a few minutes, debating with herself. She doesn't speculate if hanging with Keating is a good idea or not, because she knows it isn't. He looks old and tired, like he's been up a few nights, not like the renewed man he appeared to be during this past week. She accepted to meet him after work when she thought he was the revamped manager, but now that she was dealing only with the assistant manager, she felt as demoted as him. *He had the nerve to cut me down on the phone the other night*, she thinks. *Now I can show him.*

Keating returns, still snorting like a horse on Kentucky Derby Day, and pulls open the menu. "I've not much of an appetite anymore," he says. "But you have something."

"Me? Are you sure?" she asks in a child-like voice, "because I wasn't sure until you told me it was okay for me to order something. Maybe you could order for me, as I'm not sure if I can do something that complicated."

Keating, now with some added energy, notices her contempt. "You know, you used to have more respect for me, or at least you used to like me more."

"And now I have more respect for myself. I can date anyone I want, and those guys would be interested in me as a person, first and foremost. Even if they weren't, they would certainly tell I'm not boring."

"I'm sorry I said that. I was kidding… "

"You were NOT kidding. You knew exactly what you were doing. I've hung out with you long enough to know what you do." Sugar takes the final sip of her sloe gin fizz and flags down the waiter for another. "And I know what I'm doing too."

The waiter is tall, young and tan, his skin is perfect, showing no signs of any marks or blemishes. Sugar looks directly into his eyes, which sit attractively proportioned on his face. "Can you bring your handsome face back here one more time with another one of these drinks in your hand? That would make me tremendously happy," she chirps.

"Yes, ma'am," he says, blushing.

"Oh, I'm certainly not a ma'am, but I'll note that you were just being sweet." Sugar notes that she has turned the waiter to putty and wants Keating to note it as well. Sugar notices the waiter walk away awkwardly, knowing she has caused this physical problem.

After he's gone, Sugar turns her attention back to Keating. "I'm thinking of going out with Woody Geyser, and I hope you'll have nothing to say about it."

"Woody Geyser? He's as dynamic as a wet dishrag."

"Around you he's like that because you're the boss and he's just trying to not get in the way. If you want my opinion, I think Woody Geyser is kind of sweet, even cute and you'll have nothing further to say about it, right?" She waits until Keating does not say anything for thirty seconds, but as each second passes his face sags a little more, his skin becomes more and more blotchy, and his eyes become puffier and puffier.

The waiter comes back enthusiastically with more physical composure and confidence.

"The manager insists, since you're such a good customer, that this one is on the house."

Sugar smiles at the waiter, then speaks to Keating, "You see how that works? Easy as pie, but you already know. You, with the way you've treated me, in every regard, know exactly what you are doing."

66. Kayak Kenny

When he was a boy, in times of distress and anger Kenny Slatts had been taught by his elementary school counselor to draw something productive and appropriate, as a form of behavioral intervention. Sunday morning, Kenny sits inside his parents' trailer drawing a picture of Joe Keating, complete with a cigarette, a smirking mouth, and a line of cocaine. Beside him is a horribly drawn waitress, who Kenny intended to portray as pretty. Then, holding the drawing up by the corner of the paper, he takes the BIC fine-point, blue, ink pen and slashes it through the paper, right through Keating's heart, leaving the torn artwork spinning away from his fingertips. Kenny, thinking of Keating's training and what Dyed-haired Bob told him, doesn't believe that there will be any change happening within Joe Keating.

Kenny takes a fresh sheet of paper and starts working his pen again, in a more appropriate manner. The yellow BIC fine-tip's point is so sharp it feels like it is not only scratching through the surface of the paper but through his mother's dining room table as well. His drawing arm swoops in an arc, and Kenny starts a picture of a kayak, which more resembles a banana. He sticks some rowers inside, which look more like giant round heads with big bulging eyes that rest on rectangular bodies with little baby arms. The ludicrous Kenny figure is holding a paddle, which looks more like a dialog balloon coming out of his arm. The Kenny figure's eyes are dark and dead looking. Kenny reaches for a red crayon but then remembers the fate of his previous red kayak, almost two weeks ago, and grabs the yellow crayon instead. Upon completion of his masterpiece, Kenny tapes the drawing of the aliens riding a banana to his mother's refrigerator.

When it is time to leave for his 3 o'clock shift, he knocks on his mother's bedroom door. It's 2:15 and his mother is still in bed. It's a good thirty-five minute drive from the trailer park in Peabody to his job at Grand Slams.

Kenny's mom comes out of the bedroom in an old, thin, rugby shirt and a pair of sweatpants she has been sleeping in. Mrs. Slatts walks past the refrigerator, and says, "Oh, that's nice," to Kenny, about the picture, then notices the shredded drawing Kenny made of Joe Keating and holds it up for Kenny to see. "Is this something we do?" she asks. Instead of showing remorse, Kenny screams at her.

"I hate him! I hate him!" Kenny yells. "He tried to get me fired just because he doesn't like me. I think he was jealous that I got the kayak and I asked one of the waitresses to go with me. He said I called the police on him. He's a jerk face!"

"Now, Kenny, none of that type of talk."

"He's an asshole. An asshole! I hate his fucking guts."

"There," his mother said. "Never use the phrase jerk face."

The purple Crown Victoria wagon, with fake wood paneling, pulls into the back parking area of Grand Slams. Joe Keating, looking thin, wrinkled, and more worn-down each day, is standing outside smoking a Camel non-filter. Kenny leers at him from the back seat in the wagon, with pure hatred, but all Mrs. Slatts sees is a non-threatening, disheveled, greasy haired man, not unlike their down on their luck trailer park neighbors. Keating looks so bad that even an impossible statistically run of good fortune would make him look healthy or like a winner. When the car door opens and Kenny gets out, Joe Keating yells a proper greeting to Denise Slatts. She waves to him, noting him to be the type of man she might have to discourage back in the day when she was still considered pretty.

Kenny's mother drives off before Kenny reaches the spot that Keating is standing in. Kenny still hears, in his head, his mother's scolding voice regarding the bludgeoned drawing he made, so instead of showing anger, Kenny's plan is to walk past Keating, hands in pockets, without saying a word.

Joe Keating wasn't advised of this plan.

"I don't see any new kayaks tied to the room of mommy's car, so if you want to get that replacement kayak launched before summer is over, don't fuck with management," Keating grins through his sweaty, drawn out face, where a strand of hair is partially stuck to his forehead and the rest of what hangs dangles over his left eye. "That is, if what you want and can have is within your control, you should use whatever means possible to get it. So from a management point of view, what you are doing, walking by and shutting the fuck up, is good work practice."

Kenny feels around the inside of his brown pants pocket for his fine-point BIC. There is nothing there, just like his life. Then he thinks, *There must be something I can do to turn the tables.*

67. Geyser's Foursome Meets The Parents

Sunday afternoons usually aren't a big time for going out, but it's a big enough day for Woody to wrestle over what t-shirt to wear with his dark blue Levis. He's nervous about plans later involving himself, Maloney, Sugar, and Debbie, on what might be considered a double date. Since none of them are working the night shift, today is the earliest time that this could transpire. It seems to be happening too early for Woody. He knows Sugar is a Country music aficionado, and Debbie, he is told, likes Punk. When Maloney clarified she likes The Talking Heads, Woody concludes what Debbie likes is more Pop than Punk, but she goes to a lot of shows and knows a lot of local bands. Woody decided on a Television t-shirt because, at least if Sugar never heard of the band, she may have watched TV.

Woody's read on the evening is one of where everyone must compromise their own tastes, except Debbie, who chose the location. Maloney told Woody that they are going to Jack's in Cambridge, where most of the bands play Cowpunk, a Punk-Blues hybrid style of music. Woody feels it's not Punk enough for him, not Country enough for Sugar, and not mainstream enough for Maloney, but Maloney will fall right in for Debbie's sake. Why is it that once a guy gets laid, what he says and does seems to change? Woody waxes up his hair so that he looks much different than he does in his Grand Slams uniform. At work, he flattens it down to look conservative, to avoid being called Woody Vicious from Keating or any of the other boring regular customers.

They've agreed to pick Woody up last, since Woody's parent's house is the closest to Cambridge. Maloney has the only vehicle that could comfortably fit the four of them. The huge Dodge Monaco could comfortably fit Woody's mother as well, if she had her way. Woody watches for the car, from his attic bedroom window, three floors up to make sure he can race down and not deal with any uncomfortable interactions with his mom. Woody curses, leaves his perch, needing to piss. Predictably, as he reaches for the flusher, the doorbell rings.

Woody zips his fly on the way down the stairs to get the door quickly. All he wants is to run out of the house with them before they get intercepted, but it is too late; his mother has already invited them in. Woody now wishes he could escape back upstairs and leave his friends sitting in the living room until they were no longer held hostage. Woody doesn't join them, standing nearby the front door, not wanting to sit.

This is an odd combination of people. Sugar looks good. She is wearing a men's white V-neck undershirt, denim shorts, and her blonde hair neatly tucked into her John Deere baseball hat so the heat and humidity won't glue the moist strands to her neck. Debbie wears a black shirt, black jeans with dark black eyeliner, looking very rock club girl yet somehow very wholesome. Maloney wears a pink IZOD shirt that matches his rosy forehead, penny loafers, and white khakis. Woody's mother offers Maloney coffee, and he accepts.

Woody is not used to having people over, but the mood is more as if his mother is having friends over. "Do you have any Sweet'N Low, Mrs. Geyser?" Maloney asks. Woody's mother brings over two pink packets just in time for Maloney to ask for more cream in his coffee. Debbie shoots him a dirty look, but when Woody's mom moves back into the kitchen, Maloney winks to all of them, his humor acting as an ice-breaker.

"This is the best coffee, Mrs. Geyser," Maloney triumphs. "Are you guys sure you don't want any? It's so good that you should get a job at Grand Slams as the coffee maker. Mrs. Geyser, people would come from miles around to drink it."

"I'll take a beer," Debbie interjects.

Woody knows his mother is a smart woman and that Maloney's jokes are not going over her head, but she is all too happy to play along. "Do you think my coffee is Grand Slams worthy Woody? How would you feel about us working together?"

Woody rocks on his feet slightly, not wanting to give this interaction any more attention. He knows he has a few outs. He could bring Debbie her beer, but that would painfully prolong this group's time here. He could open the front door and pray they would all follow him, or he could suddenly cut in with an enthusiastic, "Let's go!" and hope they would fall in line, which is what he decides to try. Sadly, Woody's interruption did not turn out as enthusiastic as he wants, releasing it with an unconfident, whiney, cracking voice.

"I'm not done with my coffee," Maloney says. "And Debbie hasn't had her beer yet. Sugar will have one too."

"Me too," Woody says, causing his mom to look across the living room at him, leave and bring back only two beers. "This is all we have," she lies. "And who's driving?"

Maloney raises his coffee cup toward her in a salute worthy of a Maxwell House commercial, and Woody's mother nods approval. "The Donato kid across the street wrapped his car around a pole on the Cape. He may not walk again," she notes. "A few years older than Woody too."

"Sorry to hear that," Sugar says to the buzz kill, placing her Bud Light can down on the coffee table after taking only one sip. "We should go," she says. Debbie places her can next to Sugar's, and Maloney chugs his coffee and brings the cup down hard enough to confirm the transition from house to car.

"I like your mom," Sugar says, noticing Woody frown immediately after. Sugar takes the flat of her palm and bounces it off the top of Woody's stiff hair. "And I like you all spiked out too."

"I thought you'd be into more of the cowboy type."

"Cowboys? Like Joe Keating? Sayid? They were *real* cowboys. Look at me," Sugar says, pointing at her own outfit. "Do I look like someone that really gives a fuck?"

"You look like someone that would turn heads at a rodeo," Maloney says.

When Debbie hears that, she slides over the car's leather bench seat to sit nearly on top of Maloney. Sugar looks over at Woody who doesn't know what to do or say, but he keeps his eye contact on Sugar. "I like your hat," he says. Debbie tries to stifle a laugh, and it comes out a cross between a chuckle and a cough, but Maloney can't keep it in and lets out a short hard burst of laughter. Sugar gives Woody a sympathetic look and slides over to him; she is close enough so that her shorts make contact with the side of his jeans, and his arm springs out, as if loaded, around her shoulders.

68. Maloney: Afternoon Show

Maloney holds Debbie's hand as they walk up Massachusetts Avenue, a few blocks to Jack's.

"I'm not going to know any of the songs, am I?" he says to Debbie.

"Not unless you know the Sex Execs and Scruffy the Cat."

"Oh. It sounds like live bestiality. "

"Listen," Debbie says with annoyance. "You agreed to come to this. I would have had just as good a time doing this on my own. I love afternoon shows."

"Okay, Okay, relax Debbie. It's just a joke."

Woody, walking silently ten yards behind them, shrugs his shoulders and tosses his hand out for Sugar to grab onto. "You seem a little more comfortable now," she says, to which he looks over and nods.

"I just hope the bands aren't too lame," he adds.

"Then we'll have fun anyway, just us."

When they walk past the large glass window, Debbie notices a decent crowd and turns back to Woody and Sugar to give them a thumbs up. She gives Sal the bouncer at the door a hug and goes in without paying. Maloney is given the complete up and down, as Sal isn't quite sure, suspicious of someone dressed so preppy. Sugar doesn't get ID-ed, but Woody, looking gangly and gaunt, is getting the full scan on his driver's license once again. Sal calls out over to another hired thug-like being, but Debbie rushes over. "Hey, Sally... he's cool. He's with me. I work with the guy."

Sal points at Debbie with a side smile, then jabs the same finger into Woody's bony chest. "You'd better not start any trouble. You just ain't worth us getting closed over. Go' won inside."

"Cool, but I'm fucking legal," Woody says, getting a little sick of the shakedown in these places as Sugar pulls him inside. She's never seen this attitude from him, and she puts an arm around his waist. "I thought you were a nice boy."

"I am nice. I'm nice to the nice, but not to the dickheads." He touches a scar on his lip. "From a bouncer," he says.

"Yeah, tough guy," Maloney adds. "I'm sure you were totally innocent when you got that."

"Well, I was throwing chairs around The Channel. Honestly, I don't remember why I did that."

"Hey!" Debbie says, "You go to a lot of places I do."

"I want to go to some of those places too," Sugar responds, feeling suddenly competitive.

"We'll go, but it's not going to be Country," Woody says.

Maloney and Debbie have disappeared, him up by the bar and her to the ladies room. From the back of the room a person wearing a suit and tie can be seen jumping ten feet in the air, in front of the stage. "People seem to enjoy themselves here," Sugar notes, looking at the thrusting jumper.

Maloney buys four beers and hands two of the bottles over to Woody and Sugar, holding the other two in his large right hand for him and Debbie. The full crowd makes it challenging to head to the front of the stage and get a good view. About twenty yards away, what looks to be a boyish and wasted businessman in a loose fitting suit gyrates and karate kicks to the music of Sex Execs. He is the jumper. "He must be blowing off steam after working hard all weekend," Woody notes. "Who else wears suits on Sunday?"

"Isn't that what we're doing?" Sugar asks. "Blowing off steam."

Woody slugs half his bottle of beer, "Yeah, but I shouldn't be doing this. I'm trying to slow down."

Woody and Sugar keep watching the suit wearing young businessman. At one point, as he leaps in the air, the contents of his glass shoot straight up, about six inches, and when he lands the liquid and ice miraculously land and are recaptured in his glass. His tie is moving freely around his shirt's unbuttoned collar, like a ribbon tied to an electric fan. The rest of his see-through, sweat soaked, white shirt is unbuttoned as well, having been forced open by his bustle. The rage

214

and fury of his dance has brought him within five feet of their group at times, and as he spastically moves away a dollop of liquid splats on Maloney's arm.

"Hey!"

The whirling dervish of a man hears him and immediately gets a few feet closer to Maloney on his next pass. He slops more of his drink, in what looks like to be an intentional act on Maloney's trousers. "Quit it, you fucking asshole," Maloney threatens, shouting over the loud music, but he feels his arms being pulled back by Debbie.

"Bobby, that guy is Billy Ruane. He's bipolar, not drunk, and he's really well known on the scene. He books the music in all these clubs and he's amazing. I've been out with him a few times… everyone knows him, so let it slide, no fights tonight. Just wait, I can introduce you."

Billy notices Debbie explaining everything to Maloney, which causes him to abandon his perceived misunderstood behavior; come over, and give her a bear hug, but also the largest grin possible. "Debbie-honey, honey-Debbie-Deb, how are you! You here for the Sex Execs?"

"Yes, Billy! And I want you to meet Bobby and some of my friends."

Billy practically leaps into Maloney's arms. "I'm sorry man. I didn't mean anything. I'll make it up to you, but first I have a present for Debbie-Deb-Deb." Billy reaches into his inside jacket pocket for a worn looking cassette, without a case, and pushes it into Debbie's hand like a bribe. "I made something for you! It's a great mix. Call me later and tell me what you think of the songs."

Billy runs through the crowd like a football running back, busting through the defensive line and coming back with five beers and five shots of Jack Daniels balancing on a brown serving tray which he slapped a hundred dollar bill on, for later payment, which he knows covers drinks and anything else that may break in the course of the evening. The waitress is right behind him, "Billy…Billy, I need the tray."

Billy's face is red, screaming for Debbie and his three new friends to take these drinks right away. He also instructs that when anyone has finished to let him know and he'd fill them up again.

Because of Billy's generosity, the Scruffy the Cat set flew by in a blur, much too quickly to even remember much of what happened in it at all. And as he does so often, Billy Ruane has touched down like a tornado and flown off into another state.

Debbie has bought Maloney a Sex Execs t-shirt, and he has slipped it on over his IZOD, the pink designer collar jutting out over the black band shirt's neckline. Maloney and Debbie look for Woody and Sugar, then find their friends sitting together, her head neatly nuzzled on his shoulder.

"Nice shirt," a woman leaving the bathroom and wearing the same Sex Execs shirt as Maloney says to him. Sugar hears the strange sounding, oddly familiar voice, and pops her head off Woody's shoulders, adjusting her John Deere hat which is now off-kilter. It takes a second, but she and the other woman try to place each other from somewhere else. Suddenly, Sugar recognizes Wendy, Sayid's date from Grand Slams.

"You're Sugar, aren't you?" Wendy says to her. "Look, let me apologize for being a bitch the other night. You were in the right to break up with that Egyptian dickhead. God, was he a jerk. I had no idea. What a weirdo."

Sugar wants to not accept the apology, out of principle, but she is also vulnerable to being seen making out at a bar with Woody, her spike-haired co-worker, after the conversations based on promiscuity she's had with Wendy.

"It's okay. I'm sorry if what happened to me happened to you," Sugar tells her, flattening her white shirt against herself and wondering why she cares, even a little bit.

"Yeah, it did, and he bought me a watch too, but I'm keeping mine!" Wendy says, showing Sugar an extreme close-up of the watch on her wrist. "There is nothing worse than a creep that cries," she adds. "I don't want to ever see him or even run into him again. He made me feel like the biggest slut."

Sugar pulls firmly on the fringe of her denim shorts. "It's okay," she tells Wendy. "You're going to be okay." Maloney sees the shyness in Sugar now which she rarely lets anyone see. Typically she wears a façade of being cool that covers her vulnerabilities at all times.

"Let's get out of here," he says, "before things get stranger." Sugar hugs Wendy goodbye and they walk back up Massachusetts Avenue, Debbie recapping the evening , while Woody and Sugar walk with their arms around one another.

"You can drop him off with me," Sugar says, quickly kissing Woody on the lips as Maloney unlocks his car.

69. Sugar Takes It Slow

They had been pretty busy with each other in the car on the way over. When they get to Sugar's door, she turns to speak as Woody goes in for another kiss, so that they bump.

"Ow," she says grabbing for her nose.

Woody is flustered and suddenly doesn't know what to do with his hands. "Sorry, sorry, are you alright?" He flaps them fanning himself.

"It's fine," she says kissing him. "Don't apologize."

She turns the key, kicks open the door, and shoves him inside. This time she coordinates the timing; her lips against his, their bodies pressing together. Woody lets out a long breath. "Are you alright?" she laughs.

"I've just never been kissed by someone who looks like you like *that*," he sighs. They move quickly for more, this time the kisses soft, often, and affecting. *If he's never been kissed like that, he's doing pretty well himself*, Sugar thinks. Her legs feel rubbery, slightly weak and she can feel the surge of him against her—and she wants him in a way that makes her throb in anticipation.

"Let's move to the sofa," she says and swats a few weeks' worth of clothes off the top of the upholstery, onto the floor. Sugar lies back and pulls him on top of her, her hips riding up around the outside of his. "Let's just kiss," she whispers. "I only want to kiss." She pushes her fingers against his short hair, making it pull and then snap back.

"I like this," he says. "We can just kiss."

"Just for now," she says, knowing that his statement is one of him liking her, not just wanting her. *And I never thought I'd like you this way*. Sugar thinks, *I feel I might want this more than I've wanted anything in a long time. This feels really different*. Sugar feels a surge of euphoria.

"I'm so turned on," she says, in between her gasps. "But let's only do this, okay? I want to take it slow."

"Just for now," he says. "I think I can manage."

"Yes, just for now."

70. Maura Greets Monday Morning

Monday mornings bring Maura into a relaxed state. Gone are the hectic weekend rushes, the unreliable early shift arrivals, and the feeling that everyone in the universe has the day off but herself. Maura has not had a day off in two weeks. *Why can't there be more like me?* she asks herself. *The restaurant would certainly run smoother.*

Maura has a difficult time with the concept of doing anything and not giving a shit about it. When Mike Homer started this place and brought it to where it is today, he had to give the ultimate shit. The Bobs only think they are committed as much as he was, and the people like Maloney or Geyser, in their weird little competitiveness around their jobs, show some sort of pride. Monday morning is usually a good measuring stick. The customers are regulars and the employees are the full-time, all season workers.

Gerry can communicate with Maura without talking, and he never has to ring his bell for her when an order is up. On the weekends, the bell becomes a constant sound, and because of that, it seems to have lost its relevance. Joe Keating also communicates without talking. Today he is communicating, with his body language, that he has been up for days and has no respect for the company vision of Mike Homer. He can barely hold a conversation without it coming to a grinding pause. Today he smells strongly of Lysol, which means that he is both dirty and germ free at the same time.

A man with long red sideburns and a tight mustache is sitting at a booth by himself, sipping coffee and holding up a menu, pointing for attention. Keating stares at him as Maura runs over to take his order.

"Doesn't he look like my father?" Keating asks Maura, as she puts the paper order slip up on the wheel.

"I don't know what your father looks like," Maura responds. "Did you know that Debbie is late again."

"Yep," Keating says quietly and mostly to himself. "He does look like my father."

219

Maura shakes her head and turns face-to-face with a struggling Kayak Kenny who is carrying a mountain of clean dinner plates—which he promptly drops. After they loudly shatter, there is the usual cheering from the room of diners.

Maura sees Keating jumping out of his trance-like stupor from the ruckus, as Kenny's miscue is a needle of adrenaline for him. Even if Keating doesn't give a shit, if the conflict involves Kayak Kenny, he chooses to confront it. "Hey, Dishwasher Slatts!" Keating yells across Grand Slams. "That was an expensive mistake. You just cost us hundreds."

Kenny feels the silent buzzing of the now quiet restaurant. "You cost me hundreds on my kayak," he counters. The Muzak version of "Theme from Greatest American Hero" (Believe it or not) is heard in the background.

"What the hell does that have to do with this?" Keating asks, pointing to the pile of shards. "Now, clean it up!"

"If you hadn't fired me, I would not have been distracted when I was paddling. I would not have hit the dock!"

Maura sees that this is an argument, like many of the arguments or conversations which take place at Grand Slams, which only makes sense if you have a frame of reference from Grand Slams, Store #509. The renewed sound of forks on china brings the normal background sound of Grand Slams to the dining room. *Conflict, kayaks, and docks are exactly what people should not be giving a shit about at breakfast,* Maura thinks.

Keating does his trademark upward nodding head jerk and then the fake smile, states with a belittling tone, "We're going to dock your pay for those," pointing again to the broken plates. "I told you to go grab a broom and dustpan."

"Fuck you!" Kenny yells, silencing the dining opus once more, as distinctly as John Williams creating a full stop at a Boston Pops concert then leaving the rostrum. Kenny, who wouldn't know a rostrum from a rectum, storms off and kicks open the swinging door to the back area.

Maura leaves Keating standing over the broken dishes, mumbling something about what his father might think of this. Maura follows Kenny to the back, to try to smooth things over, in her maternal way, for the benefit of the rest of everyone here. She passes Debbie at the break area, chatting it up about her date, still sporting slightly smudged eye-liner from yesterday. She shoots Maura a judgmental look regarding the crying Kenny behind the dish station. Maura gives Debbie an indifferent one of her own, as not to side with either of them, as both are demonstrating unprofessional Grand Slams behavior.

Maura ducks into the enclosed dish station the inconsolable Kenny resides in. She knows the exact way to approach this subject so that Kenny's tears don't suddenly morph into anger or rage. She lightly places her hand on his back. "It's going to be okay," she says. "I'm sure it'll work out. Assistant Manager Keating is only the assistant now, so he is not able to automatically dock your pay."

"Mama, I'll never get another kayak. My next few checks will be nothing. I want a yellow kayak."

"It's okay. Assistant Manager Keating is just in a bad mood. I'll put in a good word for you with Manager Boolay," Maura says. "Don't worry. I'll say it was all an accident... "

Maura disappears into the cleaning supply locker, returns with a broom and dustpan, and heads out to the front to take care of it herself.

71. Keating: Close To The Expiration Date

After the adrenaline wears off, Joe Keating's sweat runs off his forehead and onto the stainless steel counter, in front of the cook's window. He's aware to not have it drip on any of the food or condiments. Keating is not feeling well, but he thinks if he is careful with his stash he might have enough cocaine to last until Wednesday, when the Convoy arrives. It's not something he knows for sure, but rather something he hopes to happen. He thinks he may run out as well, so with either option, Keating is in a bad way.

His head is muddled, hollow and echoic, but at the same time Joe clearly reflects on the plate incident and is proud of himself for his confrontation with Kenny. It brings Kenny a step closer to being fired, or to quitting, either being a desirable outcome. Even in conflict, he feels that he has acted in The Grand Slams way, adjusting for costs and making up for losses. Plus, he gets to twist the knife into that fucker a bit. Keating doesn't even understand Kenny's argument about blaming him for wrecking his kayak, which is fine, as Keating, up for days, is in no shape to completely understand and connect to anything that is told to him.

"Assistant Manager Keating, are you alright?" Gerry asks him through the window. "You've been standing there for five minutes." He rings the bell for Debbie. "ORDER UP!" he shouts.

Debbie leaves a table she is answering questions from and rushes over. "This order of Cream of Wheat is getting cold and lumpy," Gerry admonishes her. "The heat lamp will put a crust on top of it, then it won't be you that'll get blamed, it'll be me."

"Yeah, yeah, yeah, quit your bitching," Debbie snaps. "They wanted grits anyway. Fucking rednecks."

Keating knows enough to know that this conversation is one that could escalate into cook versus waitress, waitress against customer, neither of these a good outcome for their work environment. Funny that Keating would even think that, but it's shit like this that his training has brainwashed into him. Joe Keating also knows, he may not have the power to stop it, being unable to string together a coherent sentence. Keating resigns himself to the fact that some interactions end up playing themselves out on their own. Unfortunately, he overhears Debbie's table yelling at her, then demanding to speak to the manager. Keating reluctantly walks over.

"Are you the manager? I want you to know that this is not grits!" the burly man states from under a trucker hat, in the exact color and style Keating swears he's seen Sugar wear.

"Where are you from?" Keating asks, trying to re-direct him in the friendly Grand Slams way from the video.

"South Carolina."

"This is not one of our southern stores," Keating says. "In South Carolina we offer grits on our regional menu, but unfortunately there are not too many of you up North that would make grits a popular choice in Bedford, Massachusetts, so it's not even on the menu."

"We were told by her," he gestures to Debbie, one table away, "that she would be able to serve grits with my fried eggs."

Debbie, who has moved onto another table, stops taking their order and confronts the southerner. "I told you that we didn't serve grits but I would bring something *similar* to grits. Do you know what similar means? Also, we don't serve possum or raccoon either, in case you wanted to order that."

The man dips his spoon deeply into the Cream of Wheat. Keating notices that at least he's going to try the crusty cereal and nods with mock approval, "Give it a try, you might like it." Keating feels a warm sense of relief that this conflict is close to being resolved.

Instead, the South Carolinian faces the spoon toward Keating, pulls it back and catapults a chunk of white cereal onto Keating's grease-spotted brown jacket. The lump of hot cereal rolls down his lapel like a tumbleweed, and leaves a trail of gritty wheat from his chest all the way down to the bottom of his suit coat. Debbie tries to cover her mouth, but she can't help squealing with laughter and has to run off. The southerner catches her reaction and lets out a laugh as well.

"Hey, honey. You're alright. That's what I think of this product that is *similar to grits*."

"I'll send someone over to help you with anything else you need," Keating says.

When three o'clock rolls in, a fresh and extremely sharp Bob Boolay bounces in carrying a briefcase and brand new clipboard. He gives everyone a big corporate smile and wave, but when he passes Keating he says, "Do you know you have something on your jacket. It looks kind of gritty."

"It's not grits, it's Cream of Wheat," Keating counters, thinking that a warm bed of Cream of Wheat would make a decent bed to finally get some sleep on.

"I know that sometimes getting down and dirty often indicates hard work, but I expect you to do something about your suit before your next shift. Maura told me all about what happened at that table. Good attempt, Joe. I mean that. I also heard about the action you took regarding the broken dishes. I'll support your call on it, even though I could overrule it. I'm glad you are taking initiative regarding the company, which is something I want to reinforce with you."

"Thank you Manager Boolay," Keating says.

Kayak Kenny rushes from the back, "Bob, Bob," he says. "I need to talk to you. I need to buy the kayak and if I have to pay for the dishes, I don't know how I'm going to save for it. I don't know if I can even handle... "

"Dishwasher Slatts," Dyed-haired Bob Boolay says. "Can't you see I'm busy at the moment. Why don't you clock out and we can talk about it tomorrow. I need to speak to Debbie about something now. Assistant Manager Keating, could you send her to my office?"

72. Sugar: The Sorry Sight of Failure vs. The Success of Shyness

Sugar hits the pre-set button to 92.9, Boston's Best Country, as her truck barrels down North Road, heading to Bedford. She's nervous about what the fallout from her date with Woody might be; but then again, Keating is no longer in the power position there; he cannot cut her shifts, give her less lucrative work stations or attempt anything which might get back to Dyed-haired Bob in a negative way. If for some reason Keating finds out, he's probably just going to be a prick about it. That, she can deal with.

What Sugar can't deal with is the sorry sight of the decompensated Joe Keating in dirty clothes, with an oily face, and greasy hair. She's seen him strung out pretty bad, but not as dejected and with as little energy as this. She places her palm against his suit, resting it on his chest, which causes some of the Cream of Wheat to fall to the floor.

"Joe, are you alright?"

"Well besides having grits thrown on me, hearing second hand from Debbie about your date, being exhausted, and maybe not being able to last till Wednesday when the truck arrives—add in a side order of being demoted, and not having any food without mold at my house… everything is just great. Couldn't be better."

"Grits?"

"I mean, Cream of Wheat. It's a long story."

"Why don't you go home and go to bed?" Sugar asks.

"I know I won't wake up till Friday. I can last. I gotta last!"

"Well, have something to eat," she says. "I'll bring you some chicken noodle soup."

"Yeah, hot soup on a July day, temperature in the nineties. You know that soup has been sitting in an insert since Friday. God, who orders soup in the summer?" Keating asks as Sugar stifles a laugh.

Dyed-haired Bob overhears them, walks over, and whispers assertively to Keating. "Don't speak about the product like that when you are on the floor. I want you to bring that insert to the back and dump it down the disposal. Right now! You've just guaranteed that we can't sell that soup to anyone who might have heard you."

Keating covers his hand with a Handi-Wipe to pull the scorching round insert up, out of the steam counter, and he carries it toward the back. "Hot stuff. Hot stuff. Hot stuff," he repeats to warn others as he passes. Sugar is right behind him, and when Keating gets to Kenny's work area, instead of dumping it down the disposal himself, he slides the entire insert across the stainless steel counter in Kenny's direction. "Hot stuff!" he shouts as the soup container doesn't decelerate; catches the lip of the counter; and spills onto Kenny's pants. "Ow!" Kenny yells and jumps a little.

"Oh sorry," Keating says and keeps walking. "I gave you some warning."

Kayak Kenny is furious and runs in hot pursuit of Keating.

"Kenny, don't!" Sugar shouts, stopping Kenny in his tracks.

"I'm going to get that asshole," Kenny says. "Just wait."

When Woody Geyser comes on shift, Sugar is happy that he is as shy and uncomfortable as a human being as he acts in work situations. She knows he won't come over; act as if they are an item; kiss her; or do even something as minor as put a hand on her shoulder. She likes him, but she wants to keep things unobservable and at a distance here at Grand Slams. Then she thinks about what Keating just said, *Christ, Debbie has already opened her mouth, so everyone must know. I need to talk to her about that.*

Tonight the rush is busier than the usual busy but the dead time is deader than dead. When everyone comes in at the same time, it's bad for tips because of the timing. Now that they're gone, the prospect for earning anything more is grim. While Dyed-haired Bob meets with Debbie, Sugar has to cover her section, which is easy as there is only one table of customers. Debbie has been gone for fifteen minutes.

226

Sugar takes a three dollar tip off a table Debbie had an hour ago and heads to the back so she can give it to Debbie. If a tip were to disappear, for any reason, she didn't want to take the blame, not that she would ever take a tip that didn't belong to her, but stranger accusations have occurred. Debbie is just closing the door behind her from Dyed-haired Bob's office when Sugar arrives. "I'm being told to go home," Debbie says. "I'm on verbal warning, because of my attitude. Fuck it, it's dead tonight anyway, I'm only missing out on about ten bucks." Debbie then turns to face Dyed-haired Bob's closed door. "Did you hear that? Fuck it!" she says to the veneer.

"Debbie," Sugar says. "I would appreciate if you didn't talk about personal stuff outside the job here. I don't want things to get around."

"Well, if you didn't get around, there wouldn't be things," Debbie says, then immediately catches herself. "Oh, hey. I'm sorry, I didn't mean to say that. I'm just pissed to be on warning."

"Oh, Debbie, that's rough and all, but I don't think I deserved that," Sugar says. "Look, just so you know, I've worked here a while and our outside life tends to acquire a life of its own. You'll find out soon enough. Talk to Bobby about it," Sugar says. "Believe me, you want to make your life easier around here. Losing shifts because of a man with fake black hair, who doesn't want to have you on at the same time as someone you're dating, just isn't worth losing money over. You're in school and you need more than one shift a week to pay your bills. Plus, those ten bucks can add up."

"Yeah, yeah, I see your point," Debbie says. "Look I'm sorry about what I said. I don't do well with other women, I tend to be friends with guys, but you are a pretty cool girl." Debbie turns to grab her bag so she can go home before Dyed-haired Bob decides to leave his office, as she'd rather not speak to him again. Sugar gives her a hug then sees Woody over Debbie's shoulder waiting. When Debbie turns to walk out the back door, Sugar turns to Woody and grins.

"On the next day we are both off, do you want to go to the beach?" he asks.

"Sure," Sugar says. "That would be fun, but please keep it between ourselves. I think it might be Wednesday, so let's shoot for that."

Sugar sees the pow-wow forming in Section 1, where the two Bobs are sitting with Maura. She is able to read their lips and see it's nothing but idle chit-chat for the moment.

"Bob," Blond Bob says.

"Bob," responds Dyed-haired Bob.

"Maura," they both say.

"Bob, and Bob," she says to both.

"Amazing interaction," Sugar says under her breath.

"Sugar, bring us some coffee," Blond Bob calls out to her from forty yards away. "I love that Sugar. I hope some of her attitude rubs off on that new one."

"Careful what you hope for," Maura counters, polishing her twenty-year pin with a paper napkin from the table.

Sugar scoots over with a steaming pot of coffee in her right hand, a small silver pitcher of cream on her left, and eight packets of sugar held tight in the crease of her palm. "That-a girl," he says. "Are there any more of you out there?" Blond Bob chants cheerfully.

"Oh, Regional Manager Bob," she responds with a forged laugh. "I wish there were more of you that came here to eat." Bob laughs in his own fake way and the interaction is aptly concluded. Maura feels suddenly invisible sitting next to the two big bosses. She watches Sugar work her ass, swaying it perfectly, as she walks away, heading in the direction of Bobby Maloney. It's a job skill which becomes second nature to the new ones, after a few weeks, whether they feel wrong about it, or not; one she used to use herself when she was younger.

73. Sugar: Bobbing for Bobs

"*Oh, Regional Manager Booooooob,*" Maloney says mockingly in a high voice, after Sugar joins him at Center Station.

"What should I have said instead? Shut the fuck up? When you're in the game, it's better to play along."

Maloney then changes to Blond Bob's voice, "*I looooove that Sugar. Oh, that-a girl. Oh. Oh. Oh.*"

"Ewwwww, gross, quit it. Anyway, listen. I saw that your girl Debbie got a warning from Dyed-haired Bob."

"That shoe-polished bastard. That must have been why she left without saying goodbye," Maloney says, causing Sugar to laugh.

"I'm sure you guys are alright, plus I don't think Debbie cares too much about the discipline around here or anything else that goes on. I had to talk to her about keeping her mouth shut about gossipy type stuff. Just mention it to her too. You don't want your shit smeared all over this place," Sugar warns.

"You know what? I don't care either."

"What do you think they're talking about?" Sugar asks, pitching her eyes in the direction of Section 1.

"I wouldn't worry. I think it's just Maura's playing her company-pride-ass-kissing-role. She likes to be held in the highest of standards." Maloney stands regally, as if he's a king talking about a queen.

"Quiet," Sugar says. "It's easier to read their lips if you shut up."

"Are they talking about Debbie?"

"No, it's something about Keating."

"You mean, Assistant Manager Keating... proper terminology, honey."

"Who's the ass kisser now Bobby? Okay, I can't see through the backs of the Bobs, but Maura is saying... she's saying... holy shit, she's saying that she'd accept the Assistant Manager position if that's the way things fall, and only if things get better."

"No shit?"

"No shit."

74. Geyser: One Or Two Things

Wednesday can't come fast enough for Woody Geyser. He's replayed every interaction he's had with Sugar from the past two weeks and is shocked how things have positively progressed with her. Even the beginning of her being nice to him was a surprise, and then innocently enough, the asking for his help seemed indicative of something. It didn't seem like they were supposed to like each other, but they did.

Today, when he gets home, he places some calls to a few colleges: Mass Bay, BU, Boston College, Tufts, and, of course, UMass. Since he knows her schedule by heart, he has set up a few interviews with admissions, which will be his surprise for her on Wednesday. He is proud of the work he's done, but he knows he needs to present it all to Sugar in a way that doesn't place any pressure on her. "*Since you happened to ask for help... I decided to do what you asked of me... So, you said you were interested in looking at colleges again... Check, it out. I made a few calls and they all want to meet with you...* " is how he'll broach it depending on how the date goes. Selling her on UMass, where Maloney, Debbie, and he attend school, would have to happen in a low keyed way also.

While he was on the phone with one of the schools his mother walked in on him. After he was done, his mother wanted to know if he were thinking of transferring. Woody, using one of the skills he had acquired in life, avoidance, told her, "I don't know, Mom. I'll let you know."

The interaction he plays the most in his head is his mouth locking on Sugar's inside her apartment, his head pushing her trucker cap slightly askew. When he twisted his head, her lips kept up with his to keep their seal airtight. Woody still feels that the entire crew of Grand Slams is going to jump out from behind the ice-machine on his next shift to scream out that this is all a prank.

Right after dinner the phone rings and Woody knows it's Maloney to firm up plans for the night. Instead it's Sugar, who called to say, "one or two things." The first thing she addressed, on the phone, was a professional thank you, to "Busboy Woodrow," for being so cool at work and not letting on to anything. The second one was a personal message. "I am looking forward to our beach trip," she tells him. *Shit, he thinks. I guess it can't be a prank after all.*

75. Maura's On a Role

Maura would be willing to take a managerial role in the event that Joe Keating got demoted to a position no higher than hers and perhaps as powerful as Kayak Kenny's. With her Grand Slams pin in her hand, like a rosary, she prays about it in order to come up with some hope.

Her Catholic parents too had prayed when Bridget was born. They prayed to not feel the shame associated with being grandparents, bringing up a child without a father. Yet somehow, what they had prayed to avoid was exactly the shame they were ladling onto Maura. Maura rejected God for many years and her parents brought up Bridget as her own.

Her current prayers weren't without images of her daughter. It helped Maura make a definitive decision about a new job, one which detached her from the self-image she held for most of her life. For Maura, waitressing was a lifelong constant she held living without her daughter. Even working extra shifts now to send money to California didn't relieve her pain. From an assistant manager's salary, she knew money would still be sent, but taking the job was more something for her own personal gain.

Maura also feels that she is a link to the original manager, Mike Homer, and by placing herself in a managerial role she would be following the Grand Slams tradition. In fact, upholding that tradition was all she had wanted for twenty years. Maura was not getting any younger, and the essence of Mike Homer in the Grand Slams Corporation seemed to be fading, much in the way that one's sense of hearing or vision decreases over time. Maura would run things the way Mike had, because she observed his leadership first hand, and to be honest, Blond and Dyed-haired Bob are not on par in the least with the visions of Mike Homer. When she was in doubt, the voice of Mike Homer runs in Maura's head, which leads her directly to The Grand Slams way.

Also when in doubt, Maura would think of the ways Joe Keating might cut corners, might do things at work to boost his ego, or might lead in a way to further Joe Keating, rather than the Grand Slams way. When she would focus on that, she would do the opposite. This was the main reason she would consider moving up into management. It was about replacing a person so infuriating that she had tried to rat on him so he could be fired. The Bobs had told her, if Joe Keating had problems she would be first in line over anyone else. It was a closed position, which would only become available if Joe Keating were to fuck up. That's the position she wanted, so each day, as much as possible, she would observe Joe Keating the same way he observed Kayak Kenny.

Each moment Joe would look increasingly worse, and infinitely tired. He'd make more absurd statements and ridiculous minor moves, which Maura knew, very soon, would lead to irrational major moves, or as Mike Homer wrote in the original handbook, terminable offenses. Currently Joe Keating was transparently trolling for Kayak Kenny, in an attempt to re-terminate him, due to an offense which, unbeknownst to him, Maura had actually committed. Keating is getting more and more frenzied in that quest, each and every minute, pointing out, on the fly, petty indiscretions, such as increased percent shrinkage abuses (Kenny ate extra French fries with his employee meal), and uniform violations by Kenny (Kenny's bowtie hanging crookedly or his grabbing the wrong colored apron).

God has made this all clear to Maura, and if the opportunity arose, the decision would now be a much easier one to make. All she has to do is mentally dot the i's and cross the t's, as there is a system for that which she and Mike Homer had worked on twenty years ago, when Mike wanted the hiring process, the trainings, the tasks, and even the firings to be standardized. They had sat in Section 1, that day in California, firing ideas off one another about pamphlets and quizzes based on pamphlets. Maura was asked to come up with the list of standardized interview questions which are still used today. Maura wrote all the questions which are asked during the interview for a managerial position. She reviews Question 1, in her head, preparing an answer. Tell me, (*say managerial candidates name*), how do you reinforce (in a non-monetary way) a behavior by an employee you want repeated?

76. Keating: Is There Anybody In There?

It's easy for Joe Keating to lose track of the days when he's been up for a number of them in a row. Not that there's a lot to keep track of, the morning shifts run about the same way they always do, the night shifts as well, only the players change. Is it Gus or Gerry, Sugar or Debbie, Maloney or Woody? If you stick with the Grand Slams way, no loose variable comes into play, as there are only so many situations which might come up, producing so many limited outcomes. For example, if an employee is constantly late, makes mistakes, or comes off as rude, the manager can either let it slide, speak to them, put them on warning, or fire them.

Life is kept simple by working in a standardized chain restaurant. If someone breaks a stack of plates, the manager can either let it slide or put in the paperwork for a payroll deduction. Keating calculates the loss at $200 using the official Grand Slams re-order sheet. Each plate is about ten dollars and Kayak Kenny may have dropped twenty of them. Using this number it's only about a week's pay charged to Kayak Kenny, which hardly seems like enough. Keating pencils in a new cost of $400 on line 5-D.

His own limited outcomes would include hiding in the manager's booth in Section 1, where he might doze off. He could also remain standing, holding himself up by the front counter. He's been going through about half a gram of cocaine per shift, so that's producing an outcome of financial burden. When he is this tired, he needs to double down, but his supply is down and demand is up. Keating is stressing about this problem, causing sweat to run down his face and his world to spin dizzily around him. He is desperate for this all this to stop.

At least Debbie isn't here at the moment, so he doesn't have to discipline her yet. She called in thirty minutes late, five minutes after she was due in. He has some time to get himself together, to prepare for a conversation with her when she comes in. This chat is something Dyed-haired Bob should be doing, but he's not in until 3 PM. Maloney is here, looking tired, after his night out, but at least he's answering the bell.

"Did Debbie call you?" he asks.

"Yes. Where is she?"

"She's at home."

"Why isn't she here?"

Maloney isn't quite sure what to do with Keating seemingly losing his mind, which is occurring right before his eyes. "Joe, are you alright? She called from home, right? She said she's going to be late. She told me to tell you that she would be a few minutes late."

"Okay, I get it."

"So," Maloney states, picturing her still curled in bed as he got up to jump in the shower, "In conclusion, Debbie will be late."

"Okay, I get it." Keating is exhausted, and the thought of helping to cover some of Debbie's tables seems like an impossible task.

Keating catches Maloney lingering longer than usual, so he raises his hand and weakly shoos him away. It's an odd and awkward movement and Maloney stands there, without leaving. "What's wrong with you?" Maloney asks and continues to stare at Keating's face. "Looks like you haven't shaved in a few days."

"I think I'm getting the flu," Keating says, his white shirt starting to feel damp and clammy under his suit.

"Maybe you should go home."

"No, I'll be okay, I just need some extra coffee."

"You don't look good."

"If I can wait it out, the truck comes today and we get paid."

"And that has to do with the flu in what way… ?"

Keating feels a burst of energy in an unbridled adrenaline jolt. His face reddens like a traffic light and his voice comes out louder than he intended, sounds unintentionally like a shout. It just takes one little thing to snap Joe Keating back into Joe Keating, and that is doubt. "Just tell your girlfriend that she is on the bubble and that she needs to fucking get here on time!"

77. Kayak Kenny

Kayak Kenny is finally having a "what am I doing with my life" moment. Living with his parents has granted him the luxury of never having that thought before, but today is different. In the past few weeks he has bought a kayak, been fired, wrecked the kayak, been reinstated, and now might work for nothing after the dish incident. The yellow kayak dancing in front of his eyes is paddling away from him so fast that he can't swim quickly enough to catch up to it. There is no potential for any immediate gratification. Kenny is stuck. It's all Joe Keating's fault, and drawing pictures of him doesn't seem to help.

Dyed-haired Bob has given him the slip signed by Joe Keating which he dutifully signs, his bill for $400. Kenny knows it's bad, but he doesn't completely get it. It's a conspiracy, having Dyed-haired Bob do the dirty work, because if Kenny gets angry at the big boss it'll cost him his job. Kenny can't help but get angry at nearly everything.

Kenny is aware of basic feelings, such as anger, happiness, sadness, etcetera. It's the more nuanced feelings such as frustration that send him into anger, without him knowing why. Also, the subtlety of someone who he hates decompensating in front of everyone else's eyes is completely missed on Kayak Kenny. While others see Keating becoming dirtier and dirtier, more and more strung out, or less and less lucid, Kenny only sees him looking more threatening, layered with danger. He becomes more like the type of guy Kenny fears who hangs out under bridges and might attack you for no reason. As Keating gets worse, it's for reasons unknown in Kenny's eyes, and the unknown is something Kenny has no control over.

Who is there to talk to about this? Certainly, he talks to his mother, but she can't do anything about it, except tell him to stop thinking. He can't call Blond Bob, because he is always on the same page as Dyed-haired Bob. Maloney would just laugh it off, but then there's Momma Maura. She usually puts it all in perspective. Kenny will make sure to draw upon some of her calm, motherly advice.

78. Maloney: Today's Blue Plate Special

Bobby Maloney has had a busy morning. Every time he runs to the back with a tub, there's another full one waiting for him up front. Gerry is ringing the bell, constantly, for Keating to pick up an order and bring it to one of the tables a waitress has fallen behind on. After a full two minutes of this, Debbie, who has just arrived, comes in from the back and grabs two Double Home Run Breakfasts and brings them to the station she assumes is hers.

Maloney can see Joe Keating standing, without movement, in front of Table 6, Section 5, teetering a bit. It looks like Keating may pass out right there. The customer asks if he is alright, and when Joe nods, they request another mini-carafe of syrup.

Maloney thinks about the time Marisimo tried to rid himself of the chore of washing a rack of plastic, dirty mini-carafes by making them disappear, pouring them down the industrial garbage disposal and flipping the switch. It cost the company $1500 to replace the unit, but Marisimo didn't have to pay that. It was punishment enough for Marisimo to have to bang the dirty dishes over the large trash can and then use the utility sink, full of soapy water, to pre-wash or soak the plates; sink out of service.

"Are you alright, Assistant Manager Keating?" Debbie asks.

"Yes, you wanted syrup. I'll bring that right up," he responds to her, thinking the concern is coming from the voice of a customer. The people at Table 6 laugh uncomfortably.

"No, Joe," Debbie says. "Bobby?"

"Why don't you come with me, Mr. Keating." Maloney grabs the inside of Keating's elbow to escort him away.

"I need to run to the bathroom first. What time does the truck come today?"

"Maybe 3 PM," Maloney says, doubting that Keating can last that long.

Joe Keating, pulls the paper triangle out of the inner pocket of his cheap suit and chops the tiniest line of cocaine, all he has left on the back of the toilet reservoir. Inhaling through a straw, he shakes off the burn of the harder crystals and has a temporary tremor, which can be best defined as a violent shaking of the head, in a back and forth direction, or better known as a "no-no tremor".

"What's up with Keating?" Debbie asks Maloney, back near Section 5.

"Obviously, how he handled the interactions on the floor shows the need for another blast, but he's been up for so long that the effect of it might only last for fifteen minutes." Table 6 is waving for more syrup.

As Debbie delivers three more mini-carafes to Table 6, Keating is back and waiting for her at the front of Section 5. Maloney is across the restaurant but sees Keating step in front of her, almost as if he is setting a basketball pick. The entire place can hear him give a non-direct message, where a concrete, direct message would have been more operative, which Keating learned from Manager's C Packet.

"Look, you've been coming in late, and when Bob Boolay comes in later, he's going to have a talk with you. Stick around for today's shift, but just warning you, I might have you fired."

"Might get fired?" Debbie's brown eyes narrow. "Like I might get fired by the likes of YOU?" she says loudly, giving Keating the once-over from top to bottom. "Fuck you, I'll quit before that happens."

"It'll be Bob Boolay... 3 PM, when you... "

Debbie doesn't stick around to hear the rest of it. She yanks the zipper down on her brown, dowdy, polyester uniform, to display a white tank top, and advances aggressively to the back. It's an angry walk, one the graveyard shift has seen before when drunk customers are about to throw down with each other, and Kenny has to rush in and break it up.

By the time Maloney heads to the back to console her, the top of her waitress dress is folded down to below her waist and she is crying.

"If I could sit here in my fucking underwear, I would! I swear, I'm just going to sit here until my check comes."

"Baby, what's wrong?"

"I just got fired," she cries. "This place can eat a dick."

"Wednesday's Blue Plate Special: Eat a dick," Maloney adds.

79. Geyser: Life's A Beach

Woody pulls his Toyota into Sugar's apartment complex and reasons that his car will come off as less of a shit box when the broken air-conditioning doesn't need to be turned on, on a day like this. It's much cooler today than the usual Massachusetts summer day. Even though Sugar has a sweet ride, he would feel more comfortable being in traditional roles, him being the driver, her, the passenger.

Sugar comes down dressed in a baseball shirt and a pair of cut-off shorts, that cover a bikini. She is perfectly prepared, carrying a cooler and a burlap bag filled with sand buckets, plastic shovels, a frisbee, and a mini-football with a long aerodynamic tail. He is wearing denim cutoffs as his swim gear; there is no bathing suit underneath. "Park over there," Sugar says, pointing to a marked 'Visitor' spot. "We'll take the truck."

"Okay," Woody says, relieved of his crappy car and immediately forgetting about his assigned sexist roles. "With all this stuff, we need to."

Woody moves the miss-firing car to the assigned spot and walks over to the Ford. When she starts the truck, Waylon Jennings is wailing in his bad-ass way. For a Country singer Woody appreciates Waylon, as that type of country is almost Punk.

'Since you happened to ask for help," Woody says, "I decided to do what you asked of me. You said you were interested in looking at college again so I made a few calls, and they all want to meet with you," Woody blurts out, all of his opening lines at once.

"So, what are you saying?" Sugar asks, picking up on the words, colleges, calls, and meet. "Usually my dates mention something about my appearance first."

"I checked with your schedule and you are free to meet with some admissions officers at a few schools. If you want, I could go with you. Oh, and you look beautiful."

"Yeah? Thanks. This college stuff is a nice surprise, but it's kind of a lot."

"They have loans these days," he counters.

"No, no, a lot to do, a lot of change," she says.

"Well, you asked for help, and not going to school is a huge regret for you. A few of the places I spoke with said that you could fall under a special case and be admitted this Fall, at the earliest—if not, the rest would take you either Winter term or Spring semester. Attendance is down at all of the schools."

"Okay, it's a bit overwhelming, but I'd never get it done without help."

"There's a meeting scheduled in Amherst on Monday. They could take you in the Fall. I'm off that day too, if are you up for it?"

"Let me think about it."

The truck rounds the ramp up to Route 3, toward Highway 495, which will take them directly to Salisbury Beach. Sugar turns up the air-conditioning and scratches her arm with vigor.

"I'm a bit nervous about going," she says.

"Why? You were much smarter than me in school. I used to think of you as both brains and beauty, but you compromise yourself. I mean, you should do this. UMass should be a piece of cake for you. "

"That's pretty sweet of you to say, Woodrow, but I'm nervous about starting and paying for it. I'm behind on a lease, but if I had to, I guess I could just leave."

"You can also give Dino a call. I'm sure you could work there. Chicopee is pretty close." Sugar, traveling fast in the left lane, misses the entrance of 495 North, curses at herself for losing focus and jumps into the right lane, in order to take the next exit and reverse her course.

"Can we talk about something else?" she asks. "Let's talk about the day and what you want to do in Salisbury. I love that place, it's so trashy. That's what makes it fun. Can we play games? Skee ball? Maybe you can win me a stuffed animal."

"Sure, we can do that. I'm pretty good at the baseball toss. Those weighted milk bottles don't stand a chance against that light as air ball they give you."

"And the rides. I want to go on the rides, because the last time I went to a carnival, it sort of ended bad."

"Of course. They don't have a roller coaster, but I kind of like the Ferris wheel. There are a lot of fun places to get a beer, too."

Sugar ponders that and to her surprise says, "I'm trying to cut down."

"Really?' Woody says. "Me too. We can party at Mr. Happy Fried Dough or Lamb on a Stick, instead."

"If I cut down, it doesn't mean cut off."

Woody nods, looks at Sugar's shorts. *Lamb on a Stick*, he thinks. *Jesus fucking Christ.*

80. Sugar: Time Tics

"Woody, I just want to say that I usually have a problem with people doing things for me," Sugar says. "Even when I lived with my parents I did everything myself, and then I just couldn't. It was too much." She feels strange that she trusts Woody as much as she does right now, as she believes it only takes one wrong path to get lost.

There was zero chance for them getting lost today. Salisbury Beach is basically a straight shot in from the exit, and during the week parking is easy and cheap. The waves are big today, and Woody rides the biggest of them. Sugar sits on the shore tanning. It amazed her that someone so serious and shy is so uninhibited playing in the ocean.

They are doing all there is to do on a beach, and it sure beats Grand Slams. When he comes in, Sugar throws him her extra towel. His cut-off blue jeans drip like a leaky faucet. Sugar laughs at how his hair spikes out in every direction, when he rubs his hair dry with the towel.

"This is a day," Sugar says.

"It sure is."

"I've not done anything like this all summer. It seems that most of my activities have been after dark."

Woody runs the towel over his already dry arm, looking down at the bleached sand.

"No, that's not what I mean. I'm not talking about sex... just stuff that happens indoors," Sugar corrects, feeling that her reputation certainly has taken a knock in the past year.

"I didn't mean to... "

"That's okay. Don't worry. I do worry what will happen to Joe."

Woody feels awkward hearing him referred to familiarly by his first name. "I think Mr. Keating is in real trouble. He seems pretty out of it."

"Yeah, he has a problem. I mean, I probably did too, but it looks like he could keel over and die at any time. I don't think I was that bad."

"Well, I think he's going to get fired first. Mr. Boolay doesn't seem to mind doing that sort of thing."

"And Kenny will get fired, by Joe, before that. Can you believe that he made Kenny pay for those dishes he dropped?"

"Really?"

"That's what Maloney told me. Joe is really fucked up and I know he will continue after Kenny. He'll go to any length to get what he wants. You should have heard the phone messages he left me." Sugar can feel her anxiety rising as she pictures the number 17 blinking on her answering machine.

"Bad?" he asks.

"Ridiculous," she says. "I need a smoke."

"I'll tell you one thing. Kenny is really scary. I mean, he might be as stupid as a stuffed animal," Woody says, pointing to the hanging bears by the Arcade, "but he's certainly not placid. Maloney told *me* that he was huffing and puffing when he was told he might have to pay. Remember how he lost it when he was fired for the first time?"

"You don't have to tell me. It was bad. Hey, do you want to get a drink?" Sugar asks.

"It's noon, isn't it?"

"Yes, but there's this place called, The Five O'clock Tic-Toc, and on their sign is a big clock, reading five o'clock. You know, it makes it five o'clock somewhere, well at least there."

"And noon, somewhere else. Sure, let's have a drink."

81. Maura: The Boss Brings Paychecks

Near the end of the morning shift on Wednesdays, at 2:30-2:45 PM, it's like a roll call at Grand Slams. Extra workers are there to help unload, as this is the day the Convoy arrives full of supplies. It is also payday, and Grand Slams workers receive their checks, so they are all milling around the restaurant as well. People like Maura, Gerry, and Sugar have bills to pay; others have tuition due or waiting. Kenny wants a yellow kayak.

Convoy day creates environmental as well as human commotion. There is a gaggle of boxes piled in the back area, all waiting to be stocked, the large obstacles to be coursed around. Maura hopes no one gets hurt. Sometimes on Wednesday bodies and boxes go flying.

Maura sees Joe Keating standing like the commemorative statue of Paul Revere on the Lexington Green. He is waiting by the office door for Bob Boolay, holder of the paychecks. In the past Keating has ordered her to cash out his check from the cash register so he can stuff the cash in his wallet. She wonders if he has the power to ask her now.

Maloney passes Keating and sings, "Standing like a statue, he becomes part of the machine." Still in the restaurant, Debbie sees Maloney and yells the Woody Guthrie quote, "This machine kills fascists." Maura knows Keating is too tired to ask her to leave. Who would have acted as security and escorted her out of the premises? Kayak Kenny?

Maura doesn't understand what Kayak Kenny is waiting for today. She knows that today, and probably next week, there won't be a check for him. Apparently he has forgotten. "Want to come out in my kayak?" he asks Debbie, before correcting himself. "When I buy the new one."

"When you buy the new one, I'll be long gone."

"Payday today," Kenny says to Debbie.

"My final one," she responds. "I was fired today."

Kayak Kenny's face flushes enough to take away his yellowy tinge and he stares at Keating, "You're a son of a bitch!" he snaps at him.

Keating continues his statuesque performance, barely supplying the energy to shake his head in disapproval.

Maura and Maloney surround Kenny and although he is still agitated, he stops swearing. "Look, Kenny, she's my girlfriend," Maloney says to Kenny, "but I'm okay with it if she wants to go kayaking with you, but I told her not to smile and give you the wrong idea, okay?"

Kenny, hypnotized by his favorite subject, kayaks and women riding in them, looks up at Bobby Maloney and says a calm and simple, "Okay." Maloney places his hand on Kayak Kenny's shoulder.

"There. You're feeling better, right?"

"Right."

Maloney steps back from Kenny and turns to Debbie. "He might be stupid, but he's a good worker" he mouths to her, who mouths back, "I'm never going kayaking," as she then laughs out loud. Maloney shrugs his shoulders as Kenny has been temporarily defused, and just in time for Dyed-haired Bob Boolay, with his special guest, Blond Bob, to enter the back area of Grand Slams.

82. Keating: The Convoy Brings Supplies

Joe Keating feels his heart beating; the adrenaline pumping; and the anticipation growing with each step the two Bobs take toward the office. Usually the managerial meeting doesn't take place on Wednesday, at this time, because there is too much going on in Grand Slams, #509, Bedford. The extra Bob is there, of course, to fire Joe Keating.

Keating needs to re-stock his personal supplies from the convoy, which has not arrived yet. At least the checks are here; first things first. Dyed-haired Bob holds the office key with one hand, the briefcase full of employee checks in the other, as a line begins to form behind the two Bobs. Joe Keating is first, Maura second, then Debbie, followed by Kayak Kenny, Maloney, and Gerry, who is tapping his foot impatiently because he has left his post on the cook's line vacant.

The briefcase isn't open yet, but Keating is in the office directly in front of Dyed-haired Bob's desk, shaking, as the rest of them stay outside. As Dyed-haired Bob fumbles through his key chain, looking for the one that will open the briefcase, Keating feels like he's a kid anxiously awaiting Christmas morning, but up for days instead of just one anxious night. He is almost psychotic.

"You feeling okay, Joe?" Blond Bob asks.

"Yeah, why?" Keating answers, both his body and his voice shaking.

"You don't look too good."

The sound of the briefcase clips springing open causes an immediate need for Joe Keating to want to scream something like "Let me find the checks for you NOW, and hurry, the fuck up." Instead he says nothing, but feels like his body is going to jump through his skin. He begins to count to take his mind off, "1... 2... 3... 4... 5." Bob Boolay, pulls out the checks, sorted alphabetically and starts to flip through them.

"A... B... C... G... J... L."

248

Finally, Dyed-haired Bob gets to M, but before he can say, "Bob and I need to talk to you after everyone has been handed their checks," Joe Keating snatches the check, runs up front, signs it, and counts out his pay in twenties and tens from the front register. When he is done, he looks out the large glass window for the last of the few thousand times he's done so today and is greeted by a flood of emotions. The Convoy is sitting on busy Bedford Street about to make the difficult, left turn into the Grand Slams parking lot.

83. Maura's Check Is More Than Nothing

Payday for a food server is pocket change, $1.75 an hour, minus taxes on her tips. In other words, nothing worth Maura sending to her daughter. It is with a sense of pride that she waits in line and takes the check for $23.73 because she could have had nothing, and she knows it. After Keating bolts out, Maura steps into the office to accept her check. Along with the check she gets an offer from Blond Bob in the form of the question, "Have you thought further about it?"

Maura says, "If it includes what we discussed about Joe Keating, I think I'm ready to accept."

"Well, we're ready to roll with it," Blond Bob says, accepting the firm handshake of confirmation from Maura.

Debbie is next and announces to Blond Bob, "Hi Bob, I was fired today." She tears open her check and yells out, easily heard by those waiting outside the office, "Woo-whooo, seventeen dollars and seventy-six cents!" Kayak Kenny, standing twenty feet behind her, lets out a strange maniacal laugh and loudly repeats the minuscule earnings as if it's the funniest punchline ever delivered.

84. Keating: On The Run

Keating, with a wad of bills in his pocket, springs through the swinging doors to the back area with more energy than he's had in days. Hearing Debbie shriek out the amount of her check makes him think that she may confront him. He sees Kenny in line. Knowing that there will be an nothing in Kenny's check, causes Keating to pick up the pace, quickly walking into the parking lot, and waiting for the cars to pass. The Convoy has just begun to pull in when he hears Kenny shouting.

85. Kayak Kenny

The rage of Kayak Kenny was louder than the sound of the Convoy's engine, and it was a rage greater than Kenny had ever experienced, much worse than when he was first fired and attacked Joe Keating's office door.

His rage was so great that he couldn't hear the words of Momma Maura trying to calm him while he let out an earth shaking howl when he whirled and left the office. This angry rage was so great that he couldn't hear the words of Bobby Maloney trying to calm him while he went into the dish station and took one of Gerry's knives from out of the rack to be washed. This angry rage was so great that he couldn't hear the words of Marisimo trying to tell him that, that knife was still dirty. This angry rage was so great that when he ran out of the office to confront Keating, he couldn't hear the words of the entire crew yelling at him to stop. This angry rage was so great that he couldn't hear the truck's horn as he dashed across the lot to attack Keating, which was warning him to not to cross in front of it. This angry rage was so great, that it made him deaf and reckless.

The final moment and sight of Kayak Kenny's life was of Joe Keating, waiting in front of the office of The Super 8, wearing a dirty looking suit, red-faced and yelling something he couldn't hear because of a blaring horn.

86. Maloney: Lost Time

Bobby Maloney had been running out of the dish area in pursuit of Kayak Kenny, but it was too late. Maloney had seen the truck, just a few feet from Kayak Kenny, yelled as loud as he could, but it unfolded way too fast, yet, seemed like it was happening in slow motion. Maloney had seen some pretty gruesome sights in the boxing ring, but Kenny bouncing off the grill, propelled back, head exploded against the black top was the worst he had seen.

Maloney knows, somewhere in the background of his shocked mind, that there are people screaming and there are people crying. All of it sounds distorted to him, like trying to hear something under water.

Maloney has no idea how a white cook's apron was now around Kenny's bleeding head, and how his own head is resting on his leg, like a pillow, blood soaking his brown work pants. Kenny's head is brighter in color than it's ever been, red over the dull green of his skin, like a broken Christmas ornament. Blond Bob's hand is on Maloney's shoulder. "Hang in there," he says. "Everyone hang in there. There's an ambulance coming."

Maloney checks his watch. It seems like it is taking the ambulance a long time. The watch says, '3:05'—impossible. It seems like it has to be at least 4 PM. How long has he been holding Kayak Kenny's legs? It seems like forever.

Kenny begins to cough and blood sprays out. Maloney doesn't know where the blood is coming from. Then the coughing stops and Kenny becomes still. One of the EMT workers begins to ask questions, the other manipulates the shattered body of Kayak Kenny. Maloney doesn't know where the EMT worker has come from, but Maloney is now standing. *How am I standing?* he thinks. *And where is Kayak Kenny?* Maloney has lost time.

A police officer talks to the driver of the Convoy, who is jabbering the same thing over and over about Kenny running out. The officer asks his name. It seems no one knows the name of the Convoy driver.

The sound of a siren is heard, and the ambulance speeds away. Maloney looks down at the blood on the pavement.

Keating is standing back on the sidewalk, near the door of the Super 8 office. "Maloney, take the hose and clean up that mess," he says, deadpan, void of emotion.

"It's okay. Don't do that," Blond Bob says. "That is a direct order from me. Keating, you're fired!"

Dyed-haired Bob arrives out back, keys jangling. It's the sound of him locking the back door. "We just closed the restaurant. Maura is telling people to leave and also, not to enter. I tried to lock the front door, but it doesn't have a lock. We've never had or needed one. I put a sign up. A Grand Slams, in this region, is closed for the first time ever."

87. Keating: A Grand Slams Goodbye

Keating doesn't know what to do. He's been fired, is unable to score drugs, and Kenny might be dead. All of these events, taken by themselves, could be life changing, That they are all happening at once is simply inconceivable. He walks around to the front of the store, and Maura is bawling, telling the customers that they can't come in. "What about him?" the father of a hungry family yells, as Keating walks past the group and into the restaurant. Keating waves at him weakly, trying to shoo him away, but his gesture is as weak and defeated as he is.

"It's alright. He works here," Maura says.

"Not anymore," Keating replies.

"What?"

"It's like this. First Kenny tries to get me busted; then I'm suspended; then I am fired because of some circumstance beyond my control. I wish he wasn't dumb enough to have made that call. Shit, he might be dead, I shouldn't complain"

"Joe, this is a very difficult day. Let's not make it about you. We should be focusing on Kenny and his well-being, but with that I need to tell you that I made the call the night of the party."

"What?"

"I made the call, to the police and to the corporate office the night of the party. I did so in the name of Mike Homer, his vision of Grand Slams, and how I promised to honor it."

"No fucking shit, Maura?" Keating doesn't have the energy to strangle her or even object.

"Given the events of today, that should all be minor. But, it was me trying to get you canned. I guess I can stop trying now. It's a done deal. As newly appointed assistant manager, I am asking you to not hang around here, so get your stuff and leave!"

88. Sugar Hears The News

Sugar lets the call go to the answering machine. She groans when she hears Dyed-haired Bob's voice; successfully blocks the information; and continues her nap.

"Maybe you should listen to it," Woody Geyser says. "It might be about work."

Sugar groans and grabs Woody around his naked waist and pulls him against her. She can displace her attention when it comes to a message on a machine, but when Woody says something, she pays enough attention to him to pull her out of the fog.

"Alright, alright," she says. "I'll listen to it. They probably want me to come in. Maybe Debbie didn't show or something."

"Are you going in?"

Sugar reaches behind Woody, and pulls him even closer, feeling him go hard against her. "Fuck that," she says, pushing her buttocks against him, so she can feel him throbbing. "Not with what's going on down there."

She moves back and lets Woody touch her, slowly pushing his fingers into her, but he wants to go too fast. "Wait," she says. "Go slow. Slow." She guides him, prompting his hands to move as slow as she wants and against the areas she craves. When he begins to guide himself just inside her, she rotates her legs to massage the very end of his penis. Quickly, she pushes him away, opens the drawer of the nightstand, and hands him a condom.

Sugar thinks that for their first time together Woody did fine, and it will only get better. Sex tends to work that way. She gets up to pee and wash up a little, and walks away naked, giving a show to Woody. On the way to the bathroom, she pulls the knob out on the small television sitting on the dresser, and Chet and Nat, the married anchor people of News Center 5, are talking over an animated graphic of a truck, with a violent red looking jagged bolt over the truck's grill area. The headline "Man Struck and Killed Outside Restaurant" is placed directly above the graphic.

"I think it's cool that they're married and are on the news," Sugar says in passing, pulling the door behind her. The television reporter is now in a live shot of the Grand Slams parking lot, where the convoy truck's grill is wrapped in yellow crime tape.

"Holy shit," Woody says. "Someone was killed at Grand Slams!"

The bathroom door flies open and bounces hard off the stopper so Sugar has to push against it a second time. "Was it a fight? It's not even the overnight shift."

"No, I think the supply truck hit someone," Woody says, sitting up in bed. "The freaking Convoy ran someone over!"

Sugar, loosely clothed, settles next to him and yells out in horror as a picture of Kayak Kenny, perhaps from a high school yearbook, is framed behind Chet and Nat, Chet reporting, "Witnesses said, Slatts was running after another employee with a knife when he was struck and killed. Nat?"

"In Danvers today, the town hosted a Teddy Bear picnic… "

Sugar flips to another channel, hoping for more coverage, but it was only the weather. She then flips on the message left by Dyed-haired Bob on her machine. *Sugar, this is Bob Boolay. You are scheduled in the morning, but you may not have to come in. I'll call you later. You didn't do anything wrong, that's not why, but you probably already know. I'll keep you posted about the schedule.*

Part Three:

"Grand Slams—The Afterlife"

89. The Afterlife

Two weeks later, on behalf of the company, Blond and Dyed-haired Bob say a few words of appreciation, along the lines of, "He was not very smart, but he was a good worker." Truth is, Kayak Kenny would have liked the proceedings: lots of friends, and most of the waitresses, all of them saying nice things about him. Grand Slams Corporation paid for everything, including the casket, one Kayak Kenny would have picked out for himself.

At McGillicutty and Son Funeral Home, they've cut the top off a yellow kayak; welded on a few hinges; laid out some bedding, and had a large photo of the ocean, on poster board, fastened onto the casket stand. This is what they laid him down in. Getting the aesthetics just right took them an extra week. Debbie cried when she first saw it. Maloney held off from laughing inappropriately, thinking that instead of putting him in the ground, all they had to do is push him, intact, out to sea; he was already dressed to be buried in his tiny life vest.

McGillicutty and Son also have caked Kenny's face up with more makeup than Debbie would wear to a rock show. Most of the guests noted that it didn't look good, very unnatural, because no one is used to seeing Kayak Kenny with a peach-colored skin.

Woody sits with Sugar gripping his arm at the elbow. Woody feels like an outsider at a party where everyone knows everyone else even when he does know dozens of people here. Every relative in Kenny's family resembles adults who could have been cast as the slow kids in *Children of the Corn*. He reaches across his body and pats Sugar's hand.

When Kenny, in his yellow kayak, rolls down the aisle, Sugar grips his arm tighter. Woody feels the tension of Sugar's emotions there, but when he turns to her, her face shows nothing. "We're not going to the cemetery, are we?" he asks.

"No," she whispers.

"The reception following?"

"Hell, no. I hear that Grand Slams catered it."

"Double Home Run Breakfasts? Did they ask Marisimo to clean the dishes at the reception hall too?"

"Shhh," Sugar says, catching the eyes of Bobby Maloney, now facing them, jerking and nodding his head in an upward direction, in honor of the absent Joe Keating.

Woody and Sugar are met outside the church by Maloney and Debbie.

"That was a *lovely* service," Maloney cracks.

"Must you make a joke about everything? I thought it was beautifully done. It did well to honor him," Debbie responds, her face stained with eyeliner.

"No, really, it was," Maloney adds, backtracking. "What are you kids doing?"

"We're figuring out the financials. Sugar's an easy in at UMass," Woody says. "We met with them earlier this week, and it's possible she'll get a partial scholarship into the School of Business. Her brain is super sexy."

"That's great!" Maloney exclaims. "We'll all be classmates."

"It's too bad you're coming in so late, because I would have loved to have you as a roommate," Debbie says.

"It's okay," Sugar replies. "Woody and I got a cheap place off campus." Maloney and Debbie look at one another, raising their eyebrows.

"Well, as far as taking relationships to the next level, there's the unhealthy one between me and Grand Slams. I talked to Tribuno and I'm going to work in Chicopee this fall," Maloney says. "I won't have to go back and forth—which means Debbie and I can hang out on the weekends. Hey Sugar, I hear they need part-time waitresses."

"Well, we can hang out on weekends, if I don't have to work," Debbie replies. "I have an in at All Nacho Al's, the place on Boltwood Walk that only serves nachos! Their entire menu is nachos! They even have stuff like breakfast nachos and tuna melt lunch nachos."

"How's the boss?" Woody asks.

"Oh, Al? I heard he's pretty cool."

"Anyone want to go to Grand Slams?" Maloney asks the group.

"Who's watching the fort there?" Woody responds. "Everyone is here. I don't want to be suckered into working a shift."

"Maura and Marisimo are there minding the place along with the emergency people Keating used to call in, Mahalia, Manouchka, and Martine. He never knew their names. He was such a racist. Also, Tribuno out of respect is covering Bedford today."

"What else is new?" Maloney says.

"Speaking of Keating, I had a dream about him," Woody says. "All of us were in it. We were at the Wonderland Dog Track."

"Is that so," Sugar says, nudging him. "You'd think your dreams would be better since you're with me."

"Shh," Maloney says. "Let him talk."

"We were all there cheering the dogs, having a good time, but over by the betting window was Joe Keating. He was wearing a 7-11 shirt, the one styled with 7-11 green and orange symbols all over it. Keating's shirt had a big yellow mustard stain on it, and he looked all sketchy and greasy."

"What else is new?" Maloney says again.

"Shh," Sugar says. "Let him talk."

"Well," Woody continues, "He was scratching a bunch of lottery tickets and had an open newspaper with the racing form for the dogs. Next to each race, in blue ink, he had written the words, *loser, loser, loser.* When we asked how he was doing, he looked up from his newspaper and said, 'You know, I just can't win. I can never win.'"

About the Author

Timothy Gager is the author of two novels and ten books of short fiction and poetry. He has hosted the successful Dire Literary Series in Cambridge, Massachusetts, for over fifteen years and is the fiction editor of *The Wilderness House Literary Review*. His work appears in over 300 journals, of which ten have been nominated for the Pushcart Prize. His work has been read on National Public Radio.